LAST SEEN ON NANTUCKET

A Novel

by Garth Jeffries

The characters and events portrayed in this book are fictitious. Any similarity to real persons, living or dead, is coincidental and not intended by the author.

ISBN-13: 979-8-9959194-0-7

ALSO BY GARTH JEFFRIES

A Drowning on Nantucket

Not All Bodies Stay Buried

Starbuck, Nantucket Redemption

Dedicated to Henry Caton

Welcome to the Family

And to the amazing women in my life

To JCT, for making it all possible

To K for her 44 years of love, support, and encouragement

And to Mads for just being the best

And to FFT, the most remarkable man I have ever known.

CHAPTER ONE

May, 1992

The island was out of balance. He could feel the vibrations, the subtle wobble under his feet. Something had to be done.

He had spent the prior few days looking for just the right person to help him restore that balance. Was there someone he could count on who could help him? He wondered if it was even possible. From what he read, if done correctly, then yes, he felt that the balance could be restored and residents and visitors alike would enjoy another lovely summer on Nantucket.

But he needed the right person. The right help. It couldn't just be anyone. The wrong person wouldn't solve the current crisis and could even further stoke the imbalance.

At first, he had struggled to find that person. Some were too old, and many were just too young. He felt strongly that only adults could help him achieve his goals. Only adults would have the right physical value and personality he needed for a Gift.

But he found the one on a beautiful, warm day at Madequecham Beach. He was part of a larger group of college-aged men and women who were enjoying the day. Scantily clad, the group threw frisbees, sunned on towels, splashed in the waves, and drank heavily. It appeared they were having a wonderful time.

The man he thought could help was tall, handsome, confident, and clearly wealthy. The others in the group circled erratically in his orbit like moths to a porch light. Despite being dressed inappropriately for the location and situation, he had managed to talk to the man to determine his worth and confirm his suspicions.

He had learned he was living on the island for the summer and claimed to be working as a sailing instructor at the yacht club. He was from the City and his parents had just bought a property near Tom Nevers. He planned to work hard, help some of the summer kids learn how to sail, and save some money for college.

But he knew better. This young man was here to have fun and party. He smelled of wealth, privilege, and entitlement. Sailing was just an enjoyable distraction to kill the hours until party time. And the only money he was saving for college was beer money. Mommy and Daddy no doubt would be paying the full ride to some exclusive East Coast University.

He walked away from his encounter with the young man with a smile on his face. He had found the right candidate. This sailing instructor would bring a new vision, a new perspective, a new position to help the island achieve balance.

Yes. He would be the perfect Gift.

A few days later, the weather had turned. The sunny, warm, and clear days had given way to a damp, foggy chill. Two beachcombers, a man and a woman, were out early in the morning and looking for unique shells and sea glass. Walking a few feet above the breaking waves, he was the first to notice the bundle and motioned to his partner. Maybe it would hold some treasure?

They stumbled through the damp, heavy sand toward the bundle but soon realized it was much more than that.

The woman screamed. She turned and vomited up her breakfast.

The man dropped to check the pulse. The body was cold.

Balance had been maintained.

CHAPTER TWO

As appeared on Nantucket in the May 28th, 1992 edition of The Inquirer & Mirror.

COMMUNITY ANNOUNCEMENTS

My Gift to You

Nature's first green is gold,
Her hardest hue to hold.
Her early leaf's a flower;
But only for an hour.
Then leaf subsides to leaf.
So Eden sank to grief,
So dawn goes down to day.
Nothing gold can stay.
Unless a gift made in moment brief
Can pause our time's silent grief
She follows those gone now, still and gray
A bequest I have done for you my dear. This day.

CHAPTER THREE

Hyannis, Massachusetts

Thursday, Memorial Day Weekend

The four diesel engines on the Gray Lady IV high-speed ferry thrummed to life under a cloudless blue sky as it readied itself for the thirty-mile trip to Nantucket. It was a stunningly perfect, late spring afternoon and the first Memorial Day weekend in several years where the weather prediction was favorable. For the past few years, the three-day weekend, unofficially the start of the summer season, had been plagued by a pandemic, rain and fog, cold temperatures, and even a rare spring Nor'easter, which disrupted travel plans for thousands as planes were delayed and ferries cancelled due to high winds and large waves.

But not this year. This year, the weather was going to be perfect. And it was in anticipation of that perfect weekend that the nearly five hundred passengers of this sold-out voyage on a beautiful Thursday afternoon buzzed with excitement.

At exactly the 2:25 p.m. departure time, the dockside team untied the mooring lines and tossed them on board, where they were quickly stowed by the crew. The captain advanced the throttles, and the 160-foot, three-deck tall catamaran eased slowly out of its berth. Clearing the final pier, the captain deftly pivoted the vessel 90 degrees and pointed her due south.

Baxter's Boathouse, a Hyannis landmark favored for its delicious menu and ideal location, was packed with smiling faces, nearly every outside chair filled. Some looked up at the ferry and waved. Many on the ferry returned the gesture. The mood on ship and shore was ebullient. It was a gorgeous day, and a new summer was about to start.

The boat accelerated and passed the historic Hyannis Harbor Light to starboard. It idled slowly through the no-wake zone until it reached Kalmus Park Beach, where the harbor emptied into the Atlantic. Passing the end of the jetty, the captain advanced the throttles, and soon the Grey Lady IV was traveling at 32 knots over a sea as flat as glass.

On board, travelers had staked out their territory for the hour-long trip. The main cabin, on the first floor, held a mix of individual forward-facing buckets as well as bench seats facing each other over a Formica table. The latter was perfect for bigger groups and visiting families. The large group near the stern turned out not to be visitors at all, but the returning Nantucket High School girls' field hockey team. They had just finished the interscholastic tournament and had taken victory from their rivals from the Vineyard. Their mood was celebratory, and they took turns passing the trophy and relishing their win.

Toward the bow, the concession stand was already in full swing as a long line of travelers waited patiently to kickstart their weekend with their preferred beverage and a snack. Of course, there was always the one, the entitled, who felt like they shouldn't have to wait in line. This time, it was an older woman clutching a pocket-sized Yorkie. Claiming her sciatica was acting up, she angled her way in front of a dozen in line and was soon being served. Those behind her rolled their eyes and shared knowing looks, but none wanted to spoil the day by confronting her.

Angling back toward the bow and up the central staircase to the second deck, an elderly couple sat in the premium seating, known as the Captain's View, and proceeded to ignore all those around them. She was lost in a book while he sat and stared out across the water and into the distance. They had the familiar comfort between them from a couple who have been together for decades. He was holding her hand.

Moving rearward, an obviously wealthy young woman was struggling to control her three children. All boys under the age of ten, they were yelling, play-fighting, and trying to wrestle each other off their seats. Despite her repeated warnings and threats, the boys ignored her. Their neighbors tolerated the noise and pandemonium mainly because they had no other choice. There simply was not another seat available.

Proceeding to the rearward deck, an exterior area sheltered by the top level, the rushing wind and engine noise increased. Here, several people were relaxed, enjoying the fresh air and their journey. Many talked animatedly with their companions, some were reading, others absorbed in their devices. A teenager, watching a movie on his phone, had the volume up for all to hear.

But it was the top deck where the party had really started.

A group of a dozen college men was seated on the port side of the stern and taking turns chugging beer to supportive chants from the rest of the group. They were all starting internships the following week in New York and were anxious to celebrate the weekend before a summer of hard work and even harder partying began. More than one would vomit before they reached their destination.

On the opposite side of the boat, a group of young women was smiling and laughing. One was clearly the focus, and it soon became apparent that she was a bride-to-be and heading to the island with her friends for a proper send-off into matrimony. There were nursing hard seltzers and talking animatedly about the plans for their upcoming weekend, new bathing suits to be worn, and where they were going to eat.

Along the back rail in a seat facing toward the bow, a well-known news personality from a major network sat in the sun and was shoving handfuls of potato chips into his mouth. The breeze generated by the boat's speed was making this task very difficult, and most of the chips were missing their intended destination, much to the delight of the seagulls who were following the boat.

As the ferry motored southward, they passed a number of sailboats practicing for that weekend's big race from Hyannis to Nantucket. Known as Figawi, it was as much about the partying as it was the actual race itself. Stories from the sixty-year event were legendary. People waking up with strangers sleeping in their homes, unconscious from a night of partying. Sailors sleeping on the benches on Main Street. Even a topless woman - who didn't realize she was topless - walking into a popular local restaurant asking for another drink.

One of the car ferries passed heading northward, its open-air top deck with hundreds of seats was devoid of any passengers. Everyone was heading to the island. No one wanted to leave.

An attractive woman toward the center of the boat was making friends with her pet duck. Kept in a canvas bag, the duck seemed content sitting and looking out while fellow passengers stroked her head and smiled at the thought of a waterfowl companion.

Behind her, a yellow Lab, smiling and tail wagging furiously, was desperate to secure some of the duck's admirers. Being ignored, the dog barked a couple of times only to be rebuked by its parent, a middle-aged man with a long gray ponytail. Reluctantly, the dog lay down, his eyes darting back and forth as the line of fans progressed by the end of his nose toward his fowl neighbor.

As the group of college men finished their second case of beer, the Grey Lady IV passed the start of the jetty where seals sunbathed on the rocks, looking at the passing ferry with mild interest. Soon, the captain closed the throttles, and the boat slowed quickly. Rounding the Brant Point Lighthouse, the captain made a beeline to the Straight Wharf, passing a half dozen mega-yachts docked stern-in at the east end of the Boat Basin. The rest of the slips were full with smaller but equally impressive sailboats, sportfishing boats, and cruisers.

The boat came into its dock quickly, the captain reversing the engines at the last moment to slow the vessel to a crawl. It eased into its berth, and the dockside crew tied her off. The luggage carts made their way from the port stern door and were pulled several hundred feet down Straight Wharf, where they would reunite passengers with their luggage. Several crew worked the gangways to the center and forward openings. Once secured, the doors opened, and a flood of passengers began to disembark.

The college men stumbled, hanging onto each other and trying to act nonchalant. That image was shattered when one of the men fell face-first the minute his feet touched the island. Three others, not in full control of their movements, couldn't avoid the prone body and followed him to the ground, briefly backing up the passenger line as they struggled to get up, regain their forward momentum, and recover their pride. Nonplussed, they dusted themselves off and made their way down Straight Wharf, anxious to retrieve their belongings and find a welcoming bar.

The bridal party followed at a distance, not wanting any part of the men's debauchery, while the yellow Lab eagerly pulled its owner, anxious to be back home. The girls' field hockey team was met with dozens of friends and family, many with balloons and banners celebrating their victory. Clutching her Yorkie, the older woman managed her sciatica just fine as she made her way quickly ashore. A tall, elegantly dressed gentleman met her with a nod, and together they walked past the luggage carts and to a waiting car.

The three young boys raced down the gangway, rudely pushing other passengers out of the way as they raced to be the first to the luggage carts. The mother followed futilely behind them, apologizing for their behavior as she went.

The lady with the duck, tucked carefully under her arm with its head looking out, was one of the last to disembark, followed by the elderly couple. They were still holding hands and exchanging glances as they looked out across the town. It was evident that they had been here many times before and had a shared passion for the island.

The mass of people merged at the luggage carts, followed by a brief frenzy of activity. Most were polite, but a few lost their patience as others stood and blocked the carts, trying to remember which cart had their luggage and which one of the dozens of black roller bags was theirs.

A middle-aged, slightly heavy-set man stood in front of the Gazebo and watched with interest as the hordes of visitors descended upon his island. He smiled and chuckled at all of the people and personalities on view in front of him. They really never changed. The fashion was different, and there was more diversity within the crowd, but the people, their personalities and their attitudes were the same as when he watched his first ferry disembark over thirty years before: the wealthy and entitled, the rude New Yorkers who thought that were in the Hamptons, college kids - male and female - looking to party and have sex, the daytrippers from the Cape, the seasonal workers, the nannies and au pairs, the young families, the older single women hoping to score, older couples anxious to enjoy another summer, and the hardworking and incredibly tolerant year-rounders.

He hadn't been born here - something he would always regret - but did feel like an adopted son, especially as he cared for the island year after year. He took that responsibility seriously as he felt there was no other place on earth as special and as near to his heart. But he knew it was a balance - it always was. The crush of visitors and Covid-era transients had eased somewhat in the past few years, but the demand on island resources remained high, especially in the summer months.

And he worried deeply about his charge. There wasn't a minute that passed that he didn't have some thought or concern about the impact these visitors had on his home. When he arrived in the early nineties, Nantucket was busy, but the crowds and the demands had been manageable. As time progressed and the island became more and more popular, those demands had multiplied. For the first time in its history, local government was talking about reaching a hypothetical maximum build-out. He worried that his efforts would no longer be enough to keep things in balance. This was his 34th year. Every year since his arrival, he had been successful in maintaining balance and ensuring the quality of life for residents and visitors alike remained high. But he felt like things were tipping away from him, that his efforts were losing their potency. That he might soon lose control.

He put a hand to his chin and surveyed the passengers as they passed. Some nodded and smiled. Most simply ignored him. He wondered which, if any, of them even thought about the impact they had on the island. And could one of them be the one, the one that might help keep the balance for another year?

A group of women emerged from the long line of blue baggage carts. Based on their stumbling and erratic footsteps, he knew they had been drinking and probably not paying much attention to the people around them. As he watched them, one in particular caught his eye. She looked strong, powerful, and smart. Very different from what he had offered in the past. Yes. This was what was needed to fully restore the balance.

He smiled to himself and fell in step behind them as they made their way down Straight Wharf.

CHAPTER FOUR

Nantucket

Friday, Memorial Day Weekend

Nature's first green is gold

Katie Chapman needed a break and some alone time.

Her footfalls fell naturally to the beat of the classic rock pumping through her AirPods. Her dad had turned her on to the genre when she was still in school, and her appreciation had grown since. Her current playlist had over two hundred songs, and she was adding to it regularly as she discovered "new" bands.

She held the stem on her right and heard the tone in her ears.

"Siri, play I Need You."

The voice responded in her ear. "Now playing, I Need You by Lynyrd Skynyrd."

The beat on the high hat and the familiar chords sent a thrill through her and brought a smile to her face, thinking of her fiancé. This was their song, and in a way, how they had first met.

She had been at a biotech conference in San Francisco, and the Saturday night entertainment had featured a classic rock cover band. The conference had pretty much been a bust so far, and she was hoping that the music might make the three-thousand-mile trip worth it. She had been sitting at the bar, sipping on a Manhattan and swaying to a decent cover of "Breakfast in America" when she felt him slide up next to her.

"You like Supertramp?"

She turned and looked into the steel gray eyes of Harrison Reid. He was slightly taller than her and was dressed in a blue striped button-down, a navy quarter zip, and tan dress pants. He stood out in a sea of men who looked like they had just rolled out of bed.

"I do. Though my favorite song by them is Long Way Home. You?" She had angled slightly toward him as she spoke, a small smile lingering as she rested her arm along the back of her chair.

"Yeah. But have to admit I'm more of a Skynyrd fan myself." He had glanced down at her, one corner of his mouth lifting, his fingers tapping lightly against the table.

"Really? I love Skynyrd!" She had smiled, instantly connecting with him and feeling a spark.

That revelation had started a conversation that lasted well into the night. They discovered they both lived in Cambridge, worked in the same industry, and had a number of shared acquaintances. Returning to Boston, they had started to see each other, and it wasn't long before she had fallen head over heels. And based on his reactions, she was pretty sure he felt the same.

The proposal had taken some time, though, despite the many hints she had dropped. But he was old school and had wanted to talk to her father before he popped the question. That had happened last Thanksgiving, and now, nearly nine months later, she was here on Nantucket to celebrate her upcoming nuptials.

She and four friends had decided to have her bachelorette party on Nantucket. Her parents had brought her here as a child for a long weekend one summer, though she remembered little of it. But Harrison's sister, Madison, also her maid of honor, had spent considerable time on the island during college working as a server in several of the local establishments. She had jumped on the idea and had taken the lead in planning, wanting to make every effort to deliver a very special weekend for Katie.

The song had finished and automatically went to the next in her playlist, "Sultans of Swing". She glanced down at her phone to double-check where she was on her run. She had planned a simple out-and-back and was hoping she was getting to the turnaround point. Although she was barely thirty years old, she had to admit to herself that she couldn't party like she used to, and she was feeling it.

They had arrived on the island late yesterday afternoon, already pretty well into the cocktails. Before their ferry, they had pre-gamed at a place on the Cape and enjoyed several rounds of adult beverages along with their clam chowder. The drinks continued on the boat, served by a couple of very attractive guys working the ferry as summer jobs. She feared things with her group had gotten a little out of hand based on the glances she saw from other passengers, and she had cringed at their behavior.

And the fun continued once they had landed. They had grabbed their rental Jeep, run out to their Airbnb in Siasconset to freshen up, and then taken the Wave bus back to Town, heading to Cisco Brewers for some good beer and live music. After that, it was off to The Brotherhood of Thieves for dinner, more drinks, and some lively karaoke at the Gaslight. They finally called it quits when they realized the last bus of the evening would be leaving at quarter to eleven. Between the bus and the walk from the Sconset rotary, it had taken them nearly an hour to get home. The others had retired to the patio for a nightcap, but she had called it quits. She needed the rest if she was going to keep up this pace.

Their "celebration weekend," as her maid of honor had called it, included a detailed itinerary, matching sweatshirts - in Nantucket red of course - and a plan to send Katie off into blissful matrimony with a four-day weekend of eating, drinking, and some light flirting.

She shook her head at the thought. She could no more cheat on Harrison than she could sprout wings and fly. She was loyal, sometimes to a fault, and had been brought up in a family where marriages lasted until death. Her parents had just celebrated their forty-fifth anniversary and acted as if they had just met a few weeks ago. They were her Northstar as relationships went, and she had every intention of achieving their level of happiness and success.

Harrison's parents, on the other hand, had divorced when he was in high school. Citing that they had grown apart and needed to pursue their own interests, Katie had thought they probably should never have gotten married in the first place. They were very different people in personality, political beliefs, and life goals. Having done some quick math, Katie realized that they probably married because they had to. Harrison, their only child, had been born eight months after they were wed.

She felt her phone vibrate and looked down at the map. She had reached the turnaround point, the trailhead for one of the many hiking trails on the island, and she slowed to a walk. Pausing her music, she stopped at a picnic table and pulled her running pack off. She set it on the table and slid out her water bottle. Flipping open the top, she took a long drink, quenching the thirst she had developed in the first three miles of her run. It was then that she heard the car entering the small parking lot adjacent to the trailhead, its tires crunching on the shells used to pave the space.

The driver, a lone man, parked the car, got out, and stretched. He was older, dressed in hiking gear, and as he caught her eye, he smiled. He had a knee brace on his right leg and walked with a slight limp to the back of his car. He rummaged in the trunk and brought out a small pack, a wide-brimmed hat, and a can of what looked like insect spray.

Being a woman, she was always on alert, especially in this type of situation. She was alone, in a quiet area with no other people or activity, and had no easy means of escape. He wasn't giving off any negative vibes, and given his age and dress, he was probably harmless. Still, she paced slowly well away from him and prepared herself for the return run. Slipping the now-empty water bottle back in her pack, she slid the pack on her back, buckled the strap below her chest, and pulled up her phone to start a new playlist, the first one that she and Harrison had curated together. They had jokingly called it the Katerson Hit Parade. The first song was "Hotel California."

She glanced up and noticed that the man was walking toward her. She felt a bolt of fear, but then compelled herself to settle down. She forced a smile.

He lifted his hand. "Hi. Sorry to bother you, but have you done this trail? This is my first time, and I've got a bad knee. So, just curious if there are any tough stretches I should know about. I went on the ACKTrails app, but there wasn't much detail."

She relaxed. "Sorry, I can't help you there. I didn't do the trail. I've just been on a run. This was my turnaround point."

"Oh, okay," he said, looking up and squinting at the sun. "Well, you certainly have a beautiful day for your run."

"Yes, it is. And a good day for a hike. For you."

He smiled. “Yes. Well, enjoy the rest of your run.”

She nodded. “Thanks,” and began to turn.

He moved quickly. He raised the aerosol can in his right hand and sprayed it directly into her face.

She recoiled as the insect repellent clouded her vision and burned her throat.

Did he just spray me in the face with bug spray?

Confused, she waved her hands in front of her face in an attempt to clear the air and get a fresh breath. She hit the brow of her new hat and sent it tumbling to the ground. Strangely, she wanted to lean over to retrieve it - *why do I care about that right now!* - but before she could, she felt a stinging in her right thigh. Almost immediately, her world started to fade. She tried to run, her brain shouting at her to escape, but her legs would not respond. Stumbling, she drunkenly pulled up her phone only to have it ripped out of her hands. Confused and dizzy, she looked at him. He shifted in and out of focus, her eyes desperately trying to assess what was happening to her. In a moment of brief clarity, she saw his smiling face had been replaced with one of determination, and she felt a terrorizing stab of fear.

So this is what it’s like. This is how it feels to be taken. This is what I have feared my entire life.

Harrison!

His beautiful face flashed through her mind as she felt his hands grab her. Her world was darkening. What had he used on her? She feared she was dying. She felt her legs weaken, and she struggled to stay upright, desperate to escape. Escape to the life she loved. Escape back to Harrison and the joy she felt at the thought of their upcoming life together. A lone tear traced its way down her cheek as she felt her consciousness fading away.

She started to collapse, but he was there to catch her. His strong grip held her upright, and he marched her toward his vehicle, her feet dragging on the shells and leaving twin trails toward his car. He scanned the area looking for potential witnesses, but the parking lot and the field surrounding it were quiet. Satisfied, he popped his trunk and carefully folded her in. She was all but unconscious now; the propofol had worked its magic quickly. Still, he pulled her ankles and wrists together and used large zip ties to bind them. He didn't bother with a gag as he didn't want to increase a possible suffocation risk. Plus, the propofol would keep her out for at least an hour, so he had more than enough time to get her home and properly confined.

He loved propofol.

He had discovered this wonder drug by accident when he had had his first colonoscopy earlier in the year at Cottage Hospital. He was amazed at how quickly it knocked him out and thought it would be a good addition to his toolkit. Further research identified some risks with direct injection, but given his intended use, he thought those risks were tolerable. Obtaining it had been far easier than he thought. This was his first use of it in the field, and so far, it was a five-star review.

Satisfied she was as comfortable as possible, he closed the trunk carefully, making sure not to hurt her in the process, after all, he wasn't an animal. She was scared, yes, he had to admit that. But he knew once she understood what this would mean in the big picture, then she would appreciate what he was doing. Maybe even embrace it. She was going to play an instrumental role in maintaining the balance of life on Nantucket.

Slipping off the backpack, he opened it to retrieve a Faraday bag. He turned off her phone, the latest iPhone by the look of it, and placed it in the bag, and then slipped it all back in his pack. Adding the bug spray, he slid the pack behind the driver's seat. Closing the door, he took a long look around to confirm he was still alone. Just a couple of things left to do, and then he could get her home.

He smoothed the tracks left by her running shoes and then grabbed her hat. He thought briefly about keeping it. What a souvenir this would make! He could relive this time again and again, and only he would know just how special this hat was. But another thought came to mind, one that would likely improve his chances of success.

Ten minutes later, he glanced around one final time to ensure he hadn't overlooked anything and made his way to the driver's door. Stealing one final glance, he slid behind the wheel, started the car, and pulled slowly out of the small parking lot. As he made the left onto Polpis Road, a pack of bicyclists pulled off the bike path and into the parking lot for Windswept Bog. They pedaled up to the picnic table and began to dismount.

He looked in the rearview mirror at the cyclists and smiled. His timing had been perfect. He was certain now more than ever that she was the one.

It was all about the balance.

CHAPTER FIVE

Three Months Before Memorial Day

FBI Agent Rick Caton was in downtown Nantucket, wearing the uniform from his days as a Community Service Officer. The streets were empty as fog curled along the cobblestones like smoke from a fire that's already burned everything down. The harbor was dry with boats stranded and leaning sideways on the cracked silt. Where the Brant Point lighthouse should have been was the much larger Sankaty Head. At the top of its arched brick body, the lantern room had been painted red, and what looked like blood dripped off the railings. Inside, its light blinked slowly like it was running off a dying battery.

He felt a throbbing underfoot as if the earth was trying to warn him of an impending danger.

Like his days as a CSO, he was walking a beat. In his dream, he made his way past the parking lot at the Stop & Shop by the harbor. Several people had gathered, grouped around something that was lying on the asphalt. As he passed, they looked up at him. Where smiling faces should have been, there was a shielded, black emptiness. A twinge of fear coursed through his body, and he quickly walked away.

As he made his way up Main Street, the normally cheerful storefronts were replaced by emptiness, with shadows swirling behind them. The signs hanging above the doors creaked in the wind. The names of the stores, as he had remembered, had been replaced with words that appeared to have been written in blood. One said TRAITOR. Another, YOU LET HER DIE.

He turned a corner and found himself outside the old police station. A single red light glowed from inside, pulsing like a heartbeat.

He tried the door. The knob wouldn't turn. Locked.

From behind him, a voice grumbled: "You should've stayed gone."

He turned, but no one was there—just the ocean in the distance, rising fast, black and unnatural. It crashes down the street like it doesn't care about maps or memories. He turns to run, but the water catches him. Salt in his mouth. Cold in his bones.

As he sinks, he sees her —arms outstretched, reaching for him —her mouth forming a word he can't hear.

Gasping, Rick woke in the dark, breath ragged, heart hammering. At first, he panicked, not knowing where or who he was. But as he regained consciousness, reality started to reassemble itself. A distant siren reminded him he was still in his apartment on Berkshire Street in Cambridge. He stared at the ceiling, trying to gather his thoughts as he watched the shadows of tree limbs stirring in the wind. He let out a long breath. Just another stress dream playing on his worries and concerns about the move back to the island.

With a start, he realized that today was the day, and probably why his unconscious brain was acting up. Later today, he was planning on meeting with his boss at the FBI, Special Agent in Charge Hanna Fines, to submit his resignation, and he's pretty sure he knows how she will react. Disappointed? Definitely. But she had always been supportive of him, and he had no doubt she would be again. What he doesn't know is how he will react once that trigger has been pulled. Sadness? Reluctance? Yes. Excitement and the prospect of being back on Nantucket with the woman he fell in love with? Absolutely. But was he making the right choice? Was he rushing things?

Maybe he should give it some more time. Stay in Cambridge for another six months or a year and make sure this was the right decision.

But Nantucket was pulling at him. And his relationship with the island was complicated.

His parents, third-generation owners of a local restaurant, had wanted Rick, an only child, to join them and take over. But he had no interest in becoming the fourth generation to run the local establishment. He had other ideas. As long as he could remember, he had had the desire to protect others, and that had drawn him to law enforcement.

After graduating from Nantucket High School, he received his degree in Criminal Justice from UMass Lowell and then returned to the island, where he joined the Nantucket Police Department as a recruit. He was sent off for intensive training at the police academy in Plymouth and, following graduation, returned to Nantucket to start his career as a police officer. He had mapped out his career path and planned to build his skills and become a detective. He had hoped to spend his entire career with the NPD, perhaps one day even assuming the role of chief of police.

That dream had been derailed by a very public falling out with his wife at the time. She was a demanding spendthrift who also happened to be the daughter of the Nantucket Chief of Police. Catching her kissing another man in a crowded restaurant, the confrontation resulted in a viral incident, which did not go over well with the NPD, the Tourism Board, or the Town Manager.

Despite his three years on the job and mostly strong performance reviews, he had been fired. Many on the island thought he had been wronged - she was the one having the affair after all - but he had left the island with his tail tucked between his legs.

He had settled on the Cape and bounced around trying on different careers, but nothing seemed to fit. At a friend's suggestion, he had applied to join the FBI and was accepted, sneaking in under their mandatory age restriction with a few years to spare. After graduating from Quantico, he had been stationed at the FBI's Chelsea Field Office. With his natural curiosity and sharp intellect, his career had blossomed at the FBI, focusing on financial crimes. He had successfully closed several high-profile cases, and his future at the Agency was bright.

But that had changed with a single phone call the prior summer. An old family friend, Charles Post, had been found dead on a local beach. While the local authorities had written it off as a terrible accident, his wife, Ann, suspected otherwise. She had called Rick and begged him to investigate. Reluctantly, he had returned to the island only to discover that Ann had died as well, and the situation was far more complex and far-reaching than he had anticipated.

With the help of one of Nantucket's best detectives, Tuna Fisch, and leveraging many FBI resources, he had wrapped up that case in a week. But it was during those seven days that he came to the realization that he wanted to come home to the island. As much as he enjoyed his career at the FBI, he missed the people, the community, and the sheer beauty of the little speck of sand thirty miles out to sea. When the new leadership at the Nantucket Police Department offered him the position of detective, he knew that it was the right move and jumped at the chance.

And then of course, there was Felicity.

She was the daughter of Ann and Charles Post, and Rick had babysat her and her older brother Scott for several years. He had remembered her as a shy, gawky, and gap-toothed first grader. But she had grown into a beautiful, intelligent, and impressive young lady who had been a huge help to Rick in solving her parents' case.

That had been over five months ago, and a lot had happened in the interim.

Felicity had left her position as the director of a non-profit in Providence and relocated back to the island. She had moved into her parents' house off Monomoy Road and assumed a new role with a local foundation focused on developing affordable housing solutions. She and Rick had casually dated long distance - he had the ferry schedules memorized - but had agreed to hold off on anything serious until, if and when, he made the move back to Nantucket.

Making that move had been a very difficult decision for Rick to make, despite the powerful pull of Nantucket and all it had to offer.

Leaving the FBI would be like leaving his work family. He had a great boss in Hanna and was surrounded by a close team of dedicated and hard-working professionals. He knew he would always have their friendship and, if needed, could lean on them for assistance if and when that would occur. But he would miss the daily interactions, the satisfaction of bringing down white-collar criminals, and the sense that he was indeed making the world a better place.

But on the See-Saw in his mind, the balance always seemed to tip toward Nantucket and Felicity.

He got out of bed and padded down the narrow hallway to the kitchen. It was late January, and sunrise was still nearly three hours away. But he couldn't sleep now. His mind was still buzzing from the dream and his upcoming meeting. He opened the cabinet and pulled out a pod for the coffee machine. He looked out the window as the machine heated up and then loudly groaned out his coffee, rudely breaking the silence of his apartment.

We can put a man on the moon, but can't make a quiet coffee machine?

He grabbed the mug and blew the steam off the top. Taking a tentative sip, he thought again for the hundredth time about the words he was going to use with his boss.

...A very difficult decision to make...It's the right time for me to go back...Will really miss working with you and the team...did some great work together...Hope you understand...I can give you six weeks' notice...

Now almost forty-five, he felt the same nervous jitters as he had when he put on the uniform of the NPD for his first day on the job. He smiled at himself, thinking of the awkward recruit he had been, worried sick that he was not going to be a good cop. But that had quickly passed, and as he gained his footing, he realized that he really did have a knack for police work. And with the exception of a couple of years pause due to the incident with his now ex-wife, he had proven that.

But this next transition was far more nerve-racking than his first day on the job. He would be leaving a successful career at the FBI for the hope, the dream, of community policing on Nantucket and perhaps, if he would even let himself think about it, the potential of a life with Felicity.

He finished his coffee and put the empty mug in the sink. Time to get going and get this done.

A light snow overnight had covered his agency-issued Dodge Charger, and it took him a few minutes to clear the windshield, back window, and door glass. He had started the car before he tackled the snow, so it was warming up nicely. He pulled away from his parking spot on York Street and made his way to Chelsea.

The office was quiet, and he was happy to be in before his colleagues. He grabbed a coffee from the kitchen and walked to his office. On his desk were a half dozen file folders from the current cases he was working on. As usual, they represented all that was wrong with people. Men and the occasional woman who were hell-bent on enriching themselves at the expense of others.

His colleague, Mia, said it was just "people peopling". Mankind had been dealing with theft since the first two humans got together, and not much had changed other than what they stole.

He reviewed the files and mentally made notes on how quickly he would be able to close them out and get what the Suffolk County District Attorney needed to prosecute the cases. He didn't want to leave Hanna or any of his colleagues with an open case. They had enough on their plates as it was.

Footsteps came down the hall, and there was a tap on the door.

"You're in early," said Hanna.

Rick smiled as he looked at her. "Yes. Just want to review these cases and make a plan for wrapping them up."

"Good. You know I love closed cases." She started to leave.

"Hanna?"

She leaned back into the doorway.

"Can I grab you for a few minutes? Just need to talk to you. Personal thing."

Hanna looked surprised. "Sure, Rick. Um, I've got a regional update meeting at nine, which should be done by eleven. Pop by then?"

"Sure. Thank you."

She turned and walked down the hall toward her office.

Rick took a deep breath and, for the hundredth time in the past week, rehearsed how he was going to tell his boss he was leaving.

...An impossible decision to make...Great opportunity to get back to Nantucket...Will really miss working with you and the team...Yes, we did some great work together...Hope you understand...I can give you eight weeks' notice... I will get all of my cases wrapped up and over to the DA...Please don't hate me...

The time passed quickly, and before long, Rick was standing outside Hanna's office, feeling like the high school student whose been called to see the principal.

Hanna was at her desk, absorbed by something on her computer screen.

He tapped on the door frame. "Hanna?"

She looked up. "Rick, please come in."

He took a seat in a chair facing her desk and put his hands in his lap.

"What's up?"

Rick paused, rubbing his hands in his lap, and then took a deep breath. He looked up intently at his boss.

"It is with a lot of regret, but I need to resign my position with the Bureau."

She paused, leaned back in her chair, and steepled her fingers. A pensive look came across her face. "You know, when you first joined us, I had some concerns about you. To be honest, I didn't think you were going to make it. Joining the Bureau so late in your career? But you worked hard, applied yourself, and had some real wins." She paused, reflecting. "You remember the Hermann Capital case?"

He smiled and nodded.

"I thought you were chasing your tail. Nothing there. But you dug in, pulled the resources you needed, and built a strong case showing how the two founders were essentially using the firm as their personal ATM machine. We clawed back millions for investors and put two shady actors in prison. That case was all you. And that's when I knew my doubts were unfounded. That you were going to be a real asset to the FBI."

"Thanks, Hanna."

She smiled softly. "You know, I was kind of expecting this. After your case there last fall, I thought maybe you had thoughts of rejoining the Nantucket Police. But then, nothing happened, so I thought you had changed your mind and decided to stay with us."

"Believe me, it has been an incredibly difficult decision to make. And I have gone back and forth on it, but in the end I know it's the right move for me."

"I appreciate that. And glad you took your time on the decision. So you are sure?"

He nodded. "I am."

"Okay, well, I have two things to say to you, Rick." She blew out a breath and leaned forward in her chair.

He looked at her anxiously, fearful for what was coming. Was she going to fire him on the spot? Tell him to pack his bags and go, never to darken her door again?

"One. If it doesn't work out, for whatever reason, you will always have a position here. I might need to juggle some things, but I will always want you on my team."

Rick let out a long sigh of relief. "Thank you, Hanna, that means a lot. It really does."

"And secondly, if you need us for any reason, we are here for you. I know there is a process for local law enforcement to access FBI resources, but I'm letting you know that all you have to do is call. We'll do what we can, within reason, of course." She smiled.

Rick returned the smile. "Thanks so much, Hanna. I really appreciate it. I'm going to miss you guys. We really did a lot of good work together."

She nodded. "We will miss you, too, Rick. So what are you thinking for your last day?"

"Well, my apartment lease is up on May first. And I still have several cases that need closure. So I was thinking end of April?"

"Umm, sure. That works. Are you going to tell the team?"

"Yes. Now that we've talked, I'll let Mia and the others know."

Hanna stood and walked around her desk. "Thanks, Rick. If you change your mind or need anything in the interim, please let me know. It's been a pleasure working with you, and I wish you nothing but the best on Nantucket." She extended her hand.

Rick shook her hand. “Thank you, Hanna. I appreciate everything you and the Bureau have done for me.”

He turned and walked out of her office feeling relieved, excited, and frightened all at the same time. Relieved the decision had finally been made, excited about his future with the NPD and Fel, and frightened that he was making the wrong call.

CHAPTER SIX

Three Weeks Before Memorial Day

Rick stood at the door to his small rental cottage with more than a little trepidation. Given the housing situation on the island, he felt lucky to have secured this little gray shingled Cape out by the island's only eighteen-hole public golf course. It was more expensive than his place in Cambridge, but worth it. It came furnished but in a style that really didn't fit that of a bachelor in his early forties. But he had no one to impress, and he didn't suspect Felicity would judge him on his taste - or lack thereof - on the interior decor.

His ferry had been delayed due to a late-season Nor'Easter, and he had spent two unexpected days in Hyannis. Fortunately, it was still the off-season, so he was able to secure a room for a reasonable rate and used the time to walk the docks, read in front of the wind and rain-battered windows of his hotel room, and enjoy some delicious meals at the Black Cat. It also gave him time to think and worry some more about his decision to leave the FBI and return to Nantucket.

Finally, the wind had died down, and the ferries returned to their schedules. After a rather choppy late afternoon crossing, Rick found himself standing at Straight Wharf with two large roller bags and waiting for a taxi. In his dream of returning to the island, he fantasized about walking down the gangplank on a gorgeous, warm day to a crowd of waiting friends and colleagues. Some had signs welcoming him home. Others had balloons. All were laughing and smiling, cheering him home like a war hero.

Reality hit him square in the side of the face.

He emerged from the ferry to temperatures in the fifties, gray skies, and a dreary mist of rain. The only person to greet him was a friendly Hy-Line employee directing him to the baggage claim area. He tightened his coat at the collar, dipped his head against the rain, and made his way to the baggage carts, where he retrieved his luggage. He cinched his backpack tight and then, grabbing a roller bag in each hand, ambled his way over the bricks and down to the taxi stand.

In his arrival daydream, he had hoped that Felicity would be sitting by the curb, her old Bronco idling, with a big smile on her face, ready to welcome him back. Instead, he found the clapped-out old minivan of a local cab company.

Sighing, he threw his luggage and backpack into the back and jumped through the sliding door.

"Where to?" asked a kindly, older woman.

"One seventy Summerville Road, please."

"Is that just past the Miacomet golf course?"

"Yes."

She nodded, put the car in gear, and pulled away, the old van swaying heavily from side to side on the cobblestones. The suspension creaked and groaned in protest while a number of plastic bits on the dashboard squeaked in solidarity.

Rick closed his eyes and leaned back into the seat. He had arrived on the island with little more than two suitcases of clothes. Following the divorce and his move off the island nearly a decade before, Rick had made a pointed effort to travel light. Even once he had settled in Cambridge, he kept his apartment simple with minimal furnishings. It wasn't the cheeriest place, but he really didn't need it to be, given that he spent the bulk of his time at the FBI offices in Chelsea. The few possessions he had managed to acquire in his years there had been carefully packed up and shipped ahead of him. He expected they were waiting for him in the small one-car attached garage in the back of the house.

The Chief of the NPD, Jodi Calpers, had requested a start date of June 1st so he could get his bearings and be fully ready for the upcoming summer season, which traditionally started on Memorial Day weekend. With his last day at the FBI in late April, the few weeks had given him the time necessary to put his affairs in order in Cambridge and get settled back on the island.

Being back on Nantucket felt weird, but knowing that it was a permanent move felt stranger still. Having been born and raised here as well as starting his career in law enforcement, he knew the island and its people well. But he had been away from the island for more then a decade, and if life had taught him anything, it was that things always change. People, places, communities, the environment. He was hoping, praying, that his decision to return was the right one.

He felt a contentment here on the island that he had never felt anywhere else. This was home with a big H, and it fit him like a well-worn sweater. His experience with the Post case the prior fall had been the key in his decision. In a way, it allowed him to take a test drive of being back on the island, to feel it out and see if it still fit. And of course, the people he had worked closely with, Tuna, Felicity, Peter Bois, and several NPD officers, including the new chief, had been incredibly welcoming and kind to him, despite the personal challenges of the case.

The minivan came to a stop and broke him out of his reverie. He looked at his rental cottage and smiled at the thought that this was his new home. No more apartment living with its narrow staircase that was such a pain to navigate, especially with his groceries. No more spending what seemed like hours trying to find a parking spot within three or four blocks. No more staring at the ceiling in the middle of the night, listening to his downstairs neighbor trying their best to quiet an infant dealing with teething.

He paid the driver, got out, and pulled his suitcases up to the front steps. This was it. After a few moments standing at the door, he summoned the courage, took a deep breath, and opened the door to his new life on Nantucket. Instantly, he was hit by the delicious smell of garlic, onion, and, he thought, fresh bread.

What the?

"Rick!"

Felicity came flying out of the kitchen and ran across the small hearth room to Rick, jumping into his arms. She kissed him hard on the mouth and embraced him intensely. It was all Rick could do to maintain his balance, but he relished the feeling of her against him. A lock of her auburn hair fell onto his face, and it smelled of lavender and soap. He inhaled deeply.

Home.

Felicity loosened her grip on him and leaned back to look into his brown eyes. "God, it is so good to see you. And you are here!" she said excitedly.

Rick smiled broadly. "I can't believe this is finally happening. It seems like it's been forever." He leaned in to kiss her again. "And how the hell did you get in here?"

Felicity laughed heartily. “I’m not sure I should share all my secrets with you. But if you have to know, since I started working with the foundation last fall, I have met a lot of people on the island who are dealing with the housing crisis here, and one of them, Yancy Garcia, also happens to own this little place. Your landlord, in other words.”

He chuckled. “You are amazing.”

She smiled warmly and pulled him in for another embrace, her head on his chest. “I just wanted to make your first moment back on the island special. Make you feel welcomed.” Her eyes twinkled.

He pulled back and looked into her face. “Thank you, Fel. To be honest, I was feeling a bit sorry for myself, what with the crappy weather and all. This? This is so sweet of you.” He lifted her chin and kissed her tenderly. He pulled back and looked around, his eyes shifting from left to right.

“What is that smell?” He turned toward the kitchen and saw smoke emanating from the doorway and trailing over the ceiling.

The smoke alarm began to blare.

“Oh god! I forgot I have food on the stove!” Felicity yelped. She ran from the room to the kitchen, where she was met with billowing smoke from the cooktop. She pulled the offending pan off the heat and quickly rinsed it under the water. Steam burst from the hot metal, but soon the smoking had stopped. She dumped the contents of the pan into the disposal.

Rick moved quickly through the living room, pushing windows up with both hands. Cool air rushed in. He grabbed a dishtowel from the counter and stood beneath the smoke alarm, waving it steadily, his arm making wide, rhythmic arcs.

The alarm stopped.

Felicity emerged from the kitchen, her shoulders slumped.

Rick lowered his dish towel and looked at Felicity tenderly. "Are you okay?"

"I'm fine," said Felicity, dejected. "But my pasta a la crema with chicken and garlic is not."

Rick pulled her into a hug. "Hey, it's okay."

She pulled back just enough to look at him, her brows knitting. "No, it's not. I wanted to make you a nice dinner. Make your first night back really special."

He smiled, reaching up to tuck her hair behind her ear. "Just you being here to welcome me is special. Dinner would have been great, I'm sure. But the important thing is you were here."

She searched his face."Are you sure?"

"Absolutely." He glanced past her toward the kitchen, then jerked his thumb in that direction. "Everything okay in there?"

"No. I need to turn the oven off. I'm sure the bread is totally burnt now." She pushed off and started back toward the kitchen.

Rick stepped aside, watching her go. "Why don't you do that, and I'll drag this luggage into my room. Then let's go find us some dinner."

She paused, glancing back at him over her shoulder. A small smile crept in despite everything. "Okay. Sounds like a plan. What did you have in mind?"

Rick thought for a minute. "How about the Tap Room?"

Her eyes were twinkling again. "Deal."

"Can you drive?" Rick asked sheepishly.

"Sure. I've got the Bronco."

Rick smiled broadly. Life was good.

CHAPTER SEVEN

2008

Known to everyone who would listen, Matilda Poole was battling a litany of ailments, including sciatica, a herniated disk, shingles, and a bleeding stomach ulcer precipitated by the constant state of financial worry caused by her incompetent husband. She was a frequent visitor to local businesses and spent more time talking about the challenges in her life than she did actually doing any kind of commercial transaction.

Not that she was particularly unpopular. She was a freelance writer who focused on selling Nantucket to would-be visitors, having her pieces published in travel magazines across the U.S., Canada, and even Europe. One of her more popular pieces, a few years back, had been published in an Irish travel magazine, resulting in an influx of Gaelic visitors the following summer. The local Irish pub, Kitty Murtagh's, did a grand business that season.

Her career of selling Nantucket meant that all of the local establishments tried to stay on her good side, hoping for a mention or positive review in one of her future destination articles. And that meant having the patience to listen to her non-stop griping about her health, her husband, and the blood-sucking editors who refused to pay her what she thought she was worth. And if it was one thing Matilda had, it was stamina for conversation. The unlucky target of her discourse would often have to suffer through an hour or more of dissection of everything that was wrong with her life, her body, and her no-good husband.

One of her frequent quarry had suggested after a particularly long-winded complaint about her back pain and sciatica that she see a specialist over on the Cape. That he had read about a new practice over at Cape Cod Hospital in Hyannis that focused on relieving just such pain, and that maybe Matilda would benefit from a visit.

Which is why Matilda was standing on the top deck of the Hy-Line one evening in late May. The eight p.m. return ferry had left just minutes before sunset, and the brilliant oranges and reds in the western sky did little to brighten her mood. The trip had been a bust. The doctor - quack really - had explained that Matilda's pain was almost certainly due to her imagination. They had run a full battery of tests and could find no physical or biological cause for her discomfort. The doctor, a spritely woman in her forties, had reflected on the power of the mind and how it can cause us to feel things that aren't really there. She suggested that Matilda take up meditation.

Fuming, she had choice words for the doctor and left the practice, slamming the door hard enough to rattle the glass in the window panes. She had buried her frustration in a bowl of clam chowder at The Black Cat and then made her way to the Hy-Line dock. By the time she was standing in line with the hundred or so other passengers, she began to feel better. She dismissed the doctor as incompetent and knew deep in her heart that her pain was all too real. Now halfway to the island and chilled in the cool spring air, she started to feel better. She turned to head inside.

The ferry made quick work of the remaining miles and soon was pulling up to its berth along Straight Wharf. The gangways were wheeled into place, luggage carts were towed to their usual spot down the wharf, and passengers soon disembarked.

Matilda was not among them.

It was several weeks before her absence was noted within the community. Her husband had been on a month-long sabbatical in Central America, where cell coverage was nonexistent. It was two of her regular victims who bumped into each other at the Stop & Shop that concluded that she was missing. Local police were called, an investigation ensued, and the realization was made that Matilda had somehow fallen off the ferry.

Given her career in promoting the island, The Inq & Mirror covered the case for a few days until it slowly faded away. No one in her circle really enjoyed her company, and her husband - the man she had complained about for years - had not yet been reached, so there was little push for more. It went down as an accidental death. How she had managed to fall off the ferry would provide years of speculative conversations among the locals. The more popular theories were that she had been pushed.

He had enjoyed some of these theoretical discussions with the local business people. It was a constant reminder to him that his work had been productive.

Balance had been maintained.

CHAPTER EIGHT

Katie Chapman regained consciousness several hours later to a splitting headache, a burning throat, and stinging eyes. It took her a moment to clear her vision and shake the cobwebs out of her pounding head sufficiently to understand where she was. She was lying on her back on a bed in a darkened room, looking up at a ceiling of wooden rafters. The air smelled dank and humid and reminded her of her parents' basement in their 19th-century home back in Rhode Island.

She shivered in the cool air and realized she was still wearing her running gear.

She sat up, swung her legs over the side of the mattress, and surveyed her position. The mattress was obviously old and heavily soiled. There were no pillows or blankets to be seen. It was thin and sat on a creaky, metal frame. Each movement she made was met with a noisy response.

She attempted to stand but was immediately pulled back down on the bed. She looked down at her hands and saw that while her left hand was free, her right was secured in a police style, bright metal handcuff. The other half of the handcuff was fastened to a red plastic-coated cable, which ran to the wall behind her.

She turned and followed the cable to its home, where it ended in a circular metal contraption that was bolted to the wall. A wisp of a memory floated into her mind, and she had thoughts of her childhood dog, Tucker.

It's a retractable dog run. I'm tied up using a retractable dog run.

A cold stab of fear flooded through her.

Lying back on the bed, she tried to remember what had happened and how she had ended up here. She had been running and had stopped at a trailhead to hydrate, retie her shoes, and load the new playlist that she and Harrison had made together. She closed her eyes, trying to remember. She'd been alone until that brown, old Chevy sedan had pulled in and parked halfway down the lot. Close enough to the trailhead entrance but far enough away to be non-threatening and respectful of her personal space.

She remembered watching the car carefully before turning back to her phone to load the new playlist. The sound of walking on the shells - the crunching - had caused her to turn back. Her memory was fuzzy; she barely remembered what the man approaching her had looked like, just that he was older and wearing a knee brace. She had been cautious at first, but his simple questions about the trails and explaining his bad leg had put her more at ease.

That had all been a ruse to get her to drop her guard, which she had. She flinched, remembering him spraying something in her face.

Bug spray! It was bug spray. That's why her throat and eyes burned. She wondered if there were any long-term health implications. She made a mental note to talk to her doctor about that when she got back to Cambridge.

When I get back to Cambridge? What if I'm dead tomorrow?

The fear buzzed through her system, and her mind started racing. What was he going to do to her? Was he going to assault her? Was he going to kill her? Torture her? Keep her here forever? She thought of all the true crime podcasts she listened to, and it didn't take long before she had multiple frightening scenarios depicting her future playing in her mind.

Stop it!

She closed her eyes and forced herself to meditate, to calm her racing thoughts. She was not going to be a victim. First, she had to clear her mind of the fear and negativity so she could think coherently and create a plan to get the hell out of here. If she could lead a team to launch a billion-dollar drug in the ultra-competitive pharmaceutical market, then she could figure out a way to escape.

She took a deep breath and forced her body to relax. Then she began to feel around and under the bed for her running pack and her phone. Nothing. It was unlikely that he'd be stupid enough to leave those with her, but it was worth a shot.

Next, she examined her clothing, noting that her socks, sneakers, and running gear did not appear to have been removed or fussed with. Given how tight her leggings were, she knew she would remember if he had tried to undress her. She quickly felt her breasts and between her legs. All normal. She sighed with relief.

As her eyes adjusted to the darkness, she started to do a visual reconnaissance of the room. Her initial impressions were correct, as it appeared that she was in the basement of a house or similar structure. The walls were cement but covered in what looked like mold or algae. The air was heavy with humidity and smelled of mildew and dirt.

The floor was also concrete and looked as if it hadn't been swept in years. Dirt, leaves, and dust bunnies covered the surface.

At the end of the bed, she noticed a five-gallon plastic bucket, a roll of toilet paper, and two plastic bottles of water. Pulling against the retractable cable, which squeaked in protest, she reached down and retrieved one of the waters. She opened it and sniffed, careful to make sure it hadn't been tampered with. Satisfied, she took a long drink and then splashed some of the water into her eyes to help relieve the burning from the bug spray. She felt immediately better.

She continued her visual recon of the room.

It was an open space unbroken by walls or dividers of any kind. And unlike her parents' basement, it was mostly empty of life's detritus normally stored in a basement - old appliances, clothing, tools, and equipment. Her bed seemed to be the only piece of furniture in the room.

In the middle of the room, a single, bare light bulb dangled from a cord. The light was off, and she wondered if even if it was on, it would provide enough light to see anything down here. She followed the cord up to where it terminated in a rusty, electrical box mounted to one of the rafters.

Probably controlled by a switch at the top of the stairs.

Across from her bed was a blank expanse of wall. The concrete block appeared to have been painted at some point in its life, but the conditions had not been kind to the surface. What paint was left was peeling off, revealing the pitted concrete block underneath. Someone once thought to try to make this space a little nicer and failed miserably.

On the wall to the left of her berth, there were two small windows near the ceiling, each a couple of feet across and a foot high. The glass was black with dirt and cobwebs, and she could just barely make out some landscaping outside. Hydrangeas? Below each window was wooden shelving, each about five feet wide with a dark gap in between. The shelves held the only items in the basement: a few small cardboard boxes and what looked like old electronics. Maybe a stereo?

She glanced to her right and studied the wall. Her night vision was improving, and she could see the dark frame of stairs that looked to lead to the first floor. There was a small landing after the first step, where the stairs turned ninety degrees and followed the wall up. Under every third step was a two-by-four to reinforce the stringer. The stairs were steep and looked only a couple of feet wide.

Is that how he got me down here?

Seeing the dimensions of the staircase, she looked around, wondering if there was a second entrance. She had seen enough of the man to know that he didn't appear to be particularly strong and would have struggled significantly trying to carry her down those stairs, especially if he really had a bad knee. She squinted into the shadows, trying to make out any opening, and, emerging from the darkness between the shelves to her left, she could just make out some concrete steps. Of course! Those steps probably led up to an exterior bulkhead door, pretty common in New England.

She felt a small tug of hope knowing she was beginning to get a feel for the space. Now, if she could only find something that would help her escape.

She turned her attention to the handcuffs and the dog cable. The metal handcuff was tight around her wrist, and there was no way she would be able to work her hand out of them. The wire rope of the dog run was secured to the other cuff with a loop and a crimped ferrule. No joy there. The plastic and steel retractable mechanism itself was anchored into the concrete block using expansion toggles with special hex head bolts. She would probably need a two-foot breaker bar to loosen those.

Katie stood up, turned, and pulled hard on the cable. How much running did she have? Tugging the cable with her right hand, she walked as far as she could across the room until the reel reached its end. With the cable stopped, she found that if she stretched herself out, pulling hard on the cuffs and the cable, she could just touch the middle step of the staircase, about eye level.

Satisfied, she walked slowly back to the bed while the reel retracted the cable. She stopped the retraction several feet before the end and tucked the excess cable under her as she sat down. Now she could sit normally and start to work on a plan.

She had no idea of the time, but her instinct suggested it had only been a couple of hours since she had been taken. So that meant she was likely still on Nantucket. That was good. She thought it would be easier to find her on this small island than on the mainland, but only if she could stay alive.

The sound of a lawnmower broke into her thoughts.

Wait? What?

She looked to the left, out of the dingy windows, and could just see some movement.

Was her captor mowing the fucking lawn? While she was a prisoner down here?

She squinted to see if she could make out any further detail of the man, but the windows were so covered in dirt and cobwebs that she could really only see the occasional movement as the lawnmower went by the window. Strangely, she thought of her dad mowing their large back yard every Saturday morning. Shaking her head of the memory, she followed the noise it made as it passed from the left to the right, and then reversed. Gradually, it got fainter and fainter as she realized the mowing was getting farther from the house.

The wooden floor above her squeaked.

She startled. Wasn't he alone? Or did he have one or more accomplices who were going to help him? Fear flooded through her, but she fought it and fought it hard.

I am not going to be a victim. Again.

She thought of her accident, her mind flashing to the large grill of the pickup truck just before it hit her broadside. She could see the face of the man driving. Older, balding, thin as a rail, and looking at his phone. He hadn't even bothered to stop to see if he had hurt her.

Bastard.

A full recovery had taken months; she still felt the occasional stab of pain through her hips and leg, especially when the weather was cold. She was not going to allow someone to hurt her again. But she also knew from listening to those podcasts that time was of the essence. She couldn't just sit around and wait to be rescued. She had to take the lead and save herself.

Her recon of the space had not identified any possible escape or even a weapon to defend herself. She looked at her shoes and clothing. Maybe she could use the laces? But what the hell was she going to do with them? Use them like a whip and maybe raise a welt on his arm? It was not like she was going to be able to tie up her captor. She shook her head. She had the dog leash. Maybe she could somehow get the cable around his neck and use it as a garrote?

Surveying the bed, she lifted the mattress to see what was underneath and was pleased to see an old-fashioned metal frame. Between the squared rails ran a metal grid that looked similar to a chain link fence. Every foot, the grid was anchored to the rails with a small spring. There might be some potential here. She fingered the springs and the grid to see if she could release them, but to no avail. She would need some leverage.

She let the mattress fall back on the frame, turned, and sat down heavily. She couldn't believe this was happening to her. This was supposed to be her special weekend, a weekend of fun, celebration, and joy about her upcoming wedding. A tear ran down her cheek.

Harrison.

She thought it cliché, but he truly was the man of her dreams. She had all but given up on the dating scene, finding most men boorish, ill-mannered, and poorly dressed. And given her job, an executive with a leading biotech firm making high six figures, she doubted any man she met would be okay with her out-earning him.

But then she had found Harrison, and completely by accident. Not only did they share the same taste in music, but they also had similar life goals and aspirations. Instead of being intimidated by her position, he found it fascinating and listened enthralled as she shared stories about product development, challenging meetings with the scientists, and how she hoped to help the lives of millions of people fighting rare diseases. On more than one occasion, he expressed how proud he was of her work and would do anything to further her career.

She sighed heavily and thought he was probably going out of his mind.

Then her thoughts turned to her parents. They too, would be freaking out for sure and desperate for answers. Katie and her mom had always been close, talking two or three times a day if not more. And when they weren't talking, they would be texting, sharing pictures, and snippets of their activities. Her dad, too, would be worried, but he was more of the get things done kind of guy. He probably was chartering a jet to get them to the island as quickly as possible. She smiled sadly.

She missed them. She missed Harrison. But she was going to get out of here. She was going to live and make this bastard pay for what he had done to her.

CHAPTER NINE

Friday

Memorial Day Weekend

The past few weeks had flown by for Rick. He had settled into a new routine quickly and had spent his time off reading, walking, and enjoying time with Felicity. He had even managed to squeeze in a couple of fishing trips out to Great Point. Felicity had loaned him the Bronco, and despite a concerning increase in engine temperature, the classic old truck had performed well.

Rick had just finished lunch when his phone trilled. Hoping it was Felicity, he was disappointed to see Detective Tina Fisch's name on his screen. He lifted the phone cautiously and tapped the answer button.

"Tuna?"

"Rick. Good morning."

"Morning. To what do I owe the pleasure? I'm not officially on the clock for a few more days."

Tuna chuckled. "I know. But we have a new case, and we really need your help."

"A case? What's going on?"

"It's a missing woman. She's part of a bachelorette party, the bride in fact, and hasn't been seen since this morning."

Rick pulled the phone back and looked at the time. "It's just past one. Couldn't she just be out for a walk? Or grabbing lunch somewhere? It seems a little quick to me to label her missing."

"Normally, yes. I'd agree with you. But this case is different."

"How so?"

"I can brief you when you get to the station. How soon can you be here?"

Rick sighed. "Well, I still don't have a car, so I'll need to call a taxi. Let's plan for two o'clock."

"Sounds good," agreed Tuna. "I'll be waiting for you there." She disconnected the call.

Rick walked into his small kitchen, a trace of Felicity's burned meal a few weeks ago still apparent to his sensitive nose, and grabbed the magnetic card of a taxi service off the fridge. He dialed the number and requested a ride. He hung up, thinking he probably could have used his ride share app, but thought a local taxi was somehow more appropriate for Nantucket.

The taxi arrived, and soon Rick was heading to the station. What had been largely a theoretical exercise - his rejoining the Nantucket Police - was becoming more real by the mile. The taxi driver, a young Black woman, had made small talk about the weather, the crowds, and the upcoming Figawi weekend.

He had heard little of it, his thoughts once again turning to his decision and feeling that nervous energy in his stomach. A feeling that gathered strength the closer they got to the station.

Ten minutes later, she pulled into the parking lot. He settled the fare with a generous tip and closed the door. He turned and looked at the building. When he walked through that door, it would be official. Until now, he had thought that if things didn't feel right, he could change his mind and head back to Cambridge and the FBI.

But things did feel right. His days on the island had reinforced his decision. The people had been welcoming, the scenery beautiful, and he had slipped Nantucket on like a well-loved robe. He was ready to rejoin his old life here and the NPD.

For the second time, he reminded himself.

He took a deep breath, opened the door, and proceeded upstairs to the detective room. Walking through the framed entry, he surveyed the space and noticed little had changed in the last ten years. A half dozen tan, shoulder-height cubicles sat in the center of the space, each not much bigger than your average walk-in closet. Along one wall, a massive copier sat next to a cabinet unit that held copy paper, office supplies, and a coffee maker. Directly across from the entry, a line of double-hung windows let in some natural light and offered an outstanding view of the parking lot. In the corner, an open door led to the chief's office. He could see the lights were on and make out the edge of her desk.

"Rick!"

He turned to see Tuna approaching quickly. She came up and gave him a big hug. "Welcome back to the NPD!"

Rick smiled. "Thanks, Tuna. It's good to be here."

"We are all just thrilled to have you back, Rick. You will be a great addition to the team, and we are all excited to work with you."

He nodded. "Thanks for the warm welcome. It does feel good to be back, although I really thought I might have a few more days to settle in. Can you tell me what's up with this case?"

A determined look crossed Tuna's face. "Yes. We will get to that in a minute. But first, I've been given the job of bringing you to the Chief. She wanted to welcome you personally."

Rick nodded. "Of course."

He followed Tuna to the corner of the room and the chief's office.

They entered a bright, well-lit space where a large oak desk sat perpendicular to the corner. Two sets of windows behind the desk looked out over Fairgrounds Road. Chief Jodi Calpers, trim, fit, and sandy-haired, was sitting behind a computer monitor, the keys clacking as she typed. She glanced over the screen and, seeing Rick and Tuna, stood quickly and made her way around the desk.

"Rick!" she said and extended her hand. "Welcome back to the NPD."

"Thank you, Chief," said Rick, shaking her hand.

"It is so good to have you here. Thank you for trusting the team and me in what must have been a very difficult decision."

Rick nodded. "It was. But I know the right one. I'm anxious to get started."

"Well, we would really appreciate it if we could have you start today. We really need your investigative skills on this one. I know your original start date was planned for June first, but, as I said, we really need your help."

"Tuna mentioned a missing woman. What do we know so far?"

"Yes, we received a call about a missing woman a couple of hours ago. She was part of a bachelorette party on the island, the bride-to-be."

"Okay. Why the concern when she's only been missing a few hours? She could be out shopping, hanging with a new friend, who knows what?"

The chief nodded. "Normally, yes, we wouldn't get too concerned, but this feels different. In fact, my gut tells me she's been taken."

"Kidnapped?" exclaimed Rick. "What's pointing to that?"

The captain sighed. "It's just a few things that have come to light, like her phone is off the grid. And her friends swear she never would have gone anywhere without telling them. Again, it's just a feeling."

Rick smiled softly. "Cop instinct. I get it. Anything else?"

Chief Calpers shook her head. "No. I'm hoping it's nothing. That my gut is wrong. I mean, we've seen it before, they meet someone, and show back up a few hours later. But…" her voice trailed off.

"Understood. How do you want me to proceed?"

"I want you to work with Tuna on this one," nodding to Detective Tina Fisch, known to friends, colleagues, and family affectionately as Tuna. "You two did such great work on the Post case last fall. She'll be the lead, though, as you still need to get your sea legs under you."

"Of course." Rick turned and smiled at Tuna. She returned the expression.

The chief continued. "I've asked Officer Downs to brief you as soon as you two are ready. He had first contact with the reporting party."

Rick dipped his chin in acknowledgment.

"Great," The chief said, stopping and looking between them. "Let me know if there is anything I can do to help you settle in."

"Thank you," said Rick. He and Tuna turned to leave.

"Oh, and Rick?"

Rick paused mid-step and looked back over his shoulder. "Yes?"

The chief's expression softened. "Welcome home. I wish it were under better circumstances. But we are happy to have you back."

Rick nodded and smiled. "Thanks, Chief."

He and Tuna left the office and made their way over to her desk in the cubicle farm.

Rick leaned one hand against the edge of her desk, his brow furrowing. "That is concerning," said Rick, emphatically.

Tuna slid into her chair and glanced up at him."What's that? That the chief suspects a kidnapping?"

Rick nodded. "Yeah. I mean, that sort of thing just doesn't happen here on Nantucket."

"No, it doesn't." She spun slightly in her chair, thinking. "I can't recall a case like this in my career. I mean, we have some child custody issues where a parent grabbed a kid. But having a young woman taken off the street? Never."

"Well, we need to work under that assumption. Which means time is of the essence." He tapped the desk lightly. "How quickly can we get the details?"

Tuna held up a finger and picked up the phone. She dialed a few numbers. Rick could hear the phone ringing on the other end.

"Officer Downs? It's Tuna." A pause. "Yes, I'm good, thanks. Do you have a minute to update Detective Caton and me on the Chapman case?"

Rick heard a murmur of agreement.

"Excellent," said Tuna. "We'll be in the conference room." She put the phone down, swiveled in her chair, and looked at Rick. "He's on his way up. Let's go down to the conference room. You need anything?'

"I wouldn't say no to a coffee. Has it gotten any better in the ten years since I left?" said Rick, chuckling.

Tuna snorted. "Um, no. If anything, it's gotten worse. But it's black and full of caffeine."

"That's all I need."

Settling into the chairs in the conference room, Rick took a sip of coffee when Officer John Downs entered. He had a manila file folder under one arm and moved quickly to Rick with his other hand extended.

"Agent Caton. Great to see you again. And welcome to the NPD."

Rick stood and shook his hand firmly. "Thanks, Officer Downs, er, John. And please call me Rick. I'm no longer an agent," he said, somewhat wistfully.

"Of course," said Downs. He pulled out a chair and took a seat across from Rick and Tuna.

"What can you tell us about this case, John?" asked Tuna.

Downs opened the manila file folder. "She was reported missing late this morning." He pulled a few pages and placed them in front of Tuna and Rick. Rick reached out and pulled them closer.

"Her name is Katie Chapman, age thirty-two. Was on the island for a bachelorette party. Her soon-to-be sister-in-law, um, a Madison Reid," he glanced at the file, "is the one who made the report."

Rick nodded. "What do we know so far?"

"They'd only been on the island for a day, arrived yesterday afternoon on the two-twenty-five Hy-Line. Apparently, they've been partying pretty hard. They've got a rental out in 'Sconset." He looked at the papers. "Total bridal party is five women. Katie, of course. The sister-in-law whom I mentioned, a prior roommate, and two colleagues from work."

"Do we have a picture?" Rick asked, looking up.

"Yes. Ms. Reid texted me one after I took her report." He pulled out his phone, tapped the screen a couple of times, then turned it to face Rick and Tuna. On the screen, a happy woman with brown kinky hair, brown eyes, and a wide, engaging smile stared back at them.

Downs pointed at the screen. "This was taken yesterday afternoon at Cisco Brewery."

Rick nodded. "Where else did the group go?"

"The pretty typical bridal party circuit. They left Cisco at closing time, seven pm, and headed downtown. They had dinner at Brotherhood and finished their evening doing karaoke at Gaslight. They grabbed the last bus to Sconset, the eleven fifteen Old South Route. Ms. Reid stated that they walked into their Airbnb around eleven fifty and had a nightcap on their patio before turning in."

"And when did they notice that Ms. Chapman was missing?" asked Tuna.

"Well, according to Ms. Reid, she was a runner and liked to run first thing, often starting just after sunrise. And apparently, she was pretty good, competing in several marathons a year. Including Boston."

Rick raised an eyebrow. "So she was a decent runner then?"

Officer Downs nodded. "Yes."

"Was anyone up when she left for this run?"

"According to Ms. Reid, no. Apparently, Ms. Chapman, Katie, was the only one up. The rest were sleeping off their hangovers."

"So we don't know exactly when she left their Airbnb, do we?" asked Rick.

"No," replied Downs. "But we know her phone went off the grid at a little after eight."

"Off the grid? How do we know that?"

"According to Ms. Reid, the entire bridal party was using an app called Life360, and each was sharing their location information with the others through the app." Downs said, tapping his phone again.

"Okay," said Rick, interested. "And when did her phone go off the grid?"

"Ms. Reid sent me this screenshot," said Downs, and once again angled his screen toward Tuna and Rick. "You can see her track here," he said, pointing. "She was running down Polpis Road, probably the bike path, until she reached this spot, the trailhead for the Windswept Bog loop. According to Google Maps, that's three point nine miles from their rental."

"And that's where the phone went off the grid?"

"Yes. According to the app, her phone went dark at eight twenty-one a.m. So, backing up, and assuming she was running an easy pace, then she likely left their rental around seven forty. Maybe a little earlier, as she could have been stretching or just admiring the scenery at the trailhead before she made her return run."

Tuna nodded. "Any chance her phone just died? Or she turned it off?"

Downs nodded. "It is. But why would she? They were using the app so they could keep tabs on each other and make sure everyone was safe. Turning it off would defeat the purpose."

"And a dead battery?"

Downs shook his head. "The app will notify the friend group when the battery gets low. None of her friends reportedly received any notification."

"Hmm," grunted Tuna. "Any chance she was meeting up with someone? Maybe she met someone the night before and was having a secret liaison?"

Again, Downs shook his head. "Unlikely. Ms. Reid said that they only had a few casual encounters during their day. Harmless flirting. And Ms. Reid was adamant that Katie was not that type of woman."

"Yeah, but maybe one of the people she met didn't like to take no for an answer," said Rick. "Do we know anything more about the men they talked to?"

Downs shook his head. "No. It sounds like they might have had some conversations with men at both Cisco and Gaslight."

"Okay, let's hold that thought for now," said Rick, and turned to Tuna. "Did she go for a hike then? Maybe wanted to take advantage of the morning and enjoy some nature?"

"Possible," replied Tuna. "But again. Why turn off your phone?"

"Maybe she just wanted to disconnect? Have a few hours tech-free. I've heard that's pretty popular right now with a lot of men and women her age."

"Okay. Then why hasn't she shown up? Or turned her phone back on?"

Rick didn't answer right away. He rubbed his chin, thinking. "I don't know. Maybe she got lost on the trail, maybe lost her phone. Now she's wandering around and trying to find her way out?"

Tuna looked at Downs. "How big is that trail?"

"There are several paths one can take. The longest is the Eastern Edge loop, which is three point two miles long."

"What type of trail is it?"

"According to ACKTrails, it's very uneven and weaves through a large wetland area."

Rick looked at Tuna. "So, let's say she runs to the trailhead. Maybe gets an email or text that upsets her, or upsets her tranquility, and decides to unplug, get some digital detox, as they say. Then, as she's walking the trail, maybe she gets hurt, or falls into a swampy area?"

Tuna looked at Officer Downs. "John, is this a popular trail? Isn't it possible that someone would have found her if that was the case?"

"Possible, yes, but it is not a popular trail. And if she went off the trail for any reason, then it's unlikely anyone would find her unless they heard her yelling for help. Which she couldn't do if she had fallen, hit her head, and been unconscious."

"Is that the only trail on the property?" asked Tuna.

Downs shook his head. "No. Four other trails share that trailhead. Plus, the entire property is over two hundred and forty acres."

"Two hundred and forty?" said Rick, whistling.

"Yeah," said Downs. "So there are a lot of places where she could be hurt and hidden from view."

Tuna nodded and turned to Rick. "We need to search that entire area. All five trails, as well as any space in between."

"Yes," said Rick. He looked at Officer Downs. "John, grab every available Community Resource Officer you can find and meet us at the trail head in sixty minutes."

"Yes, sir." Downs nodded and retreated from the conference room.

He turned to Tuna. "Any chance for some aerial assets?"

Tuna nodded. "We don't have a helicopter, but we do have the Small Unmanned Aircraft Unit. They call it the Soohah. These guys - and gal - are FAA-certified drone pilots and have the full spectrum of capabilities, including search and rescue. They have thermal imaging, but not sure there's enough temperature differential today to make that effective."

"Probably not. It'll be in the eighties by the time we get out there. Can you make that request?"

"On it," said Tuna. She picked up the phone at the center of the conference table and dialed four numbers. "Kurt? We need the Soohah to help with a missing person. Can you or one of the other pilots meet us with your equipment at the trailhead for the Windswept Bog?" She listened intently, nodding her head. "Terrific. We will meet you there."

She hung up the phone. "Okay. Officer White will meet us there in ninety minutes. Said he had to retrieve his equipment from storage."

"That's good news. Who's this officer White? Is he new?"

"Kurt? No. He's been here longer than me. I think he started in the late nineties. You don't remember him from your first time here?"

"Name doesn't ring a bell. But then again, I was a lowly rookie and just starting in the force. I'll probably recognize him when I see him."

"You ready?"

"I am. You driving, I hope? As I mentioned, I don't have a car yet."

"Of course, Rick. Anything for our newest officer. Happy to make your entry to the NPD as smooth as possible," she said with a chuckle.

Rick smiled wanly. "Thanks. But let's just hope that Katie is sitting out there with a twisted ankle and a dead phone waiting for someone to come rescue her."

"I hope you're right," said Tuna.

"Me too, Tuna. Me too."

CHAPTER TEN

Rick and Tuna pulled into the parking area for the trailhead for Windswept Bog. The long, narrow lot was lined on one side by a split rail fence and on the other by the dense brush and trees of the moor. A large red-framed map of the property stood at the end, close to the entrance to the trails. Nearby, a lone picnic table was surrounded by a dozen patrol officers and CSOs, probably wondering why they had been dragged here.

Tuna pulled her trusted old Ford Explorer in next to the last car on the lot and got out. Rick took a look at the gathering of police and then went back to Tuna. "Is it me, or are the CSOs getting younger every year?"

"Um, it's you. Hiring guidelines for the CSO haven't changed since the program was initiated. They are all eighteen years or older. Most are college kids getting degrees in criminal justice."

Rick stole another glance at the gathering. "They look like they should be in junior high school," he said sadly. "God, I hate getting old."

"Um, you're barely in your forties. You are most definitely not old!"

"Uh huh. Tell that to my aging body."

Rick's attention was diverted as a pickup wearing the livery of the Nantucket Police pulled in and parked. A man, probably a few years older than Rick, wearing khakis and a white button-down, got out of the driver's side and went to the back of the truck, where he opened the tailgate and slid out a steel cargo tray. It was metal, with arms cradling two large drones. The man pulled out the first drone and began to prep it for launch.

“Is that Officer White?” asked Rick, pointing his thumb at the new arrival.

“It is,” confirmed Tuna.

“Give me a minute,” said Rick and walked briskly over to the pickup.

“Good afternoon,” said Rick. “Officer White?”

The man turned. “I am,” he said pleasantly. “And you are?”

Rick introduced himself, extending his hand. “I’m Detective Rick Caton, just back on the force after a bit of, let’s say, leave of absence.”

White shook his hand enthusiastically. “Nice to meet you, Rick, er, Detective.”

“Please call me Rick. No need for formalities here. And that’s a hell of a piece of equipment you got there,” said Rick, pointing at the nearest drone.

Officer White smiled like a proud father. “It is. We’ve only had it for a few weeks, so I’m still learning a lot of its capabilities, but it is pretty impressive. It’s a Flock Safety DFR.”

“DFR?”

“Drone as First Responder,” said Officer White. “It’s designed to be on scene quickly to assess the situation and provide critical information to determine the most effective response from a resource and personnel perspective.”

“Really? That’s amazing. I thought drones just provided aerial video.”

White shook his head. "That was the case a few years ago. But now? These drones feature incredible technologies, including real-time evidence capture, a license plate reader, speaker communication, weapons detection, and more."

"That is impressive," said Rick, letting out a low whistle. "I'm so glad you are here to help with our missing person."

White nodded. "I'll do what I can."

Rick, still entranced by this new technology in front of him, said, "So what does it take to learn to fly one of these things?"

White pulled out the controller and showed it to Rick. "Honestly, it's pretty easy. The drones and their associated software do all the heavy lifting. My job is to pretty much tell it what to do and then monitor it to ensure compliance."

"Do you need special training for this?"

White nodded emphatically. "Yes. I am a Certificated Remote Pilot with the Federal Aviation Authority for a UAS."

"UAS?"

White smiled knowingly. "Unmanned Aircraft System."

Rick nodded. "Pretty cool stuff. Anyway, nice to meet you, and thanks for getting here so quickly to help out with the search."

White nodded and turned back to prepping his drone. Rick walked back to Tuna, who was standing in a fog of bug spray. She was spraying up and down her legs and across her back. When she saw Rick approaching, she stopped and handed him the can.

"Don't be skimpy. Make sure you wet your clothes at least waist high."

Rick nodded. "Officer White seems to really know his stuff about drones." Rick started spraying his legs.

Tuna looked across the lot where the officer was getting ready to launch the drone. "Kurt? Yeah. He's definitely a tech geek and knows the drones inside and out. But as a cop, I'd say he's pretty average. In addition to being part of the drone unit, he runs the usual Pitman schedule as a patrol officer."

"Never promoted?"

"He made police officer years ago, but nothing further. He has the field experience but has never really demonstrated the ability to run a successful team or investigation. And he seems happy where he is. I mean, I don't know him particularly well, but when I see him at the station or in the field, he always seems to be doing well."

Rick smiled and handed back the can. "Thanks. Now, let's go brief the troops."

They walked towards the picnic table, and when they got close, Tuna spoke loudly. "Everyone? Can you join me over here by the trail map? Thank you."

The officers and CSOs stood and walked over. Tuna was standing by the map and addressed the gathering as a teacher would her class.

"Thanks so much for being here. We have an urgent case on our hands. As you know, thirty-two-year-old Katie Chapman went missing early this morning. According to her friends, she was on a run from Sconset. We think she intended to turn around here and head back to their rental cottage. But Katie didn't make it back to the cottage, and her phone, which showed her here in this parking lot at eight twenty, went off the grid one minute later." She turned to Rick.

Rick stepped forward. "That's what has us concerned, but it also might help explain where she is. Our thinking is that she decided to go for a hike on one of these trails," he said, motioning toward the map, "and something happened. Maybe she dropped her phone in the water or broke her phone somehow. She might be lost; we are talking several hundred acres of pretty dense brush. Or maybe she fell and injured herself. Regardless, our hope is that she is out on one of these trails with an injury and a broken phone, just waiting for someone to come find her. That's where you come in."

"Thanks, Rick. So, we will break into pairs, a patrol officer with a CSO, and check these trails closely. Officer Downs, you and your CSO will take the Turtle Tracking Trail. Officer Smith, you'll take the Bog Circuit Trail." She divvied up the remaining trails. "Finally, Officer Coffin, you and your CSO will take the eastern side of the Stump Pond loop. Detective Caton and I will take the west loop. Finally, Officer White will have the drone up on a grid search. Between us, we should be able to locate Katie. Any questions?"

"Do you have a description of the missing person?" It was asked by a new CSO who was in his first week on the job.

Tuna smiled. "Sorry, I should have started with that. Thanks for keeping me honest. Um, she's thirty-two, caucasian, brown hair and eyes, wearing light tan leggings, navy top, and white joggers."

The young CSO nodded.

"Anyone else?" She waited. "Okay, then. Please contact me with any findings whatsoever, no matter how small. Got it?"

All heads nodded.

"Great. Let's go find Katie."

The team dispersed, and soon cries calling out for Katie could be heard throughout the property.

Rick and Tuna headed down their assigned trail. It started easily, just walking through an open field. They made their way over a long boardwalk, which carried them above a boggy area. They looked cautiously down but were relieved not to see the body of Katie Chapman or anyone else, for that matter.

They looked up at the distant buzzing of a drone. They could see the unit above them, black and menacing, as it flew quickly to the east. Rick watched it intently as it flew away, saw it pause briefly, and then made its way eastward. To his eye, it was following a standard grid search.

Amazing stuff.

The open field narrowed down to a more defined trail that cut through the trees. Just a few feet wide, Tuna and Rick had to walk single file, being careful not to trip over the many roots exposed on the path. A mulch of the leaves from the previous fall littered the ground. The path angled downward, and soon they were close to the edge of Stump Pond. A small sandy beach gave way to bright blue water that spread out in front of them, the light ripples radiating diamonds in the bright sun.

"That is way bigger than I expected," said Rick, impressed. "And way more beautiful."

Tuna nodded. "I know, it's gorgeous. And sadly, so few people ever get to see it. This trail probably only gets a few thousand hikers a year. As for the size?" She shrugged her shoulders. "I'm going to say it's probably 20 or 30 acres? The good news is that it tends to be shallow. So if she's in there, she should be easily visible from above."

Her radio crackled. "Detective Fisch?"

She pulled the walkie-talkie and held it up. "This is Tuna."

"This is Noah Coffin. We've found a hat near a witch's tree. We are about 500 meters south of the start of the loop."

"A witch's tree?" asked Rick. "What the hell is that?"

Tuna held up a finger. "Ten four, Noah. Any sign of disturbance or struggle?"

"Negative, Detective. But there is a jon boat nearby. And it looks like it was used recently, as there are drag marks leading from the pond to where it is sitting."

"Copy. On our way."

Tuna lowered her walkie-talkie. "That sounds ominous. Why would they only find a hat?"

Rick nodded. "Yes. And what is the witch's tree?"

"Oh, a witch's tree is local slang for an American Beech. Often, when they grow in the swampy areas on the island, they take on very sinister shapes. They are definitely kind of creepy for sure."

"Interesting."

Rick and Tuna hustled back along the route they had already walked and made their way down the eastern loop. They quickly found Office Noah Coffin and his CSO, a young lady by the name of Blair Huber, who seemed very excited at their find.

"Office Coffin. Good work."

"Thanks. But it was really CSO Huber, um, Blair, who saw the hat and called my attention to it."

"Nice work, Blair," said Tuna.

The CSO nodded with pride. "It's from Cisco Brewers. One of their new designs this season."

Tuna looked at her intently.

"My boyfriend and I like the place. Even though we can't drink, they have great music. And I noticed the design of this hat. It's the same as the one I saw being promoted at their merch shop last week."

Rick looked at the young CSO. "Good job." He turned to Tuna. "Do we know if this hat was Katie's?"

"We will have to check with her friends. It wasn't in their general description of her, but they could have easily overlooked it given the circumstances. Or it could belong to another hiker." Tuna turned to Officer Coffin. "So, I'm assuming you haven't touched the hat?"

"No ma'am. But we did a quick survey of the area around it. There was no sign of a struggle. The grass appears untouched, and the area is littered with sticks and twigs. None of them showed any breakage."

Tuna pulled out her phone and tapped on the camera app. She was nearly ten feet away, so she zoomed in, framed the hat on the screen, and snapped a picture.

"Should we call in the crime techs?" asked Rick.

Tuna chuckled softly. "Don't take this the wrong way, Rick, but your last few years of detective work have been mostly behind a computer screen. And with a tremendous amount of resources at your disposal, right?"

Rick winced at the comment but had to admit to himself that it was true. He nodded.

"We don't have a crime scene unit. We would need to bring them over from the Cape, and at great expense. Not sure the value proposition is there, especially given how long it will take."

"Makes sense. Sorry. Old habits."

Tuna put her hand on Rick's shoulder. "No biggie. We are lucky to have you back, and I know you'll get used to our style of police work."

"Thanks, Tuna."

Tuna continued, "Look at this," she said, pointing at the hat lying flat below the tree. "There is no disturbed grass, no footprints that I can see, no sign of any activity. It's like someone threw the hat like a Frisbee from the path."

"You think it's an intentional distraction? To mislead us?"

Tuna nodded. "It's what my gut is saying, but until we know any differently, we need to keep this as a priority." She turned to Officer Coffin. "You mentioned a jon boat?"

"Yes," said Noah. "It's right over here."

He guided Rick and Tuna to the boat. It was obviously old, its aluminum body dented and scarred. Algae grew along the inside gunwales. A red, well-worn nylon rope was tied to the bow cleat and led to a small tree where it was roughly knotted.

"Any idea whose boat this is?" asked Rick.

Noah nodded. "I called the Nantucket Conservation Foundation. They're the ones that manage this property. They said it belonged to them and was used to do monthly surveys of the pond."

"Surveys?" asked Rick.

"Yeah. Many of Nantucket's freshwater ponds have experienced harmful algae blooms or HABs. The NCF uses this boat to take water quality samples at multiple spots around the pond."

"Did they know when it was last used?" asked Tuna.

"Last week. The surveys are done on the first and fifteenth of the month."

"Looks like it was used today," said Tuna.

"It does," agreed Rick. "Do you think someone could have used it to move Katie?"

"Dump her body, you mean?" asked Tuna.

Rick nodded solemnly.

Tuna raised her walkie-talkie. "Officer White? Come in?"

The radio crackled. "This is White."

"Kurt, how are you doing on the search?"

"About 50 percent complete with the first pass. It's following an east-west pattern and currently just south of the bog."

"Have you searched the pond yet?"

"Negative, detective. At the current pace will probably have the first pass in ten to fifteen minutes."

"Ten four. Thanks, Kurt. Please keep me in the loop."

She turned to Rick. "Okay. Probably another hour or two until Kurt fully recons the pond. Let's cordon off the area for now. My gut tells me this is a dead end, but let's hold off on any further work here until we get confirmation from the friend group that this is indeed Katie's hat. Okay, let's finish our loop. You two as well," she said, pointing to the other team.

They backtracked to the west loop and resumed their search. They found no evidence of any activity on the trail except the odd piece of trash. Katie was nowhere to be seen. It took nearly half an hour to finish their section, and then they made their way back to the trailhead. The other groups had been there a while and were clearly restless and frustrated.

She made her way to the center of the group. Tuna gathered them around. "Anything to report?"

The collected groups shook their heads. "Sorry, Tuna," said Officer Downs. "The trails were clear, and there was no response to our repeated calls."

"Thanks, John. Office White. Anything from the air?"

Officer White stepped forward. It was clear he was a bit nervous speaking in front of the group, even though he had worked with them for years. "Negative, detective. But I'm planning to rerun the grid tonight when it has cooled off. The thermal imaging didn't have enough temperature variance to be effective."

Tuna nodded. "And the pond? Anything?"

White shook his head. "Nothing visible. But several spots were deep enough to hide a body. I'd suggest we bring in the marine unit to investigate those areas."

"Okay, thanks, Kurt. I'll make that call. Anything else?"

"What should we do about the hat?" It was Officer Coffin.

Tuna thought for a moment. "I'd like you to glove up and bag the hat as evidence. If we can get confirmation from her friends that it was hers, then I'd like you to hand-deliver that to the Cape ASAP. The Staties have a satellite lab in Bourne."

"Got it, Tuna. Just give me the word, and I'll get it over there."

"Thanks, Noah. And if it comes to that, please ask them to put a rush on it. We may be able to lift some prints or some trace that might give us some idea of who has Katie."

"Yes, ma'am."

She surveyed the group. All eyes were on her. "Anything else?"

The only sound was the hush of wind through the trees and the squawking of a seagull in the distance.

"Thanks, everyone. I appreciate all your hard work."

The team started to disperse.

"Damn," said Tuna, turning to Rick. "I had really hoped we would be able to locate her, that your theory of her being hurt with a dead phone was spot on."

"What's next?" asked Rick expectantly.

"The bridal party. They are expecting us. Let's see if that's Katie's hat. Maybe they'll know something else that will help."

CHAPTER ELEVEN

Rick and Tuna left the Windswept Bog feeling both disappointed and frustrated. They had been hopeful that Rick's theory of Katie being hurt with a dead or broken phone would have been correct, and Katie would now be on her way to Cottage Hospital for a quick check and then back to her friends and family to enjoy the rest of her bridal weekend. Instead, they were no closer to understanding what happened to her than they were a few hours before. Missing persons cases were some of the most challenging, as they had to work with the crushing pressure of time on their backs. There would be no breaks, no rest, no other priorities, until she was found. The survival of the missing could very well depend on how well and how quickly they did their jobs.

"Did you connect with Ms. Reid?" asked Rick.

"Yes," said Tuna. "They are expecting us now at their Airbnb. I'm not sure what more we will get from them, but maybe we can learn a little bit more about Katie. Maybe that will lead somewhere…" her voice trailed off.

"Let's hope. This is just so damn frustrating. Young healthy women don't just fall off the face of the earth."

"I've been afraid to say it out loud, but you're thinking the chief's instinct is right. That she was grabbed?"

Rick looked out of the window as they proceeded down Polpis Road. "Unfortunately, yes," he said without turning. "It's the only thing that makes sense. But again, that's not the type of crime I ever associated with Nantucket. Boston? Cambridge? It's rare, but it happens. But I don't think it's ever happened here, has it?"

"No, certainly not during my career." She hit the brakes and swerved to the left to avoid a startled deer that had jumped out in front of them. The deer scrabbled on the pavement, and just as quickly as it had appeared, it vanished into the brush.

"Goddamn deer," said Tuna, muttering.

"They really are a problem here, aren't they?"

"Yeah. Unfortunately, they have no natural predators on the island. So they can pretty much breed at will. Current population estimates are around ten thousand."

"Ten thousand?" said Rick, whistling. "That is crazy."

"It is. Especially with the damage they do to landscaping, car collisions, and disease. Nantucket is now the number one area for tick-borne diseases like Lyme Disease. So never walk in the grass without spraying with a good tick deterrent first."

Rick looked at Tuna and could see she was very passionate about the subject. "Okay," he said. "I promise, Mom. Anything to know about the bridal party?

Tuna smiled weakly at his joke. "Officer Downs said nothing jumped out at him. Just four very upset women who want to know what happened to their friend."

"I'm sure they do. Hopefully, they might know something."

Tuna shook her head. "I doubt it."

They pulled into the shell driveway of a rambling, gray shingled house and parked behind a red Jeep sporting a spare tire cover with the Young's Bicycle Shop logo. They had followed the exact path that Katie's phone had recorded earlier that morning, but beyond a few deer and a handful of rabbits, they saw nothing that would help them in their investigation.

They got out and walked to the front door. Rick took a deep breath and knocked.

A young woman, thirtyish with curly brown hair and brown eyes, answered the door. Her hair was pulled back into a ponytail, and her eyes were red from crying. She was wearing gray leggings and a baggy sweatshirt that featured some band that Rick had never heard of.

"Ms. Reid?" asked Tuna.

The lady nodded. "Yes. Thank you for coming. Please," and motioned for them to come in. "The rest of the party is in the kitchen. We can talk there."

"Thank you." Rick and Tuna followed her down a long hallway that opened into a bright, sunlit space. The mood in the room did not echo the beautiful late spring day that was visible through the many windows that lined the space. Three other faces looked up at them expectantly as they stepped into the room.

"Hello," said Tuna. "I'm Detective Tina Fisch. This is Detective Rick Caton. Thank you for meeting with us."

"Have you found her?" asked a young woman anxiously.

"And you are?"

"I'm Jen Mueller. I work with Katie at Drury Biotech." She had her hands in her lap, clutching her phone.

"I'm sorry, Jen, but we haven't located her yet," said Rick. "Detective Fisch and I are hoping you might have some ideas on where she might be."

"If we knew where she was, then we wouldn't need you now, would we?" said a heavy-set woman acidly.

"I understand your frustration, Miss?"

"Mrs. Duncan," emphasizing her marital status. "Joan Duncan."

Rick nodded. "And how do you know Katie?"

"Best friends. We went to school together and were roommates until I got married last year."

"And did you ever see Katie exhibit this type of behavior before?"

"This type of behavior? I'm not sure what you are referring to," she said angrily.

Tuna held up her hand. "I'm sorry. We don't mean to offend, but we don't know Katie. All we know is she is missing, and we are hopeful that something you might tell us about her could help us solve what happened."

Joan let out a deep sigh, and her shoulders slumped. She played with a piece of tissue in her hands. "I'm sorry. I just can't believe this. We came here to celebrate her wedding, and now she's gone." Tears welled up in her eyes. "But to answer your question, no. She has never disappeared on me in the nearly ten years I've known her. She has always let me know where she was going and when to expect her back. It was our girls' code."

Tuna nodded. "And what did she say about where she was going this morning?"

"She didn't, at least directly. We were all still sleeping. Bit of a rough night, I'm afraid."

A new voice said, "She texted the group that she was off on a run. Probably be gone a couple of hours and not to wait for her to have breakfast."

Rick turned to face the speaker.

“I’m Lindsay Harper. I also work with Katie at Drury.”

“So she sent everyone a text?”

Lindsay nodded and tucked a lock of her black hair behind an ear. “Yes. Madison,” nodding to the maid of honor, “made sure that everyone knew all of the plans and were all connected for this weekend. We all loaded the Life360 app to share locations, we have a group text running, and we even have a group shared drive to document the whole experience. She was going to have it made into a book as a wedding present.” She sniffled.

Tuna looked impressed. “Can I see a copy of that group text?”

The maid of honor tapped her phone and then handed it to Tuna.

Going for fun run. Back by 10. You guys eat something. 

She read the text and then handed it back. “What did she mean by a ‘fun run’?”

“Katie is a competitive runner. But a fun run is just that. No pushes or goals. She was just running for the pure pleasure of it.”

“And when she didn’t come back by ten? What did you guys do next?” asked Rick.

Joan got up and walked to the window. “We gave her a little grace period, you know, maybe she was running slowly or decided to walk a bit. But by ten thirty, we started to get worried.”

“That’s when I noticed her phone was off the grid,” said Madison. “She never would have done that. Ever.”

“The app showed us where she went, so Madison and I took the Jeep and went up there looking for her,” said Lindsay. “But there was nothing. No sign of her. It’s like she vanished.”

Tuna nodded as she scribbled quickly in her notebook. “And then what?”

“Then what? We freaked out!” said Lindsay. “We got back here and talked it out and agreed the best approach was to call you guys.”

“And what time was that?” asked Rick.

“I don’t remember,” said Lindsay, frustrated. “Don’t you have that information?”

“We can check with the Communications Center and track down your call. But it would be a lot easier if you could just tell us,” said Rick, soothingly.

Lindsay nodded and pulled out her phone. She tapped and scrolled and then looked at Rick. “My call to nine one one was at five after eleven.” She clicked her phone shut and slid it into her back pocket.

“Thank you,” said Rick.

“Anything else you can tell us about Katie?” asked Tuna.

The group looked back and forth at each other, unsure what to say. Somehow, talking about Katie was admitting there was an issue. And none of them wanted to think there was. Finally, Jean spoke up.

“She was a fighter. I mean, you hear that a lot about some people, but Katie has a will and determination like no one else I know.”

“Can you expand on that? Maybe an example?”

“An example?” harrumphed Jean. “Sure. She used to be a big biker. Bicyclist, that is. During her first summer in Cambridge, a pickup truck ran a red light and struck her broadside. She was thrown up and over the roof of the truck and landed headfirst on the pavement. She should have died on the spot. Skull fracture, concussion, broken hip, broken femur, massive bruising. I think you get the picture. She had three surgeries and spent nearly two weeks in the ICU."

"Wow," said Tuna.

"Yeah, wow, but that's only the half of it. She was back to work within a month of her accident and ran her first 10K six months later. Her doctors said it was a miracle recovery. But, I, I mean, we," said Jean, pointing to the other women looking at her intently, "we just know that's Katie. That's how she is. So, if someone grabbed her, if that's what you're thinking, she will fight with all her heart to stay alive."

Rick looked at Jean intently. "Thank you for that. Sounds like an impressive woman."

"She is," agreed Jean.

"What can you tell us about her fiancé?" asked Tuna.

"Harrison?" said Madison. "He's a sweetheart. And also my brother, if you didn't know. He was crazy about Katie. They met by accident at a concert at a biotech conference in San Francisco. Hate to be so cliché, but it was love at first sight for both of them. The crazy thing was they lived just a few blocks apart in Cambridge. Went to the same coffee shop, gym, and grocery store but had never met. Had to fly the entire width of the country to bump into each other." She laughed sadly at the thought.

"Can you tell me more about Harrison? What does he look like, personality, that sort of thing?" asked Tuna.

"Harrison is thirty-three, just over six feet, curly brown hair, gray, almost light blue eyes, pale skin with lots of freckles. He's pretty fit too, also a runner."

"Any chance that he might have something to do with this?"

"What are you saying?" said Madison, indignantly. "He would never, ever hurt Katie."

Tuna put her hand up. "Sorry, I didn't mean to infer anything. But could he maybe have surprised her? Talked her into eloping or something like that?"

"I wish," said Madison, looking down at the floor. Her body shook with a sob, and when she looked back at Tuna, her eyes were filled with fresh tears. "I called him after we called nine one one. He's in a panic, as you can imagine, and is on his way here. He was trying to catch a Cape Air flight from Logan. All the flights were sold out due to the holiday weekend, so he is on standby. His last text to me said he was hoping to be on the five-thirty flight tonight."

Tuna nodded. "You mentioned you were documenting the weekend. I assume that means pictures?"

The women around the room nodded.

"Any chance you could share all those with us? We'd like to look through them and see if anything jumps out."

"Sure," replied Madison. "If you give me your email, I can grant you access to our shared drive. All the pictures we've taken so far are there."

"That would be great," said Tuna. "One last question. Do you guys know if Katie was wearing a hat this morning?"

The women looked at each other, unsure.

"Maybe one from Cisco Brewers?" prompted Rick.

Joan smiled. "Yeah, now that you mention it. Katie bought one yesterday when we were there as a memento of our weekend. Had some new design she thought looked really cool."

Tuna pulled out her phone, tapped the screen, and then showed a picture to Joan. "Is this it?"

"Yes!" said Joan, excitedly. "You found it? Is that hers? Where did you find it? And where is she?" She broke into tears again.

"I'm sorry. It is probably from another hiker on the path, but we are investigating all possibilities where Katie is concerned."

Joan's crying stopped, and she nodded.

"I think we have everything we need." She extracted a business card from a pocket in her notebook and handed it to Madison. "This is my card. My cell, email, and desk phones are all on there. Please don't hesitate to reach out for anything. And I do mean anything. We are here for you. And if by chance you think of anything that might be helpful, we would love to hear from you."

Madison took the card and nodded slightly. "Thank you," she whispered. "And I'll add you to our shared drive."

Tuna stepped forward and put a hand on her shoulder. "Thank you. We will do everything we can to help Katie. This is our department's number one priority, and we will put every available resource toward finding her as soon as possible."

"Thank you, ladies," said Rick and motioned to Tuna. She followed him down the hall and out the door toward her cruiser. Rick leaned up against the car and looked back at the house. "What do you think? Anything there?"

"Just four very upset women at the thought of losing their friend. Clearly, they have no idea what happened to her and are thinking the worst."

"Honestly, Tuna. So am I. Right now, everything we know points to a kidnapping. Someone grabbed her while she was on that run. Now we need to find her as quickly as we can."

Tuna nodded and pulled out her phone. She tapped on the screen and waited a few moments. "Noah? It's Tuna. It's a go. We got the confirmation that Katie was wearing a hat that matched the one you found." She paused, listening. "Good. And please remind them of the urgency that we have a missing persons case dependent on it."

She tapped the screen, slipped the phone in her pocket, and turned to Rick. "Let's get back and brief the chief. We have a lot of work to do."

CHAPTER TWELVE

Nantucket Police Chief Jodi Calpers sat at her desk, her eyes intent on the screen in front of her. She had been recruited to this position a few years before with the intent of maintaining the public trust and accountability with the NPD. And she had done that in spades. If she were honest with herself, it really hadn't been that difficult a task. The department was filled with talented officers and support personnel who just needed consistent, predictable leadership to excel in their positions.

She had a few wrongs to right, including the dismissal of Officer Rick Caton nearly a decade earlier after a public incident that hadn't truly been his fault. Only after he returned to Nantucket and solved a suspicious drowning did she realize the department's loss—and eventually convinced him to come back as a detective.

Now six months later, Rick Caton tapped twice on her door before pushing it open. Tuna stood just off his shoulder, arms folded loosely as they stepped inside.

The chief looked up. "Rick, Tuna, please come in," she said, motioning to a couple of chairs that faced her desk. "How are you two holding up?"

Tuna let out a long sigh. "Honestly, it's been very frustrating. When we received the case from you about the missing woman this morning, we both thought it would be cut and dry. But the more we have uncovered about the case, the more we believe a crime may have occurred."

The chief leaned back slightly, fingers steepled. "Okay. Tell me why you think that."

“According to her friends, she went for a run this morning and didn’t return. They have a tracking app on their phones - so they can keep an eye on each other - and hers stopped sharing her location at eight twenty-one.” She glanced briefly at Rick, then back to the chief. “Concerned, her friends went to look for her, and when they couldn’t locate her, they called nine one one.”

The chief shifted in her chair, brow furrowing. “Any chance she could have been injured or hurt and went to the ER?”

“No. We checked with Cottage Hospital. They have no record of a young woman with any injuries coming in this morning.”

“What about her phone? Could the battery be dead? Or just a bad signal? Certainly, we have pockets on the island where cell coverage is horrible to non-existent.”

Rick nodded. “Yes, we thought maybe she had gone on a hike and had been injured, her phone dead or broken, and she was waiting to be rescued.”

The chief tilted her head slightly. “So nothing there?”

Rick let out a small breath, glancing at Tuna before answering. “No. We conducted a full search of the Windswept Bog area, both on the ground as well as an aerial survey with the drone officer, and found nothing but what we think is her hat.”

“Her hat?” The chief straightened, eyebrows lifting.

“Yes,” said Tuna. “Her friends confirmed she had purchased one just like it at Cisco’s yesterday. We are not absolutely certain it’s hers, but are proceeding under that assumption.”

The chief leaned forward now, interest sharpening. “Where did you find it? In the parking lot?”

Tuna shook her head. "That's the thing." She exchanged a quick look with Rick. "It was a few hundred yards down one of the trails, near Stump Pond."

The chief's fingers drummed lightly on the desk as she processed that. "Okay, that's a bit strange. What about prints and trace?"

"In process, ma'am. I've got Officer Coffin hand-delivering the hat to the crime lab in Bourne. I hope we will know something later today or first thing tomorrow."

"Good. What about the trail and the area around the hat? Anything there?"

Tuna shook her head. "Nothing. The trail was clear of any signs of a struggle, as was the area around the hat. It looked like someone threw the hat like a Frisbee. It was a good twenty feet off the trail, but there were no footprints or other signs."

"But there was the jon boat," said Rick.

"Jon boat?"

"Yes," said Tuna. "Just down the trail from the hat was a jon boat that looked to have been used recently. It belongs to the NCF. They use it to do surveys of the pond. One possibility is that it was used to move a body into the pond."

"But nothing showed up in your search to support that, did it?" asked the chief, concerned.

"No. Surveillance video from the drone was negative on anything that looked to be a body, at least in the shallow areas. There are a couple of deeper pockets that I've asked our marine unit to investigate."

"Divers?"

Tuna nodded. “Yes. If she’s down there, that team will find her.” She glanced at her watch. “They should be there now. I expect we will have confirmation one way or the other shortly.”

The chief nodded. “So,” she said, drawing the word out. “We have a hat that is sitting off the trail, devoid of any signs of struggle, and an old boat that may or may not have been recently used. What is that telling us?”

Rick took a breath. “I think it’s been staged.”

“Really?” said the chief. “You’re thinking it’s a diversion?”

“That makes the most sense.” Rick paced a few steps across the room, then turned back, running a hand through his hair. “But what I don’t get is why? If he’s already grabbed her, maybe she’s in the trunk of the car. Why go to the trouble of planting the hat and dragging the boat around? Why not just take off and avoid the risk of being seen?”

“Good question. Maybe he wanted us to know he had her?” asked Tuna.

Rick stopped pacing, glancing over at her, one brow lifting slightly. “I guess, but why? Why would he want to advertise the fact?”

“To assert his dominance? Show that he’s in control?”

“That’s one possibility. Or maybe he just wants to toy with us. Maybe he gets a kick out of us chasing our tails trying to find her.”

“Regardless of his intentions,” said the chief. “We need to find her. And quickly.”

“Agreed. We need to assume that she’s been taken and likely being held captive,” said Tuna.

The chief let out a long sigh. "A young woman visiting the island to celebrate her nuptials is jumped on a run. Kidnapped. It could also be a possibility that she's been a victim of sexual assault. That would be a nightmare scenario for us."

Rick nodded. "Yes, especially now with the holiday weekend. The island is going to be packed with seasonal residents and tourists. It would be a terrible stain…"

The chief cut him off. "I agree it would not look good for tourism, but that's the least of my concerns. This is a nightmare for her family. Her friends. This has become a living hell for them, not knowing where she is. Or even if she's alive. We need to find her."

"I'm sorry, chief, I didn't mean to infer you didn't care."

She held up her hand. "It's okay, Rick. Yes, it would be bad publicity for Nantucket. But we have to put her family first. So how do we proceed?"

Tuna and Rick looked at each other.

"What? What are you thinking?"

Tuna replied confidently. "First, we need to talk with everyone she might have encountered after they landed on the island. It sounds like they did some heavy partying, so it's entirely possible she met someone, and the others either didn't see it or may have forgotten. I know what her friends said, but people aren't always what they seem. Maybe the idea of getting married scared her, and she wanted to have one last fling? It's the least likely, but we need to close that line of inquiry."

The chief nodded.

"Second, we need to notify the public and call for their help. This is a small island; maybe someone saw or heard something?

I've got a friend who manages the programming at True Island Radio. If you agree, I'd like to ask her to put out an announcement immediately."

"Great idea," said the chief. "I'd also suggest getting coverage in the daily email newsletters from the Current and the Inquirer and Mirror. Have them call nine one one if they know anything."

"Nine one one?" asked Rick.

The chief nodded adamantly. "We need to keep it simple. Most people can't remember a phone number, but everyone knows nine one one. And we don't normally get a lot of emergency calls, so it shouldn't impact anything."

Rick nodded.

"Great," said Tuna. "Then we need to check the passenger manifests for the ferries and airlines. One to see if she left on her own. Maybe she's upset or wants to get away for some reason. But also to determine if her kidnapper has or is trying to take her off the island. There's only been a handful of car ferries so far today."

"Good plan," said the chief, nodding as she leaned back in her chair. She lifted a hand slightly, as if to pause them. "One suggestion."

"Sure," said Tuna. "What's that?"

The chief folded her hands on the desk, her expression softening a touch. "I talked with Katie's mom about an hour ago. She and her husband live in Rhode Island - Bristol, I think - and are very upset, as you can imagine."

Tuna exhaled quietly, her posture easing just a bit. "I'm sure. This is a parent's worst nightmare."

"Yes. Well, they are on their way here. Have offered to help with anything we need."

Tuna shifted her weight, arms crossing again as she thought it over. "Not sure there is much they can do at this point."

The chief nodded. "I agree. But I think it would be beneficial to their mental health if we could make them feel like they are contributing. Maybe ask them to coordinate with the friend group and do another search of the trail? Have them put together and distribute some fliers?" She paused, tone softening. "I don't want to call it busy work, but anything that will help them keep their minds off the situation."

Rick and Tuna nodded in unison.

"Detective Fisch, as the lead on this case, I did give them your contact information. I expect you'll be hearing from them as soon as they hit the island."

"Thanks, Chief."

The chief leaned forward, her voice laced with concern. "Thank you both. I know this is a tough case, and I appreciate everything you're doing to solve it." She paused and turned to Rick. "How are you settling in? Anything we can do?"

Rick shook his head. "Thanks, Chief, but I'm okay. Tuna and I have been through worse. We'll find her. I promise."

The chief nodded, satisfied. "Good. Anything else?"

"No, ma'am."

"Okay. Thanks again for the hard work. Please let me know if there is anything you need to help find this young woman. She is our number one priority."

"Absolutely."

They excused themselves and went to Tuna's office. The clock on the wall said it was nearly dinner time.

Tuna sat down heavily and let out a long sigh. "I'm starving. Do you want to grab a bite?"

Rick looked at his watch. "Actually, Fel was making me dinner. It was supposed to be a welcome home meal, but now it will be a quick eat and run."

"Okay. Can we plan on meeting back here in an hour? I'd like your help with the computer work, checking the ferry and plane manifests, see if there is anything pointing to Katie leaving the island."

"You really think she would have left on her own without telling anyone?"

"From what we've heard about her? No, not likely. But you never know. Maybe the focus on her wedding made her have second thoughts. Maybe she had an argument with her friends that they are hesitant to tell us about. And despite what they say, Katie could have met someone. You never know."

He nodded. "True." He looked at his phone and back at Tuna. "I'll be back by seven."

* * *

Rick took a taxi over to Felicity's family home on Monomoy Road. It had been months since he had last been there, and wasn't sure how he was going to feel.

Felicity met him at the door, her auburn hair radiating the late afternoon sun. She took one look at him and could tell something was very wrong. "Are you okay?"

He shook his head. "Rough case." He leaned in and kissed her. "But that helps."

She smiled softly. "Come in and relax. Let me try to get your mind off things."

He followed her down the long hallway to the kitchen, where a delicious aroma of butter, garlic, and herbs confronted him. Immediately, his mouth started to water.

"That smells absolutely delicious."

Felicity smiled. "Thanks. It's my mom's chicken piccata recipe. Always a family favorite, although I wish she were here to enjoy it with us. And dad too. "

He pulled her into a hug. "I know Fel. We lost your mom and dad way too young."

She pulled away. "Why don't you make yourself a drink. And would you mind pouring me a glass of the sauvignon blanc?"

Rick walked over to the sink and looked out the big windows at Nantucket Harbor. While he was dealing with the challenges of the case and its associated burdens, the rest of the island was bustling with activity. A small fleet of sailboats was racing off Coatue Point while a number of larger boats were powering around Brant Point toward the Boat Basin. He could almost feel the energy pulsing off the water at the start of the holiday weekend and the unofficial start of summer. He wished he could relax and allow himself to enjoy being here for his first Memorial Day as a resident, but Katie weighed heavily on his mind.

Felicity, leaning in the doorway, studied him for a beat before stepping closer. “Talk to me, Rick.”

He rubbed the back of his neck and turned slightly toward her. “Sorry. We are working a missing persons case. A young woman. Over for the weekend for a bachelorette party.”

Felicity’s hand came up to her mouth, her expression shifting immediately. “Oh my god, no. When did she disappear?”

“On a run this morning.” Rick pushed off the counter and paced a couple of steps, then stopped. “Went out early before the rest of her friends had gotten up and didn’t return.”

Felicity folded her arms loosely, concern deepening. “What do you think happened?”

Rick hesitated, his gaze dropping for a moment before he looked back up. “I hate to say it, but we think she might have been grabbed.”

Felicity’s eyes widened as she took a step closer. “Grabbed? You mean kidnapped!” she exclaimed.

Rick gave a small, grim nod. “I know. Hard to believe something like that could happen here.”

“I’m so sorry, Rick.” She reached out slightly, then let her hand fall, searching his face. “Do you have any leads?” she asked hopefully.

He shook his head slowly. “Nothing. It’s like she vanished off the face of the earth.”

Felicity shifted her weight, trying to follow his thinking. “What about her phone?”

“It disappeared off the grid this morning. We thought - hoped really - that it was just a dead battery. Or maybe she had dropped and broken it. But we did a thorough search of the area where it went off the grid and found nothing."

Felicity looked intently at him. "I'm so sorry, Rick."

Rick nodded once, absently rubbing his jaw. "We did find a hat on the trail, which her bridal party thinks might be hers. But it just doesn't make a lot of sense to me."

Felicity tilted her head slightly, brows knitting. "Why not? Couldn't that be a lead?"

He nodded. "It could. And Tuna had one of the officers hand-carry it over to the crime lab on the Cape. But it just doesn't smell right to me."

Felicity leaned against the edge of the counter, studying him. "Why? What are you thinking?"

He reflected for a moment. "Her phone went off the grid at the Windswept Bog trailhead." He lifted a hand, mapping it out in the air. "Her hat was found about a quarter of a mile down one of the trails near Stump Pond."

Felicity shifted her weight, arms folding loosely. "And you don't think she might have lost it in a struggle with someone?"

"That's just it. There was no sign of a struggle anywhere. We had over a dozen officers and CSOs on site searching the area, and all we found was a hat in an otherwise undisturbed area." He gestured faintly, frustration creeping in. "I think it was just a diversion."

"Huh," said Felicity, thinking. "Do you think she's still alive?"

Rick hesitated, then gave a small nod, his expression tightening. "Right now, I do. Her friends say she's a fighter and had been through a tough accident a couple of years ago."

Felicity looked back up at him, searching his face. "So now what do you do?"

Rick glanced toward the clock, then back at her, already shifting mentally to the next step. "I'm meeting Tuna at seven to explore other options - travel manifests, video, et cetera to see if she may have left the island. Or the captor left the island with her."

Felicity straightened slightly, a flicker of disappointment crossing her face. "Seven? I thought we had plans tonight."

He pulled her into a hug and stroked the back of her head. "I know. I'm disappointed too, but time is critical right now. We need to find her fast."

She pulled away, smoothing her hair back as she regrouped. "I know. I was just looking forward to it. Let me get you a plate. How about that glass of sauvignon blanc?"

"Right. On it. I wish I could join you, but I need to have a clear head this evening."

CHAPTER THIRTEEN

Tuna and Rick regrouped after dinner at the station and set up camp in the conference room. The chief had granted the space as their war room as well as access to every available officer and CSO. Every resource was at their disposal until Katie was found.

Katie's parents had made it over from Rhode Island, having taken the Seastreak ferry from New Bedford earlier in the day. Being the Memorial Day weekend, hotel rooms and short-term rentals were completely booked, so they had moved in with Katie's bridal party at the cottage in Sconset. Tuna had briefly talked with Katie's mom, Brenda, and briefed her on the case. She had wanted to meet with Tuna and Rick immediately, but remembering the chief's word, Tuna had suggested a bigger help would be another search of Windswept Bog and the jogging trail that Katie had taken to get there.

They had also connected with her fiancé, Harrison, who was in a state of panic and anxious to do whatever he could to find Katie. He had finally made it onto the island after paying several hundred dollars to an unsympathetic traveler to give up his late Friday afternoon seat on a Cape Air flight and was eager to help. He had eagerly shared Katie's password to her iCloud account so that the NPD team could get all possible information off her phone.

With the password, Rick and Tuna had spent an hour doing a deep dive on Katie's digital life: her texts, emails, photos, workout schedules, and nutrition planning.

What they learned was that Katie was a kind, generous, hard-working woman who was deeply loyal to friends and family, supportive of her peers, a mentor to other colleagues at work, and just an all-around good person. The only thing they dug up that could be considered even slightly negative was an email she had written complaining about a flower delivery she had ordered for her mom on her birthday. And even in that email, she was courteous, professional, yet firm. She had not only gotten a full refund but a significant discount on her next order.

That life continued until the moment her phone went off the grid at eight-twenty that morning.

Although the case was not even a day old, the room had already taken on an air of intensity. Tuna had used the large white board to document what little they knew so far and to manage the timeline of Katie's actions from the moment she boarded the ferry in Hyannis on Thursday afternoon until that morning. She had also made a detailed list of all the personnel involved and what activities they were currently executing.

Officer Coffin was hand-delivering the hat to the crime lab in Bourne. All twenty of the Community Service Officers the NPD had hired for the summer were canvassing the island restaurants, businesses, beaches, and tourist spots to see if anyone had seen Katie. Officer White was repeating the aerial grid search of Windswept Bog now that he had a greater temperature differential for the thermal imaging of his drone. The marine unit had completed its sweep of the deeper areas of Stump Pond and, fortunately, had come back negative.

The Inquirer & Mirror had put an announcement out on their digital platforms as well as their daily email. True Island Media had ads running every thirty minutes on all three of their radio stations, as well as their daily email. Given the local media coverage, the CSO canvassing, social media, and word of mouth, it is likely that everyone currently on the island knew about the disappearance of Katie Chapman.

Meanwhile, Rick had taken ownership of the bulletin board and had used it to visually document everything about Katie and the case. On it, he hung pictures of Katie, an aerial of the Windswept Bog, a map of the route Katie had taken jogging, and pictures of everyone in the bridal party. He also included images of the trails, the hat they had found, as well as the jon boat. Printouts of the Steamship Authority, Seastreak, and Hy-Line ferry schedules hung next to those from Cape Air, JetBlue, Tradewinds, United, and American Airlines. Since Katie's disappearance, there had been dozens of options to leave the island. But there was no evidence suggesting that Katie had been taken off.

He stepped back and stared intently, hoping something would stand out that they had missed.

"You okay?" asked Tuna.

Rick sighed. "Yeah. It's just so frustrating. I feel like we are missing something."

"I know."

"How about you? What are you thinking?" asked Rick, concerned.

"Well, none of the airline or airport personnel claim to have seen Katie. The same goes for the Hy-Line and Seastreak. In some ways, we are lucky it's the Friday before Memorial Day, as everyone wants to get to the island, but no one wants to leave. So not a lot of outbound passengers."

Tuna walked up and tapped on the Steamship Authority's traditional ferry schedule with her pencil. "This then, short of a chartered plane, would be the only way to get off the island with Katie."

"The car ferry?"

"Yeah. She could be tied up and in the back of a van or the trunk of a car, and no one would see her."

"True. But how likely do you think that is?"

Tuna sighed. "Honestly, not very. My gut says she is still somewhere on the island, but we just need to check that box. The Steamship Authority sent over the vehicle manifests for all the ferries today. I've got Officer Downs running through them and checking plates. Again, with the holiday, most of the vehicle traffic off the island is commercial, not passenger, so it shouldn't take him too long to complete that."

Rick nodded. "When will we hear back on the hat from the crime lab?"

"Officer Coffin was on the three o'clock high speed, and he confirmed that he delivered the hat to the lab just before five. As you know, even with overtime, some of the tests can take a few hours, so we probably won't hear anything until late tomorrow morning."

"Do you think I should see if any of my old colleagues can help at the FBI?" asked Rick.

"Honestly, right now I'm not sure what they do. But hold that thought. We may need their help before this is over."

Rick nodded. "So what you are saying is we have nothing new on the case. That we are no closer to finding Katie than we were this morning."

"Sadly, yes."

Tuna's phone rang, the sharp vibration breaking the silence. She slipped it from her pocket, glanced at the screen, then angled it toward Rick. "Four oh one area code. Probably Katie's mom."

"Put it on speaker?"

Tuna nodded and tapped her screen. "Hello? Mrs. Chapman?" There was a pause. "Um, can you hold that for just a second? I'd like you to put you on speaker. I have my partner, Detective Rick Caton, here with me. Thank you." Tuna pulled the phone from her ear, tapped the speaker icon, and laid the phone on the table. Both she and Rick leaned in.

"Mrs. Chapman?"

A faint rustle, then, "Yes, I'm here."

"Would you mind repeating what you just started to say to me?" asked Tuna, compassionately.

"Sure. Of course." A shaky breath crackled through the speaker. "As I was saying, my husband and I, along with Harrison and Katie's friends, went back to Windswept Bog. We spent several hours searching all of the trails and didn't see anything. It was so very frustrating." The sound of quiet sobbing came through the small speaker.

Rick's jaw tightened. He leaned in a fraction closer, one hand braced on the table. "Mrs. Chapman, this is Detective Rick Caton speaking. I promise you we will find Katie. I worked a number of these cases early in my career at the FBI, and the odds are in our favor."

There was a beat, then the voice came back sharper, breaking. "The odds are in our favor? What the hell are you saying?" exclaimed Katie's mom. "My daughter is gone! Gone!"

Tuna looked at Rick sympathetically.

Rick didn't pull back. He stayed leaned in, voice calm but firmer now. "Mrs. Chapman. Katie's friends called nine-one-one within a couple of hours of when Katie was probably taken. We also have every resource available to us, working leads, investigating possibilities, and showing Katie's picture to every business on this island. I promise you, we will find her."

The speaker was quiet, save for some sniffling. "Thank you, detective." Her voice wavered. "We appreciate everything you are doing for us, we really do. It's just so hard to think of my little girl out there, alone, with some monster. Thinking of him touching her? Assaulting her? It scares me to death!"

"Mrs. Chapman," said Rick assuringly. "I know we've only been working this case since this morning, but if there is one thing I have learned about your daughter, it is that she is a fighter." He glanced briefly at Tuna, then back to the phone. "We heard about her recovery from the hit and run a few years ago, and this is no different. Katie will fight back. She will survive this."

"You're right. She is a fighter. I just want her back in my arms."

Tuna rested her hand lightly on the table, her tone calm and even. "And Detective Caton and I will make sure that happens, Mrs. Chapman," she said, her voice calm and reassuring.

"Thank you."

"Of course. Now I'd suggest you try to get some rest. And why don't you plan on meeting us here at the station first thing tomorrow morning?"

"Get some rest? Are you kidding me? When Katie is out there?"

Tuna softened, leaning in a fraction closer to the phone. "I know, I know, Mrs. Chapman. But you need to be rested, all of you. There's nothing you can do right now except take care of yourself for Katie. That's what she would want."

"You're right." The speaker grew silent.

Tuna waited a beat, her brow knitting slightly. "Mrs. Chapman?" asked Tuna.

"Sorry." A faint breath came through the speaker. "Just remembering the last phone call I had with Katie. She had called me from Hyannis and was worried about the weekend."

"Worried? How so? Like she was in danger?" asked Rick, pointedly.

"Oh no, nothing like that. She just didn't want to be the focus of attention for three days and didn't know how she was going to manage it."

"She prefers a lower profile?" asked Tuna.

"Yes. She's never wanted to be the center of attention." A light chuckle came from the speaker. "Now that I'm thinking about it, she would absolutely hate this."

"Hate this?" asked Tuna, curiously.

"Thanks to you and your efforts, she probably has the attention of almost everyone on this island."

Tuna glanced over at Rick, a small, knowing smile tugging at her lips.

“Okay then,” said Katie’s mom. “We will see you in the morning. Eight a.m.?”

“Yes. You can call or text me when you arrive. Or let the desk sergeant know, and he’ll bring you up to us.”

“Very well. Thank you, detectives.”

“Goodbye, Mrs. Chapman,” said Tuna, and reached down to disconnect the call.

“I can’t imagine what she is going through,” said Rick, looking at Tuna.

“Nor can I,” said Tuna. “I go crazy when one of my dogs is missing. She must be out of her mind with worry.”

“Yeah,” said Rick, and turned back to the bulletin board. ‘It’s just…”

“What,” asked Tuna.

“I’m still struggling with her phone going off the grid.”

“What do you mean?”

“She had the latest iPhone, right?”

“She did.”

“So even if she shut the phone off, or her kidnapper did, it would still be findable. The Bluetooth keeps working in low power mode. But in her case, it just vanished off the grid.”

“The kidnapper could have smashed it. Maybe with a hammer?”

“Maybe. But we found no evidence of that in the parking lot. Surely there would have been something if that was the case.”

“Faraday bag,” said a voice from the door.

Tuna turned to see Officer Kurt White standing in the doorway.

"A what?"

"A Faraday bag. It's a container designed to prevent all incoming and outgoing electronic signals. Bluetooth, cellular, wifi, GPS. Essentially everything. People use them all the time to prevent unwanted tracking or skimming of their credit cards."

"Of course!" said Rick. "Why the hell didn't I think of that? We actually use them at the Bureau when we make arrests to preserve evidence. Using the Faraday bag prevents someone from remotely erasing a phone."

"Interesting. And what would this Faraday thingie look like?" asked Tuna. She shrugged her shoulders. "Sorry, I'm not a very technical person."

"It could be almost anything. They come in all shapes and sizes. But it's probably a small pouch that would hold a phone or two," replied Kurt.

"How do you know so much about this?" asked Tuna, jokingly.

Office White laughed. "I'm just a tech geek. I love all things electronic."

"Do you have a Faraday bag?" asked Rick. "That you could show Tuna?"

"Me, no. I just read about them recently in one of my drone magazines. They recommend having one on hand to protect the memory cards."

"Okay, then," said Tuna. "Speaking of drones, anything on the aerial recon with the thermal imaging?"

Officer White shook his head. "The imaging was working perfectly. But the only visuals were of deer. Lots, and I do mean lots, of deer. But negative on a person."

Tuna shook her head. "Damn. I was hoping that our theory that she was just hurt and unable to respond would be the one."

"Me too," said Rick. He turned to Officer White. "Thanks, Kurt. We certainly appreciate the help."

"Of course. Is there anything else you need me to do?"

"Right now, no. But we'll probably need your expertise again tomorrow. We may want to run some more grid searches depending on what leads we can generate."

Officer White nodded. "Okay. I will make sure the drones are charged and ready to go. Just let me know the when and where."

"Will do, Kurt. Thank you," said Tuna.

Officer White nodded and walked down the hall. Tuna turned to Rick.

"I don't know about you, but I'm exhausted."

Rick glanced at his phone. It was nearly eleven.

"Okay. I know we need to get some rest, too. Meet you back here in the morning? Say six?"

Tuna nodded. "I'm usually up with the sun, which this time of year is just after five."

Rick turned to leave. "Damn."

"What?" asked Tuna, concerned.

"I forgot I still don't have a car. Give me a ride home?" asked Rick, sheepishly.

Tuna laughed. "Of course. As long as you don't mind getting dog hair on your clothes. Blue and Striper are usually the only passengers I carry."

CHAPTER FOURTEEN

Saturday Morning

Tuna couldn't sleep, and despite her habit of waking with the sun, today she beat the sunrise by over an hour. Rather than waste that time flipping channels, she thought she would get a head start on the day and perhaps track down some clue that would lead to Katie. Still dark, she walked through the front door of the NPD and made her way up to their war room, where she found Rick deep in thought in front of the whiteboard.

"Morning," said Tuna. "I guess I'm not too surprised to see you here so early."

"Morning, Tuna. Yeah. Well, I could say the same about you," replied Rick with a slight smile. "Couldn't sleep?"

Tuna nodded. "I managed to get a few hours, but the thought of Katie out there just kept my mind on overdrive. I just couldn't stop thinking about possible scenarios, locations, motivators."

"Pretty much the same for me. I woke up at three thirty and just felt the need to do something, make some progress. So I headed here."

Tuna smiled. "I hate to ask, but how the hell did you get here without a car?"

Rick chuckled. "I biked."

"What? You rode a bike? At three frickin' thirty in the morning? Wasn't that a little slow and dangerous?"

He shook his head. "Actually, it was surprisingly efficient. My landlord had an older E-bike in the garage that she said I was welcome to use. Honestly hadn't thought much about it, but when I got home last night, thanks to you," he said, motioning to Tuna, "I saw it leaning against the wall and realized it might be my only option for a while. So I plugged it in and this morning made it here in less than ten minutes."

"Wow, okay. Glad you didn't get run over or hit by a deer. To be honest, I'm not a big fan of those things. I've been called to too many accident scenes involving them. They are just dangerous, and I want you to promise me you'll be careful."

"Thanks, Mom, I promise," said Rick with a wry smile.

Tuna gave him a stern look. "I mean it, Rick!

"Okay, Tuna. I promise. Jeez, sorry. Hopefully I'll have a car next week." He motioned to the whiteboard and changed the subject. "Anyway, what's our plan for the day?"

Tuna glanced at her phone. "We have a team meeting at seven to review findings and discuss plans for the day. Then the Chapmans will be here at eight. We should probably review what we want to share and what our plans are for finding her. They are going to be emotional and want answers."

Rick nodded. "Yes. We also need to think about what we can assign to them. Keeping them busy will make our job easier."

"Yes. Any thoughts on that?"

"Well, let's partner them with some CSOs and have them complete the canvass. They probably aren't even halfway done yet, and they could really help there. They'll bring an urgency to the canvass that the CSOs can't and will no doubt create stronger engagement with the community."

"Good idea. Maybe they can also make some fliers and post them at the businesses as well as at the public notice boards."

He nodded. "Good. Now what about us?"

"We need to go talk with everyone who saw Katie on Thursday. That means the bartenders at Cisco, the servers at Brotherhood and Gaslight, and even the bus driver for the Wave, anyone and everyone who interacted with Katie in some way. We got to shake something loose," she finished emphatically.

"We will. Any news yet on the forensics on the hat? Or the ferry manifests?"

"Nothing on the hat yet. That's going to be late morning at best. But Officer Downs texted me last night that he had completed the review of vehicle departures and nothing stood out at him. He was going to chase a couple of plates that he couldn't immediately clear, but he didn't think they would add up to much."

"And today's ferries? There's one leaving at six-fifteen this morning."

"On it. The Steamship Authority will search every vehicle before it is allowed to board the vessel. The airlines have also posted a picture of Katie at each of the departure gates."

"Excellent," said Rick, yawning.

"You look like you need a coffee."

Rick nodded. "Coffee and some food. What's open now?"

"We've got a couple of options, but I'd suggest Stubby's on Steamboat Wharf. Good coffee, bagels, sandwiches. They open at six."

"You driving?"

"I sure as hell ain't riding tandem on your goddam bike," said Tuna, laughing.

* * *

Rick and Tuna had grabbed coffee and a sandwich and walked around the corner to Easy Street. They made their way to a bench and enjoyed their breakfast while watching the harbor come to life. The sun was already well above the horizon, and Rick, his stomach satisfied, closed his eyes and let the warmth play across his face. He was ready to fall asleep.

"We gotta' go," said Tuna.

"Oh, right," said Rick, sitting up. He rubbed his eyes. "Okay."

They made their way back to NPD and walked into the war room just before seven. The team had already assembled, and there was a low yet energized murmuring in the room. They quieted as Rick and Tuna entered, and a couple of dozen faces turned to them expectantly.

"Good morning," said Tuna. "Thank you for being here on time."

Heads nodded.

"I am sorry to report that nothing has changed with this case overnight. Katie Chapman is still missing. And we need to do everything we can to find her."

She walked over to the whiteboard, picked the eraser from the tray, and quickly cleared the right side, eliminating the tasks she had assigned the day before. She grabbed a marker and turned to the team.

"Here's the plan for the morning. CSOs." She looked at all the faces and silently marveled at how young they all looked. "You will be completing the canvass. We want to make sure we talk to every business, every restaurant, every waiter. The same procedures as yesterday, but this morning you will have some help. Katie's family and her fiancé arrived on the island late yesterday, and we want to keep them busy. So a few of you will have some company. I'll leave it to you to sort it out, who goes with whom. But please remember what they are going through."

Heads nodded, and a hand went up. It was CSO Huber.

"Yes, Blair, isn't it?"

The young CSO nodded. "I'd like to volunteer to accompany Katie's mom."

"That is kind of you, officer. Can I ask why?"

Officer Huber was quiet for a moment, a tear forming in her eye. "When I was fourteen, my older sister was kidnapped during her spring break trip."

"I am so sorry, Blair. I hope it turned out okay," said Tuna, hopefully.

The young CSO shook her head slightly. A tear trickled down her cheek. "I just think I can be helpful to Katie's mom. I saw what my family went through and know what she's probably feeling."

Tuna looked at her softly. "That is a very kind and very brave thing for you to do, Officer Huber. Of course, that would be immensely helpful. Thank you."

The CSO nodded.

Tuna took a moment to gather her thoughts. "Okay. Officer White?"

"Yes?" Kurt was standing to the side of the CSOs and dressed in his typical khakis and NPD button-down.

"I'd like you to continue aerial surveillance. We have over ten thousand acres of open space where Katie could be. Plenty of possibilities there."

"That will take some time, Detective Fisch."

"Agreed. Let's prioritize those closest to the kidnapping site." She walked over to the map of the island that Rick had tacked to the bulletin board, slipped on her reading glasses, and studied it closely. "Why don't you focus on the Middle Moors and Altar Rock areas for now?"

Officer White nodded. "Can I also suggest the Serengeti? Those three properties are fairly close to each other and would make for an efficient grid search plan."

"Terrific. Yes, let's do that."

Kurt nodded in agreement.

"Officer Downs?"

"Yes, Detective."

"Have you completed the investigation into the ferry manifests?"

Downs nodded. "Yes. I cleared the last of those vehicles. Katie Chapman did not leave the island on a car ferry."

"Great, thank you. Today, I'd like you to focus on Katie's digital life. Talk to her bank, see if anything is happening there. I know it's a long shot, but maybe someone is using her credit card. Also, please take a look at her iCloud account. We didn't spot anything unusual, but I'd love to have your eyes on it as well."

"Ma'am," said Downs, nodding.

She turned to Rick. "Did I miss anything?"

Rick stepped forward. “No, I think you covered it.” He turned to the team. “I will be the first to admit that these are very difficult cases to work on. It’s hard not to think of what this young woman must be going through and wanting so badly to help her.” He scanned the room. “But focus on your jobs. Keep your eyes and ears open. If you find or hear anything, and I do mean anything, no matter how small it might seem, please let Detective Fisch or me know.” He stepped back.

“Thanks, detective. Any questions?”

The room was quiet.

“Great. Let’s plan on meeting back here at two o’clock. Thank you. Dismissed.”

The team filed out, and Tuna waited until the room was empty before turning to Rick. “I feel like I missed something.”

“You didn’t, Tuna, I assure you. But this type of case always leaves you second-guessing yourself. They are the most difficult cases to work because the time pressure is just so intense. You feel like you can’t waste a minute, or it could impact finding our victim.”

Tuna nodded. “Sorry, I just don’t have much experience with these.” She paused for a minute and added. “Thankfully.”

“What makes it even more difficult is that we are sitting here on Saturday morning of the Memorial Day holiday. Everyone on this island will be having fun today: boating, swimming, partying, and celebrating the start of summer. Everyone will be having fun except us, those looking for Katie and her family.”

There was a knock on the door. It was the desk sergeant, Tomas Santos. "Detective Fisch? The Chapman family is here. Did you want me to show them up?"

Tuna looked around at the whiteboard and the images on the bulletin board. The visuals would do little to comfort the grieving family.

"No. Please show them into the cafeteria. We will be right down."

The sergeant nodded and retreated.

Tuna looked at Rick. "Any words of advice?"

"No. Just be yourself."

She nodded. "Ready?"

"Yep."

Tuna and Rick made their way down to the cafeteria. It was a fairly large space with a half dozen round tables, each with eight chairs. The Chapmans, her fiancé, and two of her bridesmaids had taken the table closest to the entrance.

Tuna walked in and stood in front of the table. "Mr. and Mrs. Chapman. Nice to meet you, although I wish under better circumstances. I'm Detective Fisch. But you can call me Tuna. This is Detective Caton."

"Call me Rick, please," he said, trying to give an air of comfort and assurance.

"And you must be Harrison," said Tuna, directing her comments to a young man with his face buried in his hands.

He looked up at her. His eyes were red, and it looked like he hadn't slept in a week. "Yes. Thank you for seeing us. We just want to know what is happening with Katie. Do you know where she is?" he asked pleadingly. He sobbed. His sister, Madison, seated next to him, put her arm on his shoulder and pulled him close.

"I'm so sorry. We are doing everything we can to find Katie. As I told you on the phone last night, the chief has made this our number one priority and given us access to every possible resource."

"Thank you, detective," said Katie's father, Larry. "But what about other resources like the State Police or FBI?"

"The Massachusetts State Police, Troop D, has been briefed on the case and will be vigilant in their patrols. But they are a small unit and really can't spare any officers to work the case exclusively," answered Rick. "And as you know, the FBI usually will not get involved unless there is suspicion of interstate travel or ransom demands."

Larry Chapman nodded his head slowly.

"But as a former FBI agent myself, let me assure you that we will utilize them as much as possible when the situation warrants."

"When the situation warrants? Does the disappearance of my daughter not warrant their attention?" exclaimed her father, angrily.

Rick held up his hand. "I'm sorry, that did not come out right. Of course, your daughter's case deserves everything we have. I spent seven years with the FBI working out of their Boston field office, and I can assure you they are primed and ready to assist us as soon as we give them the word. But it's not an open checkbook. We need to request specific resources based on collected evidence. And unfortunately, right now, evidence is the one thing we are lacking."

"So you are telling me you don't know anything more today than you did yesterday?" asked her friend, Joan, acidly. "What have you been doing all this time?"

"Ms. Duncan, I…"

"Mrs., please."

"Mrs. Duncan. I appreciate your frustration. We are all frustrated," said Tuna, empathetically. "But we are doing everything we can to find her."

"Okay. So what do we do now?" asked Katie's mom, her arms crossed, trying and failing to show she was in total control of her emotions.

Rick answered, his voice strong and assuring. "We search. We knock on doors. We talk to people. And we need your help."

"What can we do?" asked Harrison, pleading.

"We would like you to join the canvass."

"The canvass?" asked Katie's sister, confused.

"I'm sorry, Madison, police term. It just means talking to people. And that's where we want your help. To partner with our Community Service Officers and go knock on doors. We think you'll add a sense of urgency, of gravity. People will want to help you."

"Of course. Glad to do anything," said Madison.

"Great. Just so you know, Detective Caton and I will be retracing Katie's steps from Thursday, talking to everyone she may have interacted with, whether it's a bartender, a server, or a bus driver. Somewhere during her day, she caught the eye of someone. I intend to find out who that someone is."

"Please find her," pleaded Harrison.

"We will do everything in our power, Harrison, I promise you," said Tuna. She pulled out her wallet and distributed her business card to each of them. "This is my card; it has all my contact information. Please don't hesitate to reach out. I'm available twenty-four hours a day."

"Thank you, detective," said Katie's dad. "Despite our frustration, we really do appreciate everything you are doing to find our Katie."

Tuna nodded. "The CSOs, er, Community Service Officers, are waiting for you in the meeting room across the hall. They are young, but they are also smart, enthusiastic, and engaged with our community. They'll let you know which group you'll be working with."

They stood and slowly made their way out.

Rick waited for the room to clear and then turned to Tuna. "That went better than I expected. I thought they might be more angry with us."

"They have every right to be."

Rick nodded slowly, wondering what Katie's family and friends must be going through. The thought energized him. His protective instincts came out.

"Ready?"

Tuna looked at him reassuringly. "Ready."

CHAPTER FIFTEEN

Saturday, the first day of the Memorial Day Weekend featured spectacular, Chamber of Commerce weather. The sky was a deep azure with temperatures forecasted to be in the seventies, along with a light shore breeze. And if the activities of the night before were an indication, then the next few days were going to be absolutely crazy with fun.

Fun that is for everyone but Katie's family and the NPD.

Tuna and Rick left the offices on Fairgrounds Road, weaving their way through large groups of cyclists heading to the beach. Turning left on Bartlett Road, they cleared much of the traffic and followed until the hard right turn, where it turned into Raceway Drive and then shortly into Somerset Lane.

"I haven't been done this way in forever," said Rick, looking around. "More houses than I remember."

"Yeah. This area has had some development over the last few years, but mostly for the year-rounders."

Rick nodded. "I used to date a girl who lived down here, off Raceway. Do you remember Clara Hurst?"

"Clara? Yeah, I think so. She was in your class at Nantucket High, wasn't she?"

"She was. A few years before you."

"Where did she end up?"

"Last I heard, she was still in Boston. Working at Brigham and Women's."

"Nurse?"

Rick laughed. "Cardiovascular surgeon, actually. She was a smart one. Way too smart for me."

She gave him the side eye. "You are a smart guy, Rick. And a great detective."

"Thanks. Anyway, what can we expect this morning?"

Tuna waited at the intersection of Somerset and Hummock Pond Road. Cars, mopeds, and bicyclists paraded by, and it was several minutes before she found a gap in traffic. She pulled out and accelerated quickly.

"Are you familiar with Cisco Brewers?"

Rick nodded. "Good beer. They have a neat spot in Southport in Boston that I've been to once or twice."

"And the brewery here?"

"Heard about it but have never been."

"Prepare yourself."

"Prepare myself? For what?"

Tuna turned onto Bartlett Farm Road and nodded her head. "Look."

Despite the brewery not opening for another hour, a long line of eager celebrants extended a few hundred yards down Bartlett Road.

"What? This is crazy," said Rick.

"It's one of the most popular spots on Nantucket, especially this weekend. They will be at capacity all day until they close at seven. And then again tomorrow. And Monday."

Tuna slowed and put her blinker on. Two CSOs, the only ones not actively involved in Katie's disappearance, were working the crowd and helping to manage traffic. Together, they parted the line so Tuna could access the driveway and enter the small parking lot. She pulled into the only spot available.

Rick got out of the car and surveyed the area. The line extended from Bartlett Road, through the several hundred feet of the parking lot, and across to the entrance. The merchandise shop where Katie had purchased her new cap sat to the right of the entrance and was absolutely teeming with people. He turned to Tuna. "This is amazing. I can't believe how many people are already here. And where do they all park? This lot looks like it could only hold a dozen or so cars."

"They have a big field just a few hundred yards down Bartlett Road, probably a couple of acres. I'm pretty sure it will be full today."

They cut their way through the line and, despite protests from the crowd, slipped inside the temporary barrier and made their way in. Framing a large cobblestone courtyard, several buildings in various colors sat facing the center. Several parallel rows of narrow tables led to a stage in the corner where a band was setting up. A few pop-up tents were scattered about, providing some shade for customers.

"Where do you want to start?" asked Rick.

"Let's try the beer shack. That's this small building over here," she said, pointing to their left.

They walked over the cobblestones and entered the small wooden structure. A wide, gleaming bar featured a few dozen taps. Behind the bar on the back wall, narrow, hand-drawn signs hung featuring the names of the available beers, the type, and the alcohol level. Rick recognized several of them, but there were quite a few that were new to him. He would need to bring Fel here and give them a try.

A tall man with a brown, bushy beard was prepping the bar for what would no doubt be a very busy day. He was wearing an open flannel shirt, an old, battered t-shirt underneath, and a well-worn cap featuring the brewery's logo.

They approached. "Good morning. Do you have a minute?" asked Tuna.

"Sure."

"I'm Detective Fisch. This is Detective Caton. We are investigating the disappearance of a young woman."

The man nodded. "I heard about it. Awful. Are the rumors true that she was kidnapped?"

Tuna nodded. "We can't really discuss the details, but yes, that's our current theory."

"Awful," the man repeated. "This is Nantucket. We just want everyone to have fun. Be kind. This monster can't be one of us."

Rick nodded. "She was here on Thursday night with four of her friends." He held up his phone with a picture taken of the group in front of the stage. They were raising their glasses, and all looked ecstatic. "Do you recognize them?"

He concentrated on the photo for a minute. "No, sorry. Doesn't look familiar. We must have had hundreds of people here Thursday. But it looks like they are having a mixed drink, so you might want to try across the yard at Triple Eight. Maybe they'll remember."

"Okay, thanks," said Tuna. Rick nodded at the man, and together they walked back into the courtyard.

Rick looked at Tuna. “Triple Eight?”

Tuna smiled. “Yeah, calling this a brewery is a bit misleading as they also have a distillery where they make vodka, rum, gin, tequila, and some absolutely fantastic bourbon.”

“Okay. Wow.”

“They also make pretty decent wines.”

“Quite the enterprise”, said Rick, impressed.

“That it is. Now follow me.”

They walked the hundred or so feet across the courtyard to another wooden building, this one a bit bigger and taller than the beer shack. Inside was a long wooden bar. Behind the bar were shelves holding dozens of bottles of the distillery’s output. A young woman with red hair was cleaning the bar and preparing for the day. As Rick and Tuna approached, she looked up, irritated at being interrupted.

“Can I help you?” she asked, slightly annoyed.

“Yes,” said Tuna. “We are detectives from the NPD and are investigating the disappearance of a woman.”

The bartender’s face softened. “Oh my god, I heard about her. What happened? Is she okay?”

“That’s what we are trying to figure out.”

The girl nodded. “Happy to help in any way. This is just so awful.”

Rick held his phone up. “Do you recognize this group of women? They were here on Thursday until close.”

“Was it a bridal party?”

“It was,” said Rick.

She stared intently at the picture. “I do remember them.” She pointed to the photo. “The lady with the curly brown hair, I served her a few rounds. They were all drinking Nantucket Reds.”

Tuna nodded. “And did you notice anything unusual? Were they talking to anybody?”

The bartender shook her head. “I didn’t notice anything. They just seemed to be having a great time.”

“Okay, thank you,” said Tuna, and turned to leave.

“Have you talked to Robert?” asked the bartender.

Rick and Tuna both turned back. “Who’s Robert?” asked Rick.

“He manages the beer garden. The outdoor space,” she said and pointed toward the stage. “He was working all day Thursday. If they talked to anyone, I’m sure Robert would have noticed.”

Tuna nodded. “Is he here today?”

“Yeah, for sure. He’s probably over at the stage right now helping the band set up.”

“Great. Thank you for your help,” said Tuna.

The bartender nodded slowly. “Just please find her. That sort of thing just doesn’t happen here. It’s definitely got all of us on edge.”

“We will,” said Rick. “We will.”

Rick and Tuna exited the bar and walked across the cobblestones to the stage. A handful of men and women were setting up microphones, amplifiers, and arranging a handful of guitars on stands. In the back, a man was placing cymbals on a stand and tightening the wingnut.

“Excuse me,” said Rick. “Is one of you Robert?”

A thin, older gentleman stood up from behind a large PA speaker. He was wearing khakis and an old Cisco sweatshirt featuring the fluke of a whale. His gray hair was thinning, and he was slightly stooped. "I'm Robert," he said with a touch of concern in his voice. "Is everything alright?"

"Yes, sir. Everything is okay. We just wanted to have a word," said Rick.

The man nodded and carefully maneuvered through the speakers and across the wires. He stepped down from the raised stage. "What can I do for you?"

"Were you working here on Thursday?" asked Tuna.

"Yeah, I was here. Ten to closing at seven. I pretty much work every day in season. We are always just so busy."

"And were you out here? " asked Rick, motioning to the tables across the courtyard.

"Yes. I'm pretty much responsible for the entire outdoor area. I mostly collect empties, make sure the trash cans are emptied, plenty of TP in the bathroom. That sort of thing."

Tuna nodded. "Do you by chance remember this group of young women?" she said, motioning to Rick's phone. He held it up.

He studied the picture intently. "Oh yeah! I remember them. They were sitting over there, close to the stage."

Rick put his phone down. "Did anything stand out to you?"

"No. They were just like every other group that was here. Talking, drinking, laughing. I think they may have gotten up to dance once or twice."

“Do you remember if they talked to anyone else? Any men, for example?”

He thought for a moment. “Actually, now that you mention it, there were a few guys who were talking to them. Seemed kind of interested, if you know what I mean.”

Rick perked up. “What can you tell us about them? What did they look like?”

The man looked back at them with a you-must-be-kidding-me expression. “They were guys, okay. Probably late twenties or early thirties. I mean, they all look young to me,” he said with a laugh.

Tuna nodded, smiling. “Did everything look okay between them? Any vibes like they were getting aggressive or not getting along?”

Robert shook his head. “The guys talked to them for maybe ten, fifteen minutes? I got the impression the ladies were definitely not interested. After that, I think the guys tried with another group of women. And then I think they left.”

Tuna was writing in her notebook and looked up. “Do you remember what time that was?”

“It was almost closing time, so I’d say probably six thirty or so.”

“Great. Thank you for your time, Robert. We appreciate it.”

The man nodded and jumped back on stage.

Rick and Tuna made their way through the courtyard and out into the parking lot. The energy from the crowd was building. Opening time at Cisco Brewery was just minutes away.

As they stepped into Tuna's old Ford Explorer, her phone rang. She looked at the screen, turned to Rick, and said, "Officer Coffin." She clicked accept and put the call on speaker.

"Noah," said Tuna. "I'm hoping you are calling about forensics on the hat?"

"I am. I just got the prelim on their findings."

"What did they find?" asked Tuna hopefully.

"They did find a number of hairs. The lab did confirm color, gender, and overall characteristics matched the vic. But we would need one of her hairs to confirm."

"The vic?" asked Tuna accusingly. "Officer Coffin, we have a missing person. Her name is Katie. Please do not call her a vic again."

The phone went silent. If one could imagine someone trying to fade into a corner on a cell phone call, this would be it.

After a minute, a voice said softly, "You're right, Detective. My apologies."

"It's okay, Noah. What else did they find?"

"They were also able to lift three prints. One complete and two partials."

"Any matches?" asked Rick, excited.

"On that, there's good news and bad news."

"Okay."

"The good news is that the complete fingerprint was from our vi…, er Katie," said Noah. "Apparently, she was fingerprinted as part of her onboarding at Drury Biotech. Part of a standard clearance process, I guess, due to the sensitive nature of their work."

"The bad news?"

"The bad news is the two partials did not match Katie or anyone in AFIS. The lab is going to continue to work on them, but right now, there is just not enough detail."

"What about trace?" asked Rick.

They could hear papers rustling. After a moment, Noah said, "Aside from the hair, the only other trace they could identify was grass, topsoil, and leaf matter. All of which was likely from the spot where we found the hat."

"Thanks, Noah. Anything else?" asked Tuna.

"They are going to run DNA, but as you know, that will take a week or more. As usual, they are pretty backed up. But I think it's safe to assume the hat is Katie's," said Officer Coffin, emphasizing the name.

Tuna nodded. "Got it. Won't hold our breath. Are you heading back?"

"Yes, I'm on the three oh five Hy-Line. Should be in the office by four-thirty."

"Good. We need you back here."

"On my way. See you shortly," said Officer Coffin and disconnected the call.

Tuna looked at Rick. "Okay. The trace lines up with where we found the hat, but the two partials? They could be from our kidnapper."

"Or they could be from the person who sold Katie the hat at Cisco. Or from someone else in the bridal party."

Tuna's face slumped. "I was hoping we finally had something to go on."

Rick rubbed her shoulder. "It is something. And we need to pursue it. But that analysis can take some time, time we don't have."

"What about the FBI? Could they help?"

"We, I mean, they, have a number of fingerprint experts at Quantico. I just don't know how quickly we could engage them. But it's certainly worth a try." Rick pulled out his phone and sent a quick text to his former boss, SAIC Hanna Fines. Tuna could hear the swoosh as the text was sent. "It's Saturday, but I know Hanna keeps her phone close at all times. We should hear back shortly."

"Thank you," said Tuna.

"Of course," replied Rick. "So where now?"

"Brotherhood."

Tuna drove her old Explorer back into town following Hummock Pond Road, continuing on Milk Street, and then slowly eased her way past the Nantucket Civil War Monument and onto the cobblestones of upper Main Street. The old Ford's suspension protested mightily as the vehicle swayed heavily from side to side.

"I think I'm going to be ill," said Rick, laughing, happy to have some relief from the tension of the morning.

"Sorry," said Tuna, chuckling.

They made their way to the top of Main Street and turned left onto Centre Street. The road turned to pavement, and the ride smoothed out immediately. Tuna followed Centre to Broad Street and turned right. Rick looked over at the Tap Room and smiled warmly. He and Felicity had just enjoyed dinner there when she had burned the surprise dinner she had planned. And then he remembered the prior fall when he had been on the island investigating the death of her father. He had shared with her his story about how he was fired from the NPD a decade before, and felt like his opening up was the start of their relationship.

"You here?" asked Tuna. She had pulled the Explorer into the small lot next to the restaurant, ignoring the no-parking signs.

"Sorry," said Rick apologetically. "Just thinking about Fel and our first real date together."

Tuna smiled. "She's a keeper, that one."

"Yes, she is," said Rick.

They made their way in and found it quiet, opening time still a half hour away. Thanks to guidance from the bartender, they found the server who had taken care of Katie's party on Thursday. She had reported nothing unusual, just five women enjoying themselves.

"Did you see anyone paying particular attention to them?" asked Tuna.

The waitress shook her head. "No. They did get loud a couple of times, laughing, which I could tell was annoying some people at the adjacent tables, but that was about it."

They thanked the server and went outside, the sunlight hitting them hard as they emerged from the dark basement of the Brotherhood.

"Well, that was a bust," said Rick. "It seems like they pretty much kept to themselves."

"Yeah. I honestly didn't think we'd get much, but got to cover our bases."

Rick's phone dinged. "It's Hanna," he said as he read the text. "If we send her the partials, she'll see what she can do with the team at Quantico." Rick tapped back with a thumbs up.

"Okay. My turn," said Tuna. She pulled out her phone and sent a quick text to Officer Coffin. "I've asked Noah to send those immediately to Hanna."

"You have her number?" asked Rick, surprised.

Tuna nodded. "You shared it with me during the Post investigation. I thought it might come in handy someday."

Rick smiled. "You never fail to impress me, Tuna."

She returned the smile. "Up for a little walk? I'll leave the car here as there's probably not an open parking spot within a few miles of here, and it's only a few blocks over to Gaslight."

He nodded. "I can use the exercise."

Together they weaved their way through throngs of summer residents, day trippers, and tourists, the uneven bricks of the sidewalk slowing their progress. They made their way past the beautiful white columns of the Athenaeum, jaywalked across the cobblestones of India Street, and down Union to the former movie theater now turned into one of the most popular late-night bars on the island.

Although they didn't open for several more hours, they could see some activity through the large windows that faced the street. They opened the door and made their way in.

"Hello?" asked Tuna.

A heavily tattooed man, mid-forties with dark brown hair and a long ponytail, emerged from behind the bar.

"Can I help you?" he asked.

"Yes, I'm Detective Fisch. This is Detective Caton. We are investigating the disappearance of a young woman."

His shoulders slumped. "Oh, man. I heard about her. So sad, tragic really. I'm Darren Ward. I help manage the place and work the bar. What can I do to help?"

"Hi, Darren. Were you working Thursday night?"

He nodded. "I was. Man, it was crazy. People were partying hard and having fun. It was insane," he said softly. "But the tips were great."

"Do you by chance recognize this woman? She was here with a bachelorette group. According to one of the women in the party, they sat at a high top and sang karaoke," said Rick as he held up his phone.

The bartender looked intently at the image. "Oh yeah. They were sitting over there," he said, pointing to a high-top table by the window.

"Anything you could tell us about the group? Or her specifically? Anything unusual happen?"

He shook his head. "Not that I recall. They sang some karaoke, which, honestly, was pretty bad, but everyone was laughing about it. They seemed to be having a great time."

"Did they stay pretty much just themselves? Do you remember them talking with anyone?"

He thought for a moment. "You know, now that you mention it, there was a guy who seemed intent on talking to them. I'm sure he was probably trying to hook up for the evening."

"Do you remember which woman he was talking to?"

"I think all of them. But he seemed pretty intent on her, the woman you just showed me."

"Really?"

"Yeah. He hung around for a while and was definitely bothering them."

"Why do you say that?"

"Just a vibe, really. I mean, I'm slammed at the bar making drinks and trying to take care of all the customers. So I couldn't watch them constantly. But every time I looked over, he seemed to be there."

"What did he look like?"

"Um. He was older, for sure. Probably in his fifties. A little heavy-set. Dressed pretty nicely."

"Have you seen him before?"

He shook her head. "Not that I recall."

"Was he alone?" asked Rick.

"I don't think so. There was a table farther down with some older customers. I think he arrived with them."

Tuna nodded, taking notes. "Did he stay with the women the whole time?"

"No. From what I saw, it looked like they froze him out. I don't think anyone was interested in him, and they just kind of ignored him. He was gone by the time they closed out."

"What time was that?"

"I think it was around eleven. Maybe a little earlier."

"And you didn't see what time he left?"

"No."

"Do you guys have video?"

The bartender shook his head. "No. Being a popular place, we tend to get a lot of celebrities here, and we want to respect their privacy."

"Any chance you could find his bill? Get his name for us."

"Sure. If he's the one who paid. And assuming he used a card. A lot of people just pay cash. They throw down a few Benjamins and call it good."

"Understood. But we'd appreciate it if you could take a look for us."

"Happy too. Just give me a minute." He left Rick and Tuna and went back behind the bar. He stared intensely at the screen while tapping repeatedly on the point of sale system. After a few minutes, he seemed to find what he was looking for and pulled out a pen and a pad of paper from under the bar.

He returned to the detectives carrying an old-school restaurant order form. "We may have gotten lucky. The tab for table twelve, which I believe was the one where the men were sitting, was paid for by this gentleman," said the bartender, handing them the paper. "Geoffrey Pierce."

Rick took the paper. "Do you know this man?"

Darren shook his head. "I don't. And I'm not sure if he was the guy or not, trying to talk to the women. But he's the one who paid the tab."

Rick held up the paper. "Thanks, Darren. This is a huge help."

"You're welcome. I just hope you find her alive and well. Nantucket is a safe place. That sort of shit doesn't happen here."

Rick and Tuna thanked him and started back to her car.

"Can we get someone working on tracking down this Pierce guy?" asked Rick.

"Absolutely. Tomas Santos, our desk sergeant. Not only does he pretty much run the place, but he has an amazing skill of being able to find out just about anything about anybody. Personally, I think he secretly wants to be in the FBI or CIA," she said, chuckling. "He's that good."

"Then let's give him the green light," said Rick, impressed.

She pulled out her phone and tapped the screen. "Tomas? Tuna here. I need you to do a quick search on a man named Geoffrey Pierce. And it's not the traditional spelling, it's G-e-o-f-f-r-e-y, last name Pierce. Find out who he is, where he's staying on the island, criminal background. You know the drill."

Tuna nodded several times. "Great. Thanks," and ended the call. She turned to Rick. "He's on it. Hopefully, he'll have some top-line by our meeting at two."

"Excellent," said Rick. "What's next?"

Tuna glanced at her phone. "We have a little time before the team meeting. Hungry?"

CHAPTER SIXTEEN

2015

The remains were found by two hikers one chilly December day near Altar Rock. Their dog had veered off the trail and returned with a bone clenched firmly in its teeth. One of the hikers, a nurse, recognized the bone as human, most likely a femur or tibia. It was hard to tell given the age and degradation of the sample. The dog's enthusiastic chewing on it hadn't helped in the identification process.

A call to the police was followed by a more thorough investigation by several officers. It didn't take them long to find the nearly complete skeleton half-buried in the sand just a few yards off the trail. Following exhumation and a comparison to dental records, the body was identified as that of Mary Ward, a long-time summer resident in the village of Siasconset and reported missing by her landscapers in May of 2002.

At the time, local authorities had led an intense search effort for the wealthy seasonal resident to no effect. The leading theory to her disappearance suggested she had dementia or early onset Alzymer's and had simply wandered off. Others surmised that she had maybe tried going for a swim off Sconset Beach and had either been dragged under by a rip current or had had a medical event that caused her to drown.

It didn't help that most of the people who had met Mary were happy to see her go.

She was widely regarded as an elitist and a snob. She had grown up the daughter of a third-generation banking scion and thought that she was above everyone else. Work was not a word in her vocabulary. Neither was kindness nor generosity. The fact that she was a spinster, unmarried at the age of seventy-two, might have contributed to her dour and unpleasant personality.

Her treatment of the staff at Sconset's local grocery store and sandwich shop was legendary, treating them as if they were her personal servants. Her reputation with the bartenders, waiters, and others in Nantucket's demanding service business was no better. She was simply never happy with anything, and no amount of effort would change her opinion.

There were more than a few rumors that her disappearance was orchestrated by the staff of one of her favorite restaurants in Town simply because they could no longer stand dealing with her, despite the many dollars she spent in their establishment. Of course, her tipping was right in line with her feelings of the staff in general, and rarely would exceed five percent. On more than one occasion, she had publicly dressed down her server and left nothing for their hard work.

The proprietor of one of her most frequented restaurants, facing a revolt by his team, had briefly entertained the idea of banning her from the establishment. Fearing her anger and the storm of fury she could unleash, he took the easier route of compensating the staff with generous hazard pay for whenever she darkened their door.

News of the discovery of her remains brought little celebration or acknowledgement. The years had scrubbed the negative image of Mary Ward from most residents, and the turnover was such that most current waiters and bartenders had never had the displeasure of dealing with her.

The Inquirer & Mirror had a front page article on the discovery with some speculation on how she died and how she had ended up miles from her Ocean Drive manse. Despite the suspicions of criminal activity, there was insufficient evidence to support any investigation. Given the lack of public empathy and no family or friends to push for a resolution, The Inq & M reported that the case would likely not be pursued any further.

Randy had read the article and smiled.

Balance had been maintained.

CHAPTER SEVENTEEN

About the time her family walked into the NPD, a shaft of golden sunlight cut through the grime and dirt of the small basement window and struck Katie Chapman squarely on the eye. She roused, her mind spinning, trying to grapple with where she was. Disoriented, at first, she thought the prior twenty-four hours had just been a nightmare, and with that came a rushing sense of relief.

Then she caught a whiff of the damp, dreary smell of the basement, and reality hit her hard. She tried to sit up only to have the dog leash pull her back down on the old mattress, the springs squeaking in protest. The cable must have tangled around her while she slept, she thought, and carefully stood and unwound the red vinyl-wrapped cable from around her stomach.

She pulled the cable out sufficiently so she could step over it and then let it retract noisily back into the spool attached to the wall. Letting her eyes adjust to the meager light in the basement, the surroundings came into focus.

Nothing had changed. The same sparse wall and old wooden shelving laden with moldy cardboard boxes were still there, as were the steep, narrow treads of the flimsy-looking staircase.

An idea hit her. Maybe?

She pulled hard on the cable until it reached its full extension, and then, like the day before, she walked slowly until she reached the limit and then stretched her hand as far as it could go. She could just touch the middle of the stringer and the end of the tread, darkened with age and riddled with fine cracks. She gathered her strength, closed her eyes, and pushed.

Her goal was to make it rock, hoping that it would sway enough so that he would lose his balance. She remembered he was neither a small nor a young man, and if she could time it right, maybe just maybe he would fall, and she could quickly get on top of him and choke him with the dog cable. Hopefully, he would have the keys on him for the handcuffs.

But that all proved moot. She pushed hard, and the stairway remained firm. She noticed now what she hadn't seen the day before. The opposing stringer was secured into the basement wall with large anchor bolts spaced every couple of feet. It wasn't going anywhere.

Disappointed, she retreated to her bed, sat down heavily, and cupped her face in her hands. She sobbed quietly at the frustration of being tied up like a dog, from the fear of what might happen to her, and the sheer anger of being a victim again of one man's repellent behavior.

It was then that she looked up and noticed that there were a couple of fresh water bottles and a small plate of food at the end of her reach.

Had he come down here during the night while I was asleep? How had I not heard him?

She shuddered.

She stood and, pulling the leash, grabbed the plate and one of the bottles of water. The plate was old, probably from the fifties, and sadly, reminded her of her paternal grandmother, Mur. She had spent many a weekend with her kindly grandmother at her home on Cape Cod, playing games, reading books, and hearing the stories of her father's childhood. Mur had made the most delicious oatmeal raisin cookies and always served them on an amber glass plate, its rim patterned with small daisies, and at its center a starburst; its indentations in the glass always seemed to catch the last of the oatmeal crumbles.

A tear ran down her cheek as she removed the plastic cling wrap from the familiar plate. Beneath it were a couple of protein bars, a banana, and a yellow sticky note with a few words written in black. She pulled the note up and tried to make out the words in the dim light.

Nothing Gold Can Stay.

What? What the hell does that mean?

She tossed the note aside and focused her energies on the food. She realized she had not eaten in almost twenty-four hours and was famished. She hated the thought of eating food he had provided, but forced herself to push that aside and instead focus on her well-being. If she were to be successful and find a way out of here, she had to maintain her strength.

She took a long drink of water and then quickly ate the two protein bars. She picked up the banana and examined it closely, worried about it being altered or poisoned. Slowly, she snapped the stem, peeled back the skin, and took a tentative bite of the tip. She ate it slowly, her senses on full alert to determine if there was any unusual scent or taste. Finding it acceptable, she quickly finished the fruit and then took another long drink of water.

The food had energized her, and she immediately felt more hopeful with her thoughts turning once again to finding a way out of this. She lay back on the bed, closed her eyes, and tried to let her mind relax. It was a problem-solving technique she had learned years before, and found that if she could just free her thoughts from the challenges of the moment, solutions would often find their way to her.

She focused on her breathing, inhaling for four seconds, holding it for seven, and slowly exhaling for eight. She could feel her belly rise and fall methodically, and a sense of calm began to embrace her like a warm hug from her grandmother.

Her mind free of stress, it began to replay images of Katie's life; a celebration with her colleagues after they had had a major breakthrough, meeting Harrison at the concert, college graduation, her parents beaming from the front row as she gave the valedictorian speech, her mom's gentle smile and deep blue eyes that always seem to radiate love, building a treehouse with her father when she was ten.

The treehouse!

Her eyes flung open, and she sat up so quickly that her handcuffs pinched her. She absently rubbed her wrist while she thought back on the treehouse. They had built it on a river birch tree whose multiple trunks they had called the five sisters. The largest trunk went through the middle of the treehouse, with each of the others holding a corner of the structure. Her father had used a clever design to anchor the corners so that the trunks could sway in the wind without tearing the treehouse apart.

Was that it? The way he attached the corners? What was her brain trying to tell her?

She closed her eyes and tried to calm her mind, to let the solution appear. She replayed images of the two of them building the walls, crafting the trap door and ladder system, decorating the walls, and even camping out in it. The visuals played through her mind.

A slight smile crept onto her face.

Her father had insisted that they have a hammock where she could rock back and forth, read her books, and even nap. When they were installing it, he showed her a couple of eye screws that were going to attach to the framing to anchor each end of the hammock. She had looked at the eye screws and asked how he was going to possibly install them. He had smiled, held up a screwdriver, and then laughed at the confused look on her face.

"Watch," he had said. He then threaded the screwdriver through the eye and then, using the screwdriver as a lever with a hand on each side, wound the screw into the wood. After a half dozen rotations, the eye was firmly embedded in the stud. Satisfied, her dad had turned to her, handed her the screwdriver, and asked if she wanted to do the other one. She had eagerly stepped in. Struggling at first, once the screw got a good bite into the wood, it was only a few more turns before her eye was secured as well. She had let out a little shout of triumph, which had made her dad laugh.

Replaying that in her mind, she followed the vinyl-wrapped cable to the wall and took a closer look at the retractable end of her confinement.

She noticed for the first time that there was raised text on the side of the frame, *Cordmatic Dog Tenda*, and a cartoonish imprint of a dog. The whole thing looked old, maybe even as old as the dinner plate her food was served on. The metal frame was pitted, and the drum's red paint was faded and chalky.

In the dim light, she examined the device closely. The frame was U-shaped, bolted to the wall at its base with two flanges extending to embrace the reel mechanism. A bolt ran from the right flange, through the center of the drum, and then screwed into a welded nut on the opposite flange.

Sometime in its life, this Cordmatic Dog Tenda had been repaired.

From the factory many decades ago, she was sure it would have been fitted by a hex head bolt, tightened to a specific torque setting to ensure proper reel operation. But somewhere along its sixty or seventy-year life, that bolt had been replaced. Maybe it had rusted. Maybe a particularly strong dog had reached the end of its run and pulled so hard it had bent the bolt. Maybe its owner wanted something shiny instead of flat gray. Regardless, the bolt hex head bolt had been replaced with an eyebolt.

It was certainly an unusual choice for a repair. But then she thought of her dad. He had an old Christmas cookie tin filled with washers, screws, nuts, and bolts collected from numerous projects over the years. She had seen him many times digging through it, trying to find the right screw or bolt, checking different thread pitches, until he would find the one he needed to fix whatever he was working on.

Someone years ago had probably done the same with her restraint and had settled on an eyebolt as the replacement. Her captor had probably paid no attention to it and assumed it would continue to work as designed.

But Katie saw her chance. Now she just needed a lever.

She stood, pulled the cable to its full reach, and scoured the basement looking for a possible device. She couldn't reach the shelving or the cardboard boxes. The only thing she could reach was the staircase, and there was nothing there that could help her.

Retreating to the bed, she lifted the mattress and examined the metal frame. It was steel with legs bolted firmly in each corner. Every six inches, a V-shaped metal rod protruded from the frame, where it was threaded through a hole in a tab welded to the frame. At each end of the V, a metal spring was hooked into a small hole in the rod. The other end of the spring connected to the metal grid via a simple split metal ring. By pulling on the spring and reducing tension on the attachment point, Katie was able to unhook the spring from one finger of the rod. She did the same for the other side and then was able to remove the rod from the metal tab.

Smiling, she held up the V-shaped rod to the meager light and thought it would just be the right size. She dropped the mattress back down on the frame and sat down on the edge closest to the wall. She grabbed the reel and pivoted it so the eye screw faced her. Remembering that time in the treehouse, she threaded the end of the rod through the eye. She was only able to get a couple of fingers on each end and prayed she would be strong enough to turn it.

Lefty loosey, she reminded herself and twisted.

The screw didn't budge.

She needed more leverage. The V shape was not giving her enough torque to loosen the bolt. She needed to straighten it.

Her first few attempts involved trying to hold the piece vertically while stepping on it. All she managed to do was step on her fingers. Frustrated, she grabbed the legs and tried to flatten them using the bed frame. All that did was gauge the metal of the bed frame and create some sharp edges on the rod.

She let out a long sigh of exasperation. She was so close. She sat down and grabbed the other bottle of water. Taking a sip, she surveyed the walls around her, hoping for inspiration. Her eyes settled on a couple of holes in the concrete, probably once used to attach a clothes line or an ironing board. She walked over to the holes and slipped in one leg of the V-shaped rod. It was a perfect fit.

Smiling, she grabbed the remaining leg and pulled. The hole held fast, and slowly she could feel the metal yielding to her pressure. She pulled it out and saw that she had made it significantly flatter, but not yet enough. She reinserted the rod into the hole and pulled with all of her strength, her feet almost leaving the floor. Slowly, the metal rod flattened out until soon it was protruding straight out of the hole.

She held it up in the meager light. Aside from a little ridge in the center, she now had a straight rod almost a foot long.

Satisfied, Katie returned to the reel and slid the rod through the eye. She was able to get a hand on each side and, twisting, felt the bolt turn. A shot of energy and excitement flushed through her body. She twisted harder, and soon she was rotating the lever freely, backing the screw out of the nut. She felt it release and, pulling the bolt out, the drum, cable, and all fell into her hands.

She was free!

Holding the reel in her hand, she ran toward the exterior bulkhead door, anxious to get out and make a break for freedom. She was just a few feet from the concrete steps leading to freedom when she heard a screen door slam. A shot of adrenaline flooded through her, and she froze. Looking up, she could almost see her captor walking across the floor, the old beams squeaking at each footstep as he made his way across the house.

Was he coming down here? Was it time for what evil he intended for her?

She almost panicked but forced herself to calm down. She had defeated the restraint and was now free to move. That opened up a world of options for her. She could hide and trip him coming down the stairs. She could use the cable and drum as a weapon, like a flail, to catch him on the side of the head. Or she could bide her time and wait for the most opportune moment to make her escape.

She walked swiftly and quietly back to the bed and searched frantically for the eye bolt that she had just triumphantly removed. She grabbed it, held the drum up into the frame, and slid the bolt through, giving it a few turns, just enough to hold it in place.

Satisfied, she sat down on the bed and waited.

And planned.

CHAPTER EIGHTEEN

Randy Evans sat and stared at the only pictures he had of his parents. It had been taken at the one and only time in his childhood that he remembered being happy. It was late summer of his seventh year, and his parents, in an unusual act of spending money on something other than drugs and alcohol, had taken Randy to the Franklin County Fair, just a few miles from his hometown of Turners Falls, Massachusetts.

He scoffed at the idea of calling his father a parent. His father had never been able to hold down a job. Never been able to provide for his family. Never had done anything that would even remotely be called parenting. In reality, he had been nothing more than the sperm donor to a fourteen-year-old high school dropout. The shotgun wedding that followed married two totally unprepared souls together. His mother, Chloe, did her best given the miserable circumstances, her lack of experience, and the poor excuse of a human she was bonded to. The other, Levi Evans, proceeded to take out his life's frustrations and regrets on the little bundle of joy that they had brought into the world.

Looking at the picture, seeing his mother's shy smile, he reflected back on that one happy day.

They had walked the fair, looking at the livestock and agricultural displays, and had even ridden a couple of rides. One was the Tilt-a-Whirl, which made him feel sick. But he was proud of himself for not throwing up. His parents had bought him a hot dog and some fries, and he thought he was in heaven. He even caught a glimpse of his mother grinning at his father. That was something he had never seen before.

It was his mom who had wanted to capture their day with a picture. She pulled him and his father into a little booth and, after feeding a few quarters into a slot, told them to smile. He had happily sat between them and smiled broadly. The day had been the best day of his life, and he hoped, prayed, that it would never end. After sitting for just a few minutes, the machine spat out a small strip of four different pictures of Randy with his mom and dad. In all four, Randy was smiling intently at the camera while next to him, his parents had made funny faces, laughing at each other, or looking at Randy with amused interest, like they were looking at a dog doing a trick.

It was the last of four pictures that deceptively showed a young, happy family enjoying a day at the country fair.

Randy was in the middle with the same eager grin that appeared throughout each take. But this time, both his parents were looking at the camera. And both were smiling. His mom had her arm around his shoulders, leaning into him, while his father had reached his hand out to rest on the back of his mom's neck. To anyone who didn't know any better, this was a lovely young family who enjoyed each other's company immensely.

Following the picture taking, his dad had wanted to do one more ride, so they waited in line for what seemed like forever until it was their turn to go through the haunted house. The acne-pimpled teenager took their three tickets and ushered them into a little train car. Once they were seated, he pulled a lever, and the car jerked forward. They followed a twisty, bumpy journey through what his father claimed was a haunted mansion. But Randy could see laughing people and blue sky outside through slits in the black canvas walls, which let in enough light so that he could see all the time-worn props and high school age actors jump scaring riders in front of them. The whole thing was far from scary, but he still had fun. His parents had never lavished this much attention on him.

If the people who created that ride wanted to see a really scary house, they should come visit me for a day.

Their day at the fair over, Randy reluctantly followed his parents back to the parking lot and into their rusted-out, primer colored Chevy sedan. His father was always saying that he was going to fix it up, and someday it would be Randy's. It was going to be so nice that Randy would be proud to cruise down the main drag of Turners Falls, Massachusetts.

His dad was big on promises but lacked severely in the delivery department.

Randy climbed into the back seat, the door closing with a rusty squeal from the hinges. His dad got in the driver's side while mom hopped onto the bench seat across from him. Randy was still radiating in his day when he heard his mom say something to his dad. He wasn't sure what it was, but it caused his dad to turn to his mom and slug her in the cheek with his right fist. She leaned over, clutching her face, and started to cry.

It took several attempts to get the car started, but it finally roared to life after a couple of loud backfires. His father slammed it into gear and lurched out of the parking lot, aiming the family sedan toward home, a very dilapidated, trash-strewn trailer located on the eastern outskirts of Turners Falls.

Such ended young Randy's happiest day.

Now, years later, sitting in his rocking chair on his porch in the Nantucket moors, Randy thought about that day wistfully. In his mind, he thought that the happiness he felt during that day could have continued forever if not for his father, and what he saw was the lack of balance. There was no balance in the relationship between his mother and father. His father always skewed the scales in his direction and always made himself the priority of the family. Little Randy needed new school clothes? Tough shit. Your father needed his vodka. Was Randy hungry? Tough shit. Your father needed his bourbon.

His mother withered away both physically and emotionally. She knew how badly they were failing Randy as parents, and it ate her up. He wished fervently he could have talked her into running away. But he was eight. He didn't know the realities of the world and the challenges his mom faced, like not having two nickels to rub together.

He stared at the old images in his hand and tried to remember what his mom's voice sounded like. In his heart, he knew that she must have loved him. She just didn't have the power to stand up to his father and defend young Randy.

Her death had been the saddest day of his life.

Just a few weeks after the Franklin County Fair, Randy had arrived home from school. His stop was one of the last on his bus route, and he knew he didn't have much time to play outside before it got dark. And being outside was critical to his survival. He spent every available moment outside, as it was his only easy means to escape his father. He often dreamed that he and his mom would steal his crappy, rusted-out car and run away. Run far, far away from the sorry excuse of a human his father represented.

His father usually spent his days with a bottle of rotgut vodka or bourbon, getting drunk and often passing out before Randy even got home from school. Looking back, he had no idea how they survived financially but suspected it was a combination of state welfare payments and petty theft. The Franklin County Sheriff's office was a frequent visitor to their house, often escorting his father out of Randy's life on a fairly regular basis. Unfortunately, his dad would often return a day or two later and would take out his frustrations with local law enforcement on Randy or his mother. Seeing the sheriff pull in their garbage-strewn driveway was a double-edged sword. On one hand, it usually represented a respite from his father's abuse. On the other hand, that abuse would be escalated on his return until his frustrations had been assuaged.

Randy thumbed the picture and thought of that fateful day.

His mother had sent him off to school on an empty stomach. He knew she wanted better for him, but with his father spending the welfare payments and whatever spare cash on alcohol, she was rarely able to buy food for him with any regularity. Fortunately, his school offered free meals and provided much of the nutrition he desperately needed.

He had arrived home, the bus dropping him off in front of his trailer. Embarrassed, he turned and waved to the driver, a kindly old woman who always had a nice word for Randy. She returned the wave, closed the door, and pulled away in a blast of diesel fumes.

Randy walked tentatively to the front door, not knowing what to expect. Was his dad already sleeping? Was he out trying to steal enough to fund his next alcohol purchase? Or was he inside waiting for Randy to come home so he could take out his frustrations for being a complete and total failure of a human being?

The trailer was quiet; the only activity he could see was a couple of feral cats picking through the remnants of trash scattered around their yard. He stepped carefully around an old engine block that his father boasted would be the heart of their restored car. In reality, it was a worthless, rusted hulk of steel that did little more than block easy access to the rotted-out front steps that led to his sorry excuse of a home.

At first, the quiet excited him. Maybe his dad was gone, arrested for good. He had often dreamed that the sheriff would come and take him away for the rest of his life. But his father's lack of ambition extended to his criminal activities. He didn't have the drive to commit a crime that would put him behind bars for any length of time.

He walked up the steps slowly, careful to place his feet on the least rotten section of treads. The screen door had long since been inoperative, hanging drunkenly by the bottom hinge, the top having been badly damaged during one of his father's vodka-fueled rages. He opened the battered door and stepped directly into the kitchen of the trailer.

He felt a sudden jolt of adrenaline seeing his mother. She was lying face down on the cracked Formica top of the family dinner table. Blood had pooled and dried around her head, and he could make out the soft buzzing of flies.

Trash and empty vodka bottles littered the floor.

He crept slowly up to his mother's body to see if she really was dead. The back of her head was bashed in, and her hair was clotted in blood. He fought the urge to vomit. He had started to cry.

A bent and bloody aluminum softball bat lay on the floor beside her.

His poor mother. She had tried to care for him, but she just didn't have the experience or resources. She herself had grown up in a toxic family and was barely a teenager when she got pregnant. She had done her best, but she was far removed from what anyone would consider a good mother.

He looked around, suddenly unsure of where his father was. He tensed, half expecting his father to barrel down the short hallway and blame him for his mother's prone body. And maybe beat him with the bat as well. He slowly backed away from the table and tiptoed down the hall to his parents' bedroom. The door was open, and peering through, he could see, lying on his back atop the bare, stained mattress, the prone body of his father.

At first, he thought he was dead. But then Randy could see his dad's chest rise and fall, his breathing heavy. His dad had gotten shitfaced - again - and beat his mom to death with a baseball bat. The bastard! He was just sleeping off another bender, not a care in the world, and completely unaware of what he had done.

Not wanting to wake him and receive another beating, he tried to approach quietly. The floor squeaked.

Randy froze, but his father didn't move.

Then he saw the gun. His dad had the gun in his right hand, the hand closest to Randy.

Maybe he had planned to kill himself? A murder suicide?

His father had stolen it a few months before and had flashed it to his son in an attempt to make his son proud of him. Look at me, boy. Your father is a real man! But all Randy had felt was a deep sadness at this sorry excuse of a human.

He pushed a finger against his dad's chest. His dad stirred, adjusted, and resumed his snoring.

Randy slowly and carefully grabbed his father's right hand and guided it up to his forehead.

His father blew out a long breath.

Randy had almost stopped right there. Almost. But he knew deep in his bones that life with his father would have been a living hell. It had been incredibly difficult before, of course, but his mother had provided a welcome buffer and had protected him as best she could. But with her gone? He shuddered.

He worked his thumb into the gun's trigger guard, forcing his dad's finger against the trigger, closed his eyes, turned his face away, and pushed.

There was a tremendous bang, and the acrid smell of gunpowder filled his nose. He slowly opened his eyes and turned.

The gun lay on the floor, just inches from the dangling arm of his father. Looking closer, Randy could make out the bullet hole on the right temple of his father's head. Blood was flowing down his face and pooling on the heavily soiled mattress. The foul smell of blood was mixed with the potent smell of alcohol. An empty handle of the cheapest vodka sold at their local package store lay shattered next to the gun.

He didn't know how long he stood there taking in the scene before him. It could have been a few minutes. It could have been an hour. He was struggling to understand and accept his new reality. His parents were well and truly gone. But he had been the one to avenge his mother's death. The sight of blood and his father's brain matter on the wall had given him nightmares for years, but taking action to rid the world of this piece of shit? That had made him proud. He had hoped his mother would have been proud, too.

Finally, Randy had left the trailer and walked to the house next door. His parents weren't exactly popular in their neighborhood, but fortunately, no one had held his gene pool against him. Most simply just felt sorry for him having to grow up in that situation. The neighbor, a kindly older woman, had called the police and had distracted him with a sandwich while they investigated the situation and eventually removed the bodies. She had hugged him and wished him luck when the social worker for the Department of Children Services had come to collect him. He would never see her again.

He had bounced around from one foster care family to another for a few months, never staying more than a week or two at each. Some were nice, others cruel, but none were as abusive and as destructive as his biological family had been. Then, at nine, he had found Mama Hickman. She had made all the difference in his life. If not for her, he was sure he would have ended up in prison or died young. It was thanks to Mama Hickman that he had learned of the importance of maintaining the balance.

Back on his porch, slowly rocking back and forth, he thumbed the strip of images and smiled sadly. It had been almost five decades since his parents' deaths. All that remained of their sad partnership was the memories in his mind and four black-and-white images taken in a penny-ante photo booth.

He looked out over the moors. Yes, he had had what many would consider a challenging childhood. But he had recovered, even thrived, despite those challenges. He had found his way to Nantucket. Had found his true calling in life, and felt the warmth of pride swelling through him as he thought of how he alone had helped maintain the balance, the stability of the island despite the rampant changes that had occurred since his arrival. Thank you, Mama Hickman, for helping me find my true calling.

The Gift he had selected this year was special. He could feel that. And he knew that the sacrifice, while unfortunate, would renew the island's fragile equilibrium.

He slipped the photo strip in his pocket, stood, and made his way inside. The Gift would be hungry, and he needed to take care of that. After all, he wasn't a monster.

CHAPTER NINETEEN

They stopped at Henry J's, ordered up a couple of grinders - Italian for Rick, and meatball for Tuna, and drove over to Creek's Preserve, the lovely park next to the Milestone rotary. They parked, walked a few hundred yards down the winding path, and found an open picnic table. Across the lush lawn to their north, Nantucket Harbor was spread out in front of them, absolutely packed with activity.

"I love this spot," said Rick. "I ate here last fall with Noah when I was investigating the Posts' deaths. It really is just beautiful."

"That it is. And it also shows that the old Nantucket," she held her fingers up in air quotes, "is still alive and well. So many people think Nantucket has become like the Hamptons, just a playground for the super wealthy, but the vast majority of the people here see it as a community of like-minded souls who enjoy the sheer beauty of the island, the diversity of our residents, and the camaraderie of living on a small, sandy speck thirty miles out to sea."

"That's funny. That's exactly what Noah had said. He mentioned that local families sold the property to the Land Bank for a fraction of what they could have gotten for it on the open market."

"They did indeed. There was no shortage of developers hoping to get it and build another monstrosity that would only be used a couple of months out of the year. Now? The community gets to enjoy this wonderful space all year long."

"Well, it's lovely. And believe it or not, it was that conversation with Noah that got me thinking about returning to the island."

"Really," asked Tuna curiously.

"Yeah," said Rick, staring out over the water. "He seemed confident, and rightly so as it turned out, that the NPD would have me back, that things had changed. I probably should buy him a beer and thank him for being the catalyst that got me to return."

Tuna smiled. "Actually, it's me who should be buying him a beer. I feel I was a little rough on him earlier. For calling Katie a vic."

"I know he didn't mean anything by it."

"Noah? Of course not. He was just being a cop. But the term really rubbed me the wrong way."

Rick nodded. "I get that, Tuma, I really do."

She smiled softly and gazed out across the harbor. In the distance, contrasted to the bright blue sky above and the graying blue water of the ocean below, were dozens upon dozens of sails. Some were stark white, others featured bright colors and broad stripes. A few even sported the brands of well-known alcoholic beverages. Beer, rum, and vodka seemed to be the most popular.

She hooked her thumb. "Looks like Figawi will be here shortly."

"Figawi?" asked Rick. "The race? That's still going on?"

"Yeah, they paused during the pandemic, but it's back and stronger than ever. Nearly a hundred sailboats will race from Hyannis to Nantucket today, and tonight they will have a huge party on the wharf. And then make their way back to Hyannis, many with some pretty wicked hangovers."

"I remember working those weekends as a CSO," says Rick. "There was some crazy partying going on."

Tuna chuckled. “That’s for sure. And if anything, it’s got even crazier. Do you remember how they got the name?”

“Figawi?”

“Yeah.”

“I always thought it was like a term from the Wampanoag tribe that was native to the island. Like a historic chief.”

Tuna smiled. “Well, actually, it got its name in one of the first Hyannis to Nantucket races back in the seventies. During the race, it was quite foggy and almost impossible to navigate. A sailor on one of the boats looked at the captain and said ‘Where the fuck are we?’ But he had a super thick Boston accent, and it came out ‘where the Figawi?’And the name stuck.”

Rick laughed. “I had never heard that.” He shook his head slowly and smiled. “Thanks for the laugh, I needed that.”

Tuna nodded. “Me too. Ready?”

The clock on the wall of their war room showed a quarter of two when Tuna and Rick entered. Rick went straight for the whiteboard and made some notes from their morning interviews. On the left side of the board was a space marked suspects.

Currently empty, Rick added the name, Geoffrey Pierce.

Slowly, the room filled, and by two, every available seat was occupied.

“Thank you all for being prompt. Anything to report?” asked Tuna. She looked across the room expectantly, but all she saw were blank looks and shaking heads. “Nothing?”

An arm went up.

“Yes, CSO Huber,” said Tuna.

The young CSO stood. “We completed the canvass of all the downtown businesses. No one reports seeing Katie or anyone from her bridal group.”

“Thanks, Blair. How is the family holding up?”

“They are doing okay, considering. But I think having them as part of the investigation helped. The dad, Larry, made some missing person flyers which we were able to print, and we posted them in several spots up and down Main Street as well as just about every business in town.”

“Terrific,” said Tuna. “Thank you.”

CSO Huber sat. Her colleagues looked at Tuna intently, ready to get back to work.

“Great job on canvassing downtown and all the local businesses. Now we need to expand the canvass to include the beaches. Talk to the lifeguards, show Katie’s picture around. Let’s also get out to Sconset, Wauwinet, Madaket, Great Point. Talk to the lifeguards, the rangers, tourists, boaters, anyone you can.”

The CSOs nodded.

“Officer Downs. Anything to report on Katie’s electronic profile?”

“Negative, Detective. Her digital presence essentially vanished at the same time her phone went off the grid, eight twenty-one yesterday morning. She has not opened or responded to any emails or texts, no new pictures have synced to her iCloud account, and her social media, as limited as it was, hasn’t been updated.”

“Anything from her credit cards or banking?”

Downs shook his head. “Nothing. Her credit card was last used Thursday afternoon at Cisco Brewers with a thirty-dollar charge.”

"Probably the hat," said Rick.

Tuna nodded. "Yeah. Anything else?"

"I confirmed with the Steamship Authority that every vehicle on the ferries today is being checked. So far, all negative."

"Could she possibly have left on the Hy-Line?" asked Rick.

Downs shook his head. "We cleared those manifests yesterday. Pretty easy, actually, as there aren't too many people leaving the island right now. And the Hy-Line personnel are actively surveying every passenger from the ticket counter to the loading gangway."

"Yeah, but that brings up a good point. The ferries tomorrow and Monday are going to be extremely crowded," said Rick. "I think we need to post observers at all ferry departures until Katie is found. It's a long shot, but maybe whoever took her is counting on the large departure crowds to be a distraction. They might even have her disguised."

"But everything we know so far about Katie is that she's a fighter. Could someone even manage to get her off the island with what I would think would be strong resistance on her part?"

"No, not unless they have control over her in some way. Maybe they threatened her family. Or have her drugged. Like I mentioned, a long shot, but one we need to cover it."

Tuna replied. "Agreed." She turned to face the team. "CSOs. Work together and pair up. Make sure you get eyes on every person leaving the island. Ask questions, don't be shy."

Heads nodded.

"Thank you. Detective Caton and I talked with servers and staff at Cisco, Brotherhood, and Gaslight. All were consistent that the bridal group was tight-knit and focused mainly on themselves.

And having fun. But we did find out there was a man who might have had a special interest in Katie. Apparently, he was trying to engage her and the group at Gaslight late on Thursday night."

She walked over to the whiteboard and tapped it with her pencil. "His name is Geoffrey Pierce. What we know is that he paid the tab for a table of men who were sitting close to Katie and her party. We think he, or one of the men at his table, was the one interested in Katie. Sergeant Santos?"

A stocky, muscled man stood up. He was in his fifties with sandy hair and a kind countenance. His voice was raspy. "Ma'am."

"What have you found out about this mysterious gentleman?"

Santos stood and walked to the front of the room. He went to the whiteboard and taped a picture of Pierce under his name, along with an image of an amazingly large yacht. He turned to the room.

"Geoffrey Pierce is fifty-four years old, six one, two hundred and forty pounds, with brown hair and eyes, according to his New York driver's license. No prior criminal record, but I did discover that he was arrested on the Vineyard when he was 23 for drunk and disorderly, and assault." Tomas looked down at his notes. "Apparently, he was at one of the popular bars at the time and made an unwelcome pass at a young woman. She slapped him, and he hit her back. Quite the gentleman," he said sarcastically.

"Were charges filed?" asked Rick.

"No," said Santos. "Apparently, neither the woman nor the bar wanted to press charges. But that was probably because his father, Norman Pierce, was a billionaire. No doubt slid the aggrieved some money to make things go away, and little Geoffrey got to walk."

"So he has a history of violence with women. Do we know where he's staying?"

Santos nodded and tapped the picture of the boat. "He's staying on that. It's called Splendor. It's a 240-foot custom yacht currently moored at the boat basin. I confirmed with the harbor master that the slip is reserved and paid for through Monday."

"Excellent work, Officer," said Rick. "Anything else?"

"Just that he is a trust fund baby. Aside from the yacht, he has a condo in New York City and homes in West Palm Beach and Aspen. Divorced twice. No record or mentions of any kind of career. Honestly, I doubt he has ever worked a day in his life."

"Thanks, Tomas. Great work as usual. Detective Caton and I will make our way over there shortly to introduce ourselves." Tuna turned to the team. "Great work, everyone. Keep it up. Please continue your efforts to find Katie. I know it can be frustrating, but we are going to find her. And again, please let us know if you find or suspect anything, I don't care how small or unimportant it may seem. Detective Caton and I are available at any time. And I mean any time."

Some soft smiles. A few nodding heads. Many frustrated stares.

"Thank you. Dismissed."

The sound of chairs being pushed back and light chatter among the CSOs filled the room. Tuna waited until the room had cleared and then turned to Rick.

"This Pierce guy is our most promising lead by far."

Rick nodded. "Clearly interested in Katie. Tons of money, so he's used to getting what he wants."

" And he could be keeping her on that boat," said Tuna forcefully. "Can we get a warrant to search it?"

Rick shook his head. "No. No probable cause. All we have is the bartender's recollection of a man talking to Katie and a paid bar tab by Pierce. But maybe we can pry something loose from him. Ready to go have some fun?"

"Fun?" asked Tuna, questioning.

Rick smiled with a hint of deviousness. "I don't know about you, but I enjoy making rich, entitled men squirm."

Tuna smiled. "Okay then, I never knew that about you. I'll let you take the lead."

CHAPTER TWENTY

It was a little after three on Saturday afternoon when Rick and Tuna walked past the Gazebo. The small building was absolutely packed with celebrants, and a long line of potential patrons flowed out across the brick towards Straight Wharf, patiently waiting their turn. The din from dozens of well-lubricated conversations nearly overwhelmed a classic rock playlist blasting from the speakers.

"Can you believe that?" said Tuna. "Three o'clock in the afternoon and the line is already incredibly long."

"Ah, Memorial Day Weekend," said Rick, somewhat wistfully. "I can't tell you how many drunk people I had to deal with as a CSO. They treat Nantucket like it's one big amusement park built just for them. Do you know I actually had someone ask me how much the admission fee was?"

"The admission fee? To what?" asked Tuna.

"To Nantucket! He really thought it had a cover charge."

Tuna shook her head. "Enough already."

Rick laughed.

They made their way down Straight Wharf, past several small shops and the Hy-Line ticket office. Passing another full restaurant, Rick paused to look at the menu tacked up inside a small glass cabinet. He shook his head and turned to Tuna. "Fifty bucks for a lobster roll?"

Tuna smiled. "Yes. But it's a really good lobster roll. Ellen and I treated ourselves for our anniversary last year and ate here. We each had an appetizer, split an entree, and had two rounds of drinks. Want to guess?"

Rick paused and looked back at the restaurant. Every table was full. Servers ran back and forth carrying food and drinks to expectant guests. The sky was blue, the sun was shining, and everyone seemed to be having a wonderful time.

"I'm going to say a buck twenty."

Tuna laughed. "Double it."

"Are you serious? Over two hundred for two people?"

"Yep. Two fifty-five to be exact. With a good tip, of course. Those servers work their butts off, and they have to pay through the nose to live here. But it is such a beautiful location, and it made some very special memories for us, so it was worth it. Maybe you should bring Felicity here?"

Rick shook his head. "Maybe if I win the lottery. But I can't afford that on my salary."

Tuna smiled knowingly and tilted her head toward the docks. "Let's go."

Leaving the happy customers behind, they stepped up onto the wide, wooden dock. Every slip was full of boats ranging in size from thirty-foot runabouts to fifty-foot sportsfishers to sailboats of all lengths and rigging. At the far end of the marina, they could just make out a half dozen mega yachts, docked stern in. Looking past the docks, several hundred boats were moored across Nantucket Harbor. Every few minutes, one of the harbor launches would power by collecting or delivering people to and from their boats.

The sheer amount of wealth floating on the water was staggering.

Tuna and Rick walked to the end of the wharf, where it turned ninety degrees and formed the eastern end of the basin. A small wooden gate stood in their way.

Yachtsmen and their guests only.

“What, no yachtswomen?” said Tuna jokingly.

Rick smiled as they pushed their way through the gate. The dock narrowed slightly, and there were boats tied up on both sides. To their right, several large boats, probably sixty or seventy feet long, were berthed parallel to the dock. They could look through the large glass windows and see people lounging, drinking, and eating.

To their left were the truly big boats. These megayachts were all over a hundred feet in length and were docked stern-in. At each boat, a brushed aluminum, chrome, or wooden walkway extended from the stern to the dock. At the foot of the walkway was usually an elaborate welcome mat featuring the name of the boat. Most featured two stanchions connected by a soft velvet rope to help discourage any unwanted visitors.

They walked slowly down the dock, staring intently at the boats surrounding them. Tuna paused and nudged Rick, pointing down at the mat in front of them.

Welcome to the Land of Splendor.

“Splendor,” said Tuna, turning to Rick. “Here she is.”

Rick looked up. “Holy shit. This thing is huge.”

“Didn’t Sergeant Santos say it was two hundred and forty feet?”

“Saying it is one thing. Seeing it makes it real. And this thing is massive!”

His eyes followed the gangway up past the stern to a large deck area that looked as if it could hold a few dozen people comfortably. Above that was another deck where he could make out the tops of lounge chairs. And above that, at the third level, he could just make out the tail boom and rotor of a helicopter. It looked to be painted to match the boat.

He pointed up. "A helicopter? I can't imagine what this thing costs."

"Um, eighty-two point five million," said Tuna, smiling. "Not including the helicopter."

"What? How did you…"

"Santos sent me the details. I told you he knew how to find things." She gazed down at her phone and continued. "Built in 2006, she has a cruising range of seven thousand miles, a crew of nineteen, and was sold to Mr. Pierce four years ago for eighty-two point five million."

Rick let out a whistle. "A crew of nineteen? Holy crap."

Tuna stared intently at her phone. "Get this, it has a forty-six-thousand-gallon fuel tank."

"Forty-six thousand gallons?" Rick did some quick math in his head. "That means at current pump prices, it would cost over two hundred grand to fill it up. Holy crap!"

"It's a different world," said Tuna.

"Yeesh. It sure is," agreed Rick. "Now let's see if we can talk to Pierce."

Rick unclipped the velvet rope from the chrome stanchion and proceeded up the brushed aluminum and wooden gangway. At the top, a uniformed crew member was polishing the shiny chrome railing on the bulkhead. Seeing Rick and Tuna, she paused.

"Can I help you?" she asked with a pronounced French accent.

"Yes. I'm Detective Rick Caton, and this is Detective Tina Fisch. We are from the Nantucket Police Department and have some questions for Mr. Geoffrey Pierce. Is he available?"

The crew member eyed them up and down. "I'll have to check. Can I ask what this is about?"

"It's about his activities on Thursday evening."

"His activities? Please give me a moment. Wait here."

She turned and disappeared into the saloon.

Rick's eyes wandered up and down the boat, taking in the teak decking, the chrome railings, and smooth white walls. A half dozen tables were set up, each with four chairs, and were scattered about the deck. To the right of the door into the saloon stood a teak bar with four matching barstools. Behind it on glass shelves, a few dozen bottles of high-end liquor were displayed. To the left of the entrance stood a massive flat screen television.

Just as he was about to climb the ladder to explore the next deck, the crew member reappeared. "Follow me."

Rick looked at Tuna, and together they followed the crew member through an elegant saloon. Floor-to-ceiling windows offered an expansive view of the harbor while a pair of large leather sofas faced each other across a glass cocktail table. Cream colored wainscoting covered the walls and framed a wide wooden floor covered strategically in large oriental rugs.

Sitting in the center of the room on its own wainscoted display was an exact miniature of Splendor encased in glass. Rick leaned in to catch a glance and was amazed at the detail, even down to the helicopter. He shook his head.

She led them to a wall and pressed a discreetly placed button. Rick could just make out a subtle whirring sound and a slight movement of air. The whirring stopped, and the wall slid open silently to reveal an elevator. The three of them entered the wood and mirrored space. According to the buttons on the panel, the elevator serviced five levels of the ship. She pressed the top button. Quietly, the elevator rose until it reached the top deck, and the doors slid discreetly open.

They stepped out into a small foyer, which led to a large open deck. Nearest to them, a small pool was surrounded by lounge chairs. Past the pool and a short bulkhead, Rick could see the cockpit of the helicopter. To his left, a man stood, leaning on a bulkhead, and eying them curiously. He fit the description on his license closely, except he was likely being a bit optimistic when he had claimed his height and weight. Rick thought less of the former and more of the latter. Typical male vanity.

"How can I help you today, detectives?" His voice was higher-pitched than expected, given his age and size.

"Mr. Pierce?"

"Guilty as charged. To what do I owe the pleasure of your company?"

"We just have a few questions for you, sir. About your evening at the Gaslight."

"The Gaslight? I'm not sure I'm familiar with that establishment."

"Um, sir, Thursday night. You and several male acquaintances were seen there by several witnesses."

"Oh. Sorry, yes. I didn't know the name. My friends pulled me there. Threatened to make me sing karaoke. I told them they'd be swimming home." He smiled, revealing yellowed and crooked teeth that didn't seem to fit his net worth. "What about it?"

Rick pulled out his phone. "Do you remember talking to this woman?" he asked and held up the picture of Katie.

Pierce fumbled in his pocket for reading glasses, placed them on his nose, and stared at the picture. He shook his head. "I'm afraid not, detective. Should I?"

"We have several witnesses who saw you talking to her, so yes, you should remember her."

"Hmm. Well, I will admit that I had had a few that night. And I'm sure I talked to a lot of women. You see, I was feeling, what shall we call it? Expectant? So just putting out some feelers and seeing if I could generate some interest among the island's, um, female visitors." He looked at Tuna, who returned his stare.

"So you don't remember talking with this woman," said Tuna, her voice on edge.

"No, I am sorry. I do not. Can I ask what this is about?"

Rick was quiet, trying to unsettle his suspect. After a minute, he broke the silence. "She is missing."

Pierce's eyes flared. "And you think I had something to do with that?"

"Well, you do have history."

"A history. What the hell are you talking about?" he said, angrily.

"You were arrested in ninety-one on the Vineyard. Aggravated assault. Drunk and disorderly. Apparently, you tried to get friendly with a young woman, and she refused your advances. She slapped you. You hit her back." Rick looked around the boat slowly and then locked his eyes on Pierce's. "I wouldn't think a man of your position would stoop so low as to hit a woman."

"That was a big misunderstanding."

"A misunderstanding? You were arrested."

"Yes. But never charged."

"Did daddy take care of things for you?" asked Tuna, accusingly.

Pierce turned to her quickly. "No, he did not! And I resent the accusation."

"Then explain to us how it was all a misunderstanding."

He paused, unsure of how much to share. "The woman in question was a close friend from Tufts. We were both econ majors and shared several classes. I ran into her at the Vineyard, and I'm sorry to say I was drunk. Very drunk," he repeated, his voice softening. "I had always thought that Janet liked me, that maybe we could be a couple. So in my drunken stupor, I told her I liked her and tried to kiss her. And yes, she responded by slapping me across the face. But I did not hit her back!"

"Why then was that in the arrest report?"

He looked across the harbor and then back to Rick. "When she slapped me, I lost my balance. I stumbled backward into a barstool and then started to fall. I was reaching out to grab something and, unfortunately, struck her on the side of the head. But the bartender thought I had hit her, which is why he called the police."

Tuna nodded. "And didn't daddy get the charges dropped?"

"No," said Pierce, firmly. "He did not. The next morning, after I had slept off my bender in a cell, I made bail and went straight to Janet. I apologized profusely and explained how sorry I was to start that conversation at that moment. She knew I wasn't trying to hit her. She was actually very sweet about the whole thing and agreed not to press charges."

"What about the bar?"

"Janet actually went with me to the bar to explain things to the manager. It took a little convincing, but with Janet's urging, he agreed not to press charges."

"That's it?"

"No. Janet and I started dating. It was looking like it was going to get serious, but then…"

"But then what?" asked Rick.

"She was killed by a drunk driver three months later," he said sadly. "Heading home for Christmas break on the Mass Pike. Drunk was going the wrong way, hit her head on."

"I'm sorry, Mr. Pierce," said Tuna.

He looked at her with watery eyes. "Drunk driver. Got to love the irony."

Tuna and Rick exchanged a look.

"Thank you for clarifying that. Can we ask again about you and our missing woman?" asked Rick.

"You really do think I had something to do with that?"

"That is what we are trying to ascertain, Mr. Pierce. You were seen talking to her. Our witness says that they were ignoring you.

'Froze you out' was how he put it. And looking around this boat, I think you are the kind of man who usually gets what he wants. So maybe their behavior pisses you off, and you decide to take matters into your own hands."

"So what are you saying? That I kidnapped her!"

Tuna chimed in. "That is exactly what we are saying. Is it true?"

"Absolutely not!" He began to pace the teak floor, clearly uncomfortable.

Rick looked at Tuna and raised an eyebrow.

"Would you allow us to search your boat, then? Or should we come back with a warrant?"

Pierce stopped and turned to them and said, "Search the boat? A warrant?" His body relaxed, and his face softened. He stepped back and leaned on the bulkhead, his elbows on the gunwale, and let out a long sigh.

"Okay, yes, I remember talking to her. Or trying to. She was with a bunch of other women, and they seemed pretty focused on each other. Didn't want anything to do with me. And yes, detective," he said, turning to Rick, "I am a man who tends to get what he wants. But not in this case. I made several attempts to engage her and then honestly, just gave up."

"So then what? After you gave up?" asked Tuna.

"My friends and I were headed back here, but then stopped in for a nightcap."

"Do you remember where you stopped?"

He shook his head. "I'm sorry. It was dark, and we had had a few. But it was just after the street turned into the wharf area. On the left side. Down there," he said, pointing towards town.

Rick nodded. "And how long were you there?"

"About an hour. We met a group of women who did seem interested. We talked for a while and then came back to the boat for another drink. And then, you know..."

"You know? You know what?"

"We all retired to our staterooms. With our guests."

"Oh. So you found some company to alleviate your loneliness?" asked Tuna, acidly.

Pierce nodded slowly. "We are adults, after all. And I assure you it was consensual."

"Do these guests have names?"

"I'm sure they do. But I did not get them."

"You slept with a woman and don't know her name?"

"As I said. Two consenting adults enjoying an evening on Nantucket. She didn't seem all that interested in knowing my name either, if that's any consolation."

"What about your friends? Can they back up your story? And are they available?"

"Yes, they can absolutely confirm the details of our evening. But no, they are not available. They chartered a boat. Fishing offshore. They aren't due back until six."

"Can you send me their information, please?"

"Of course. Happy to. Do you have a card?"

Tuna pulled one from her wallet and handed it to him. "I need those names as soon as possible so we can eliminate you as a suspect."

"Yes, detective. I will have that to you within the hour."

"Thank you, Mr. Pierce. We appreciate your time."

"Of course. I'll have Camille show you out."

CHAPTER TWENTY-ONE

Randy knew the time was coming. He could feel it in his being. The vibrations from the island were getting stronger, losing their cohesion, getting out of sync. Like the many times before, he knew what he needed to do to protect the balance, to save the island. His Gift was ready.

In the years that he had been maintaining the balance, he was most proud of the fact that his work had stayed out of the spotlight. He was never one to draw attention to himself or his work. He was happy to undertake this responsibility thanklessly, without any need for public adulation or acknowledgement. Knowing he was maintaining the stability of this lovely island was in itself more than adequate.

He thought of the poem Mama Hickman had read to him every evening. She had found the Robert Frost piece beautiful, but also told him he had to understand the balance. She had said it was up to him to be the good person, to save the gold. To maintain the balance.

When he first heard the poem, it really didn't connect or resonate with him. It just sounded like a bunch of words. But Mama Hickman was patient, and by reading it to him every evening, he started to understand. His life had never experienced the beauty referenced or a moment in time in his life worth savoring. Perhaps that day at the fair, but any beautiful moment there had been crushed when his father had punched his mother. He had corrected that imbalance.

He heard Mama Hickman again in his head, her soft voice reciting the poem with emotion and feeling. By the time he turned eighteen and left home to make his way in the world, he could recite the piece by heart. He mumbled it again softly to himself, imagining her reading it to him, her breath smelling of tobacco and alcohol.

Mama Hickman had encouraged him to make his way in the world, and at first, he wandered, bouncing from one hostel to another, trying to find some purpose in life. Then he found Nantucket.

Its natural beauty, tranquility, and utter charm captured him in a warm embrace that he had never truly experienced before. Mama Hickman had tried, but she couldn't break through the wall that he had built following his parents' deaths. Nearly twenty years of his life had passed by; twenty years of pain, of sadness, of worthlessness. If his mother couldn't love and protect him, was he even worth protecting?

But then he found his purpose. Nantucket would love and protect him as long as he loved and protected her. It was a symbiotic relationship that deep in his core he knew he had been born for. Those twenty years of pain, of loneliness, had prepared him for this. And once again, he was ready.

And as the island had embraced him, he had begun to understand the poem and Frost's intent. Life was beautiful and fleeting and must be protected. It was as if the poet had been to Nantucket and had seen what was happening with the development, the crowded season, the disrespect visitors showed to her, the unchecked growth that skewed the natural balance. He understood.

Nothing gold can stay.

Balance must be maintained.

As the island had embraced him, he embraced the poem and saw it as his trust. But he saw it as incomplete, as if Frost had been interrupted before he could finish it properly. He had taken it upon himself, even with his lack of higher education or understanding of poetry, to add four lines to give the full meaning of his charge.

Unless a gift is made in a moment brief.

My Gift is ready. And willing.

Can pause our time's silent grief.

The sacrifice will heal the island and restore its equilibrium.

She follows those gone now, still and gray.

His Gift will follow those who have preceded her and maintained the balance for over three decades.

A bequest I have done for you my dear. This day

Sunrise tomorrow. A celebration of life as the sun broke the surface of the Atlantic, he would slip his tribute into the surf at Great Point, his most special spot on the island. He had been saving this spot for something special and knew that this year's tribute would be spectacular.

He smiled, relishing the upcoming embrace he would feel when this gift was done.

The squawking of a seagull broke him out of his reverie. Yes, tomorrow will be a wonderful day, but he had work to do first in preparation.

The time and place were set. He knew from experience that the Point would be quiet. Even with the thousands of visitors on the island for the holiday, few, if any, wanted to get up a couple of hours before dawn to make the journey. A lot of people would probably still be up from the night before. And in the off chance that there would be someone there, he did have an area of special access that ensured his privacy.

His truck was ready. He had made sure to put a thin foam mattress pad in the bed to provide her comfort; after all, he wasn't a beast.

The propofol was ready. He still had several unopened vials in his pantry and had put two in his backpack. His research had identified a few issues that he had addressed, namely disposing of any open vials, as bacteria could grow quickly once the medication was exposed to air. He wanted the formulation to be at its maximum efficacy to ease any distress his tribute may feel.

Her phone was ready. He had placed the Faraday bag with her phone in the garage and would dispose of it at the Nantucket landfill when he ran his garbage and recycling trip there early next week.

The one acknowledgement of his work he allowed himself would be his annual printing of his poem in the Inquirer & Mirror. He felt it was important to do this when the tribute was fresh, out of respect for their sacrifice. He had already placed the ad, electronically, of course, using the free wifi at the Atheneum and the virtual private network on his laptop to mask the IP address. The ad was scheduled to print in next Thursday's paper edition, but would be available online on Monday.

Memorial Day.

His last job would be to sweep the basement of any clues or evidence after the offering. He had been successful in maintaining his low profile through the years and wanted to ensure it stayed that way.

Satisfied that his offering preparation was complete, he wanted to have one final visit with his Gift before he went back to work. With everything going on this weekend, demands on him were high, and he knew he must fulfill his obligations.

He went into the kitchen and pulled a plate from the cabinet. He had bought his little cottage furnished and loved the vintage feel of the dishware, cutlery, and furniture. The seller had lived here since the mid-fifties, and when she passed away, the family had put the house on the market. Just a year on the island, he had quickly snapped it up, anxious to get out of the hostel and happy that the salary of his new job was adequate to secure a mortgage.

Setting the plate on the counter, he pulled a banana from a large wooden fruit bowl on the counter and added a couple of the nutrition bars he had purchased at Stop & Shop for this purpose. He added a package of candy, thinking that maybe she would want something special this evening.

He also wanted her to know how special she was to him.

Pulling a yellow sticky note and a marker from the top drawer, he quickly wrote a few words. He held out the note and admired his text.

Grabbing a couple of bottled waters from the mint green refrigerator, he balanced the plate on his forearm and opened the door to the basement.

* * *

Katie's heart froze when she heard the door open, and a shot of adrenaline burst through her system. She was sitting on the edge of the bed and mentally preparing herself to fight if it came to that. She thought briefly about unscrewing the eyebolt from the dog run, but was concerned he would see it and secure her another way.

The basement was dark, the only light coming from the two dingy windows and now from the open door at the top of the stairs. A shadow fell over the treads, and her heart skipped a beat. She was about to meet her captor. What was he going to do to her? Was he going to rape her? Beat her? Kill her?

She forced herself to stay calm and pushed the thoughts out of her mind.

I will not be a victim. I will not be a victim.

The tread squeaked as the first footfall landed. He came down slowly, taking seconds for each step. At first, she thought that maybe he was trying to make an entrance, to build tension or terror in her, but then, when he reached the bottom, she realized he was only balancing the plate on his arm while carrying two bottles of water. She forced herself to relax.

She waited until he had taken a few steps closer, her jaw tightening, anger pushing through the fear. "Why the hell have you kidnapped me? What are you going to do to me?" she said angrily.

He paused several feet from the bed, his face in shadow. His voice was soft and assuring. "Nature's first green is gold."

She blinked. "What?" Her brow furrowed. "What do you mean?"

He didn't move."Her hardest hue to hold."

"What are you saying? I don't understand."

"Her early leaf's a flower."

In the dim light, she could just make out his clothing, light colored trousers and shirt. But his face was hidden. He was wearing a balaclava pulled tight over his nose and a ballcap that looked older than she was.

"Who are you? And why are you doing this to me?"

"Nothing gold can stay."

She thought of the note on the plate from this morning. "I'm sorry, I don't know what you are trying to say. If you release me now, I promise I won't press charges. I just want to go home."

He slowly approached, placed the plate and bottles at the foot of her bed, and stepped back.

"What do you want from me?" she asked, pleading.

"Nothing gold can stay," he repeated.

"Please release me. I promise I won't tell anyone. Your secret is safe. I just want to see my fiancé."

"Nothing gold can stay." He turned and walked slowly back to the staircase. He glanced over his shoulder at her and then proceeded up the stairs, each tread squeaking as he passed.

She shook her head, relieved the confrontation was over and that she was still safe and unharmed.

But what the hell was he trying to say to her? Nothing gold can stay? What does that even mean?

She followed his footsteps over the floor above, heard a door open, and then slam closed. A few moments later, she heard a vehicle start and then drive away.

Through the dingy windows, she could see that the light was fading, the sweet, soft sunlight of the final hours of the day. The golden hour, as many photographers called it. She turned away from the windows and looked down on the plate where a flash of yellow caught her eye.

She leaned over and grabbed the note, and holding it up in the dim light, she could just make out the words.

Nothing gold can stay.

Unless a gift made in moment brief.

What is up with this guy?

She opened one of the bottles and took a long drink. She thought while she ate one of the nutrition bars. She reread the note and then slipped it into the band of her leggings.

I am getting out of here tonight.

Confident, she lay on the bed and stared at the old wooden beams crossing the ceiling. She would give it a couple of hours, make sure darkness had fallen, and then she would make her break.

Exhausted from the emotional and physical stress of the past day, and against her better judgment, she fell asleep.

* * *

She awoke with a start, unsure of where she was. She sat up in the bed and looked around her. The basement was nearly pitch black, with just a meager amount of light filtering through the small windows.

Quickly, the realization of where she was came flooding back to her and what she needed to do.

The house was quiet, save for the muted sounds of crickets outside the windows. She reached behind her and felt for the dog reel. Her fingers found the eyebolt, and she quietly unscrewed it until the reel fell soundlessly into her waiting hand.

She stood and stretched. She had made a mental map of the basement just for this moment. Using the dim light from the windows as a reference, she angled silently across the basement to the dark corner where the bulkhead door provided access to the outside. What she couldn't tell during her captivity was how the bulkhead door was secured. She felt around the frame until her hand came across a knob. She twisted and pushed. The door opened a fraction before it stopped.

It was locked. But how?

Her hands again groped the frame, looking for some sort of locking mechanism. She prayed it wouldn't be a deadbolt that required a key. If that were the case, she would have to try to escape up through the house. She forced herself to stay calm, her hands feeling out the wood of the frame until they came across a long, thin metal barrel, its steel cool to the touch. She felt it with her fingers and recognized it immediately.

A barrel lock!

Again, her experience with the tree house and her dad proved fruitful. They had explored various options to secure the entry door and had decided on a barrel bolt. She had enjoyed locking the entry as closing the barrel had a very satisfying sound as she sent it home into the keeper.

She smiled, grabbed the raised grip on the barrel, twisted it thirty degrees, and slid the barrel out of the keeper. Her hands moved back to the doorknob, turned, and pushed the door up and over until it was resting on the shingled siding of the house.

Katie let out a quiet whoop of excitement and stepped up out of the basement and into the fresh air of a beautiful Nantucket evening. The temperatures were cooler, but she relished the scents and sounds of her freedom. Looking around, she realized that the house was isolated; no other structures were visible. She listened for any sound of activity but was only rewarded with the distant hoots of a barn owl.

The crunch of tires on a shell driveway interrupted her examination, and she froze. Headlights splayed across the green of the lawn and then stopped on the opposite side of the house.

No!

She heard the car door close and could imagine him walking up the front steps into the house. The screen door opened, its spring squeaking in protest, before it slammed back against the frame. He was in the house. But would he notice that she was gone? Was he going to go to bed? She had no idea what time it was or how long she had slept, but figured it had to be past midnight.

Cradling the reel and handcuffs, she turned and walked quickly behind a hedge, hoping that he wouldn't be able to see her from the house. She waited, forcing herself to stay still and quiet, and anxious that her captor would remain ignorant of her escape.

The front door burst open. "Gift!" a panicked voice shouted out. "Where are you?"

She turned and ran, running as fast as she could, pushing her way through scrub brush and small pine trees. She struggled to maintain balance with the reel and handcuffs in her arms as if she were holding a baby. She put one arm over the handcuffs to keep them from clanking and giving her away.

She could hear him crashing through the brush behind her. “Gift! Where are you?”

Gift? What?

The night was dark, the only light from a glorious blanket of stars above. Given her hours in the gloomy basement, her night vision was strong, and she could easily pick her way through the brush. She kept pushing, moving as quickly as she dared, and his voice, still calling out for her, started to fade.

She paused, breathless, and tried to get her bearings. She found a gap in the trees and looked up, scanning the skies. Quickly, her eyes settled on the constellation Orion, his sword clearly visible dangling below him.

Ok, Orion is south.

She turned 180 degrees and refocused her attention skyward.

There!

The Big Dipper was clearly visible, its seven stars shining brightly against the ink-black background. Her eyes followed the two stars on the right edge of the cup and traced a line from there to Polaris, the North Star.

Now that she had her directional bearings, she closed her eyes and tried to remember the shape of the island and the roads they had taken to their rental cottage. She recalled that there was a main road, the one their bus took to town and back, and that seemed to hug the south side of the island. That road would likely be her best at getting help.

She found a fixed point in the southerly distance, a large stand of pine trees, and walked as quickly as she could toward them, being hyper aware of the noise she was making. Coming into a clearing in the brush, she heard a stomping sound. Had he found her? Was that the sound of his boots hitting the ground?

Suddenly, there was a loud snort, and three deer bolted from behind a grove of scrub oaks and ran into the distance, their large white tails documenting their path.

Despite her racing heart, she had to smile to herself, relieved. She slowed her breathing and again focused her attention on the sounds of the evening. Where was her captor? Had he been able to follow her? The night was quiet.

Satisfied, she set out and worked her way through the tall grass and scrub using the starlight to help guide her way. After what seemed like an hour, she came out of the scrub and onto a vehicle trail, its twin tracks extending southward in the dim light.

The tracks were sandy and quiet, so she felt comfortable running, thankful that her captor had never removed her sneakers. She fell into an easy pace, the handcuffs jingling lightly in her arms. Looking to her left, eastward, she could just make out a slight glow over the horizon. Sunrise was not long away. The thought of seeing a sunrise energized her, and she upped her pace. She was going to make it. She was free!

The trail came to a split rail fence line with a wooden gate blocking her path. She unlatched the gate and slipped through the gap and into a parking lot. To her left was a large signboard that looked to have a map of the property. To her right was a small parking lot suitable for only a few cars. Beyond the lot was a paved road.

But was it the right road?

She walked closer and paused by a tree to survey the road. She was sure it was the one they had driven to their rental cottage, and the one the bus had used to take them back to town. That meant she could go left and head back to their rental or turn right and head toward town. Given how small the village was where they were staying, she thought her best chance of finding people - and help - would be to head west toward town.

She emerged from behind the tree and approached the road. It was then that she noticed another, narrower road running parallel. The bike path! Yes, this was certainly the main road. She pumped her first in the air and sprinted across the road and on to the bike path, her pace quickened at the thought of seeing Harrison, her mom and dad, and of course, her friends.

Behind her, the sky had turned a dark purple, smudges of ink from the coming sunrise.

For the first time since she had seen the man in the parking lot, she felt happy and free. She was in her element, running hard, and already starting to put the last forty hours behind her.

Lights appeared in the distance. For a moment, she feared it could be her captor, that he had somehow gotten back to his vehicle and had followed her here.

No. No way.

She stopped running and rushed to the edge of the main road. As the car approached, she jumped up and down, waving her arms, trying to get the driver's attention.

The car flew by, and then a bright flash of red as the brakes were applied. The tires squealed as the car slowed quickly to a halt.

She turned in time to see the whites of the reverse lights and could hear the car accelerating back to her. It stopped next to her, and the window rolled down. A young Hispanic woman was driving.

"Are you okay?"

CHAPTER TWENTY-TWO

Early Sunday Morning

Rick had tossed and turned all night, running through Katie's case and trying to determine what he had missed. His mind kept replaying every scene of the investigation, from getting the call on Friday afternoon, to searching the trails, the interviews with all of the people who had seen Katie, to Geoffrey Pierce on his massive yacht, and most recently to the late-night session with Tuna last night reviewing their notes, trading theories, and if he was honest with himself, pissing into the wind. Nothing they had done was helping Katie be found.

His mind had finally quieted out of sheer exhaustion, and he had slipped into a troubled sleep around four. He was still sleeping when his phone trilled at half five. He didn't wake.

"Rick?" said a sleepy Felicity. "Are you awake?" She gently nudged him.

"Huh," said Rick, groggily. "What?"

"Your phone."

"My…"

"Your phone. It was ringing. Might be important."

Rick threw back the covers and sat up. He rubbed his eyes and reached for his phone on the bedside table. The screen lit up, and he saw a missed call from Tuna along with a text: Call Me Now!

"What is it?" asked Felicity.

"It's Tuna. Sounds important." He tapped the screen. Tuna picked up on the first ring.

“We got her!” said Tuna, enthusiastically.

“What?” asked Rick, his mind still struggling to wake.

“Katie. We’ve got her. She’s safe.”

Rick sat bolt upright, his ears refusing to believe what he had just heard. “Are you serious?”

He could hear Tuna laugh. “Yes. Damn serious.”

“Is she okay?”

“Thankfully, yes. She has some scratches and bruises from running through the moors at night. But otherwise she’s in perfect shape.”

“Where is she now?”

“She reunited with her fiancé and her parents. They took her over to Cottage Hospital just to make sure. But she wants to talk.”

“Has she shared anything yet about what happened? Who was it that grabbed her?” asked Rick.

“No. I think right now she is just happy to be back with her friends and family. But she will be at the station by eight. So, you need to grab a coffee and get your butt over here now. We’ve got work to do.”

“Thanks, Tuna. On my way.” He ended the call.

“What is it?” asked Felicity, concerned. She had propped herself up on the bed on one elbow and had only heard one side of the conversation.

Rick smiled back at her broadly. “They found her. Katie. She’s safe.”

Felicity sat up, leaned over, and gave Rick a big hug. "That is wonderful news. I know how much this case has been eating at you."

He returned the hug. "Yes, but I have to go. Katie is coming down to the NPD to talk with us. Hopefully, she'll give us enough to identify the bastard that grabbed her."

"I hope so. Can I make you some coffee?"

Rick leaned in and gave her a kiss, letting it linger and savoring her soft lips. "That would be wonderful," he whispered. "And do you mind giving me a ride?"

- - -

Katie, Harrison, and her parents arrived at the Nantucket Police headquarters fifteen minutes ahead of schedule. Tuna, Rick, and the rest of the team welcomed them with a cheer, happy to have Katie returned safely as well as to have their lives back. The pressure and tension of the last two days had been incredibly demanding on them all.

After the reception had died down, Tuna looked at Katie and asked, "Are you sure you're ready to talk?"

Katie nodded and looked back at Tuna with an intensity in her eyes. "I am. I wanted to share everything I remember while it is still fresh. I want you to catch this asshole."

"We will do everything we can. Let's go upstairs. Did you want Harrison or your parents to join us?"

Katie shook her head slowly. "I'd prefer it were just me. It will be easier for me to speak freely. I mean, nothing happened, if you know what I mean. But I just want them to be able to forget the whole thing."

"I understand," said Tuna. She led Katie up the stairs to the conference room where they had set up their base of operations. And it was just as they had left it the night before. Katie walked in and paused, staring at the images and notes all around her. She walked to the whiteboard and read through all the text, the comments captured by the team. She walked over to the bulletin board and took in all the pictures: of her, the wedding party, her new Cisco hat on the ground, the parking lot, and aerial views with her running route highlighted in red.

Rick and Tuna sat and let Katie absorb the information around her.

She was immediately struck by the thought of how hard all of these people had worked trying to find her. She turned and looked at Rick and Tuna intently, a tear trailing down her cheek.

"Thank you," she said gratefully. "Thank you for all you did to try and find me."

"Of course," said Tuna, gently. "I'm just sorry that we didn't find you sooner."

"I just didn't realize how many people you had involved. And honestly, I'm sorry to have put everyone out."

"Put everyone out?" exclaimed Rick. "Katie. You were kidnapped. Your fiancé, your parents, your friends? They were beside themselves with worry. Fearing the worst. And honestly, so were Detective Fisch and I," he said, nodding at Tuna. "And for good reason. I'm sorry to say that too often crimes like this don't usually end well."

Katie shivered at the thought of what could have happened to her. Of what everyone around her was expecting to happen to her. She thought of the man who had taken her and would likely kidnap again unless she could stop it. She nodded, walked over, sat down at the head of the conference table, and looked intently at Tuna and then Rick.

"I had stopped at the trailhead to hydrate and change my playlist. The parking lot was empty. Then he drove in and parked. He approached me, asking some harmless questions about the trail difficulty, claiming to have a bad knee or something. Then the next thing I know, he had sprayed me in the face with bug repellent and then stabbed me in the thigh with a needle. It must have been a pretty potent drug because I started to black out almost immediately. I tried to get to my phone, but he grabbed it out of my hands, and then I felt him lift me into the trunk. That was it. The next thing I remember is waking up in a basement."

They were both taking notes.

"Can you describe the car he was driving?" asked Rick.

Katie nodded. "It was an older Chevrolet. Brown. With a light tan vinyl top. It was a sedan, four doors with a trunk. I remember him grabbing his things out of it, the trunk that is. It's missing a hubcap. Driver's side front."

"That's very observant," said Rick, letting out an appreciative whistle.

She smiled. "My dad's a car guy. Grew up wrenching with him, going to car shows, and F1 races."

Tuna looked up from her notes and asked, "Do you remember anything about your attacker? His dress, appearance, or facial features?"

"He was older, probably fifties or early sixties. Had a wide-brimmed straw hat on. I think he had on olive colored cargo shorts with a light beige top." She thought for a minute. "He was wearing a black knee brace, you know the kind you see advertised on TV with some sort of metal in it. Copper, maybe?"

The note-taking continued. "Anything else?"

"Yes. He had a backpack. A slim one like my running pack. I think it was light blue. Maybe lime green?"

Tuna nodded approvingly. "Any facial features you recall?"

Katie shook her head. "He approached me with the sun behind him so his face was backlit. I really didn't get a good look."

"Did he touch you in any way?" Tuna asked, then paused. "I'm sorry, Katie, but I have to ask. Did he force himself on you?"

"It's okay. No, I don't think he touched me, and I know he didn't rape me."

Tuna nodded slowly, relieved.

"What about at the house, the basement? Did you ever see him there?" asked Rick.

She nodded. "Just once," and paused in thought. "That would have been last night, maybe an hour or two before sunset. He came down with some water and food."

"And?" asked Tuna expectantly, "Did you get a good look at him?"

"No. He was wearing a balaclava pulled up over his nose and an old baseball cap. Plus, it was dark; the only light came from a couple of really dirty basement windows."

"Clothing?"

"He was wearing pants, khaki colored, or maybe a light tan. Plus, he had a pale blue shirt on. And boots. He was wearing those military-style tan boots that lace up over the ankle."

Tuna looked at Rick and raised an eyebrow.

"Okay," said Rick. "Did he say or do anything?"

Katie perked up, remembering. "I didn't think of it at the time, except that it was really weird, but he said a few things that really made no sense to me. 'Nature's green or was it nothing gold?' It was just strange. I tried to get him to talk, to let me go, but he just kept repeating those words."

"And he didn't respond to you at all?" asked Tuna.

She shook her head. "No. But I did get this," she said, and pulled a wrinkled yellow sticky note from her pocket. She handed it to Tuna. "This was on the plate of food he brought me. There was another one, but I didn't save that one and can't remember what it said."

Tuna looked at the note and read it aloud. "Nothing gold can stay. Unless a gift made in moment brief." She looked at Rick. "Any ideas?"

He shook his head. "Makes no sense to me either. But we'll have the team look at it and do some online queries."

Tuna nodded and turned back to Katie. "So, how did you manage to escape?"

Katie smiled. "He had me tied up using an old dog run, you know, the retractable kind with a plastic-covered cable?"

Tuna and Rick nodded.

“It was old, probably from the fifties, and it had been repaired sometime in the past. Someone had replaced the hex head bolt with an eyebolt.”

“You know your hardware,” said Rick, admiringly.

Katie nodded and smiled. “Again. From hanging with my dad when I was younger. Anyway, I was able to fashion a rod from the bed springs and unscrew the eyebolt. Then I just waited for the right time.”

“What can you tell us about the house? Do you think you could lead us there?”

She shook her head. “I never saw much more than the basement. When I escaped through the bulkhead, I did notice it had shingled siding. And I think it was smaller, maybe one story with a porch.”

“And you don’t know where it was?”

“No, sorry. I can tell you it is north of the main road.”

“Milestone Road?” asked Tuna.

“Is that the one that runs from town to where our rental is?” asked Katie.

Tuna nodded. “Yes.”

“Okay, then, yes. The house was at least a few miles north of Milestone. After I got out, I lay low for a bit to make sure I was safe. But then I heard him calling out. ‘Gift.’”

“Gift?” asked Tuna, confused.

“Yeah, Gift. I thought that was so weird. But really, everything about this guy was weird.”

“So, then what?”

Katie continued. “I holed up in a stand of brush. Scared a few deer.”

Tuna looked at Rick knowingly.

“But then once I was sure he wasn’t close to me, I found a clearing and was able to find the North Star, and remembering the main road on the map, I headed south.”

Rick looked impressed. “How long did it take then to get to the road?”

Katie thought for a minute. “At first, I was walking quickly, but then I came upon a vehicle track. It was open and sandy, so then I started to run. After that? It was about twenty minutes or so until I got to the road. Came through a small parking lot. Then I ran down the main, er, Milestone Road for maybe another five or ten minutes until that nice young lady stopped.”

“Mariana Lopez,” said Tuna.

“Is that her name?” asked Katie, excitedly. “She told me, but I was so jazzed to be free it didn’t stick.”

“It is. She works as an aide to an older family in Sconset. She was heading there when you flagged her down.”

“Can you give me her number? I’d like to give her a proper thank you.”

“Of course,” said Tuna.

“Is there anything else you can remember that might help us find this guy?” asked Rick. “Anything at all?”

Katie thought. “He has a lawn.”

“A lawn? How do you know that?” asked Tuna, surprised.

"Because he was mowing it. It was right after I woke up in the basement. I couldn't believe he could do something so mundane after kidnapping me."

Rick took a note. "That could be very helpful. Anything else?"

She shook her head. "No, nothing is coming to me."

"Very well, Katie. Thank you for sharing what you did. This is incredibly helpful."

Katie started to stand. "Do you think you'll find him?"

Rick looked at Tuna and then back to Katie. "It's a small island, and you've given us a lot to go on. So, yeah. I think we will get him."

Katie smiled. "Good. Let me know if there is anything more I can do. Maybe I can work with an officer and try to backtrack the route I followed? It might be helpful."

"That's an excellent idea, Katie. Are you sure you are up for it?"

"Absolutely, Detective. Just let me know when and I'll be ready."

"Thanks, Katie. That could be immensely helpful. Can we show you out?"

"No, I'm good. Thank you," Katie said and walked confidently out of the room.

Rick watched her leave and then turned to Tuna. "Amazing woman."

"Isn't she?" agreed Tuna. "Not many people would have figured out how to escape a situation like that and have the internal fortitude to meet with us a few hours later and recall the whole affair. And offer to retrace her escape route."

"For sure. Now we need to leverage her information and find this guy."

Tuna nodded vigorously. "Let's gather the troops."

CHAPTER TWENTY-THREE

Ten minutes after Katie Chapman had walked out of the front door of the Nantucket Police Station on Fairgrounds Road, Officers Downs, Coffin, and Santos were seated in the war room looking expectantly at Detectives Fisch and Caton. The Community Resource Officers, as useful as they had been during the initial search for Katie, were not chartered to be part of an active criminal investigation and had resumed their normal seasonal duties of managing traffic, helping tourists, and keeping order.

"Is it true that she's okay?" asked Officer Downs, expectantly. "All we heard is that she was found."

"Yes, she is okay. Aside from a few scratches and bruises from her escape through the moors, she's completely unharmed. Physically, at least. Emotionally, she may need some time to fully process what happened to her."

"That is terrific," said Officer Coffin. "Did she ID the kidnapper? Can we go arrest this bastard?"

Rick shook his head. "Unfortunately, she never got a good look at his face. More of a general description. She thinks he's older, caucasian, mid-fifties to early sixties, average height, and heavy-set. Clothing was mostly khaki and light colored shirts."

"You just described half the men on this island," said Officer Downs. "And probably five or six of us on the NPD," he added, chuckling.

"Sadly, yes. And the description of where she was kept isn't much better. She only saw the basement, which, by what she observed, sounds like it is probably fifty or sixty years old. And the outside she only saw at night when she made her escape."

"Anything there that is useful?" asked Santos, hopefully.

"It was shingled, no surprise there, and she thought one story, with a porch. And to her it seemed isolated, but Tuna and I think it could also have just had some thick landscaping, preventing her from seeing anything."

"Do we at least have an idea of where this house could be to narrow things down a bit?" asked Coffin, exasperated.

Tuna shook her head slowly. "We did our best to estimate the distance using Katie's description of her escape. We," she said, motioning her pen at Rick, "think it was three to four miles from where she was picked up on Milestone Road, just to the west of the Serengeti."

An arm went up; it was Downs.

"Yes, John."

"Three to four miles means a lot of possibilities. That brings a lot of the houses in the northern parts of Sconset into play, as well as those along the south side of Polpis. That's easily a few hundred houses. Or more."

There was a murmuring from the team. The gathered officers had thought they were planning for an arrest, not a further investigation.

"Guys, settle down," said Tuna. "I know we want to get this guy. He created a nightmare for our community, but thanks to a strong, young woman, nothing more."

"You don't think he might try to grab another woman? Maybe out of anger or frustration from Katie's escape?"

Rick nodded. "It's certainly a possibility, but given the island is on high alert, and how well publicized Katie's disappearance was, that should make it pretty difficult for him."

Officer Coffin let out a long sigh. "So what do we know? Anything that might help us get this guy?"

"We know he was driving an old brown Chevrolet sedan. Katie thought maybe from the nineties. We need to check RMV records. There can't be many of those on the island. And maybe we can correlate the car to the perp."

"I'll look into that, Detective," said Santos. "Is there anything else? Any other evidence?"

Rick looked at Tuna and then back at the officers around the table. "The one physical piece of evidence we do have is this," he said and pointed to the yellow note he had pinned on the bulletin board, and read it aloud. "Nothing gold can stay. Unless a gift made in moment brief."

"What does that mean?" asked Coffin.

Officer Downs was busy on his phone, his fingers tapping away on the screen.

"We don't know what it means," said Tuna. "The kidnapper also mentioned a few lines similar to this to Katie when she tried to talk to him. So, clearly, they must mean something to him. That's what we need to determine."

"Shit," said Officer Downs, astonished, staring at his phone.

"John? What is it?" asked Tuna, surprised at the tone of his voice.

He cleared his throat. “I thought I recognized that line. Especially the ‘nothing gold can stay.’ It’s been a bit of an urban legend in the community for years.”

“An urban legend? What are you saying, John?” asked Tuna.

He shifted in his chair. “Every year after Memorial Day, someone has run the same poem in the community announcements section of the Inquirer and Mirror. I’ve been with the NPD for over twenty years and can tell you it’s run every year I’ve been here. I always thought it was someone honoring a veteran or someone they had lost.”

“And you think this yearly poem is coming from our kidnapper?” asked Rick

“That I don’t know. But, wait, hang on.” He tapped his phone, found what he was looking for, and handed it to Tuna. She glanced down and read:

COMMUNITY ANNOUNCEMENTS

My Gift to You

Nature’s first green is gold,

Her hardest hue to hold.

Her early leaf’s a flower;

But only for an hour.

Then leaf subsides to leaf.

So Eden sank to grief,

So dawn goes down to day.

Nothing gold can stay.

Unless a gift made in moment brief

Can pause our time's silent grief

She follows those gone now, still and gray

A bequest I have done for you my dear. This day.

Tuna handed the phone to Rick, who read the lines intently. Finally, they looked up.

"My gift to you," said Tuna. "Do you know who wrote it? I'm not much of a reader, I'm afraid."

Sergeant Santos put his hand up.

"Tomas?"

"I just Googled the first couple of lines. It's from a poem by Robert Frost, written in 1923."

"Okay. 1923? That's over a hundred years ago."

"Yeah, but."

"But what?"

"I have the poem pulled up. The Frost version ends with the line 'nothing gold can stay'. Those remaining lines, the last four, don't appear to be part of the original poem. And it certainly wasn't titled My Gift to You. Frost named his poem Nothing Gold Can Stay."

Tuna looked back at the screen on Downs' phone and read, "Unless a gift made in moment brief, can pause our time's silent grief, she follows those gone now, still and gray, a bequest I have done for you, my dear, This day."

She handed the phone back to Officer Downs. "So whoever placed this ad, our kidnapper, maybe, changed the title and added these four lines. Strange," said Tuna, stumped.

Downs cleared his throat.

"Something to add, John?" asked Rick.

"What I pulled up? The poem. That was the one from last year. Last Memorial Day."

"Okay. What are you thinking?"

"Not sure if you remember the case, but we had a death last May. A drowning off Surfside. If I remember right, it was the Tuesday or Wednesday before Memorial Day."

Tuna looked at Rick, her eyes sparking. "And?" she asked. "You think these cases are somehow connected? That's a bit of a stretch, John."

Downs shrugged his shoulders. "They're probably not related. It's just that last year the victim was a young man, about Katie's age, who was from New York. Very wealthy. He had rented a house off Polpis and invited a bunch of his friends for the week. We received a couple of complaints from the neighbors about the partying and the noise they were making."

Santos raised his hand. "Yes, Tomas?"

"Peter Carlson. He died the year before, also just before Memorial Day."

Tuna thought intently. "Peter Carlson, wasn't that ruled a heart attack?"

Tomas nodded. "It was, but maybe?"

She shook her head. “People die all the time, Tomas. That doesn’t mean it’s all one big conspiracy,” said Tuna, patiently. “And a guy drowning? That’s certainly tragic for his friends and family, but I don’t see how it relates to Katie or even this poem,” she said, pointing at the note. “Right, Rick?”

Rick nodded. “Right. We need to follow the facts on this one and find the man who abducted Katie. Maybe it’s as simple as he’s a Robert Frost fan. Regardless, we need him found.” He looked at Tuna for direction.

She nodded at him and turned to the team. “Okay. Gentlemen. I appreciate all your time and effort in helping us find Katie. Now we need to complete the job. For her sake as well as the safety of the community.”

“John?”

“Yes, Tuna?”

“I’d like you to start with a property search. Access the tax collector database and see if you can narrow down our suspect houses a bit. Consider everything south of Polpis, west of Sankaty Road, and north of Milestone. My guess is there aren’t as many houses that fit Katie’s description as we think.”

“I’ll do my best, but as you know, so many houses are in Trusts, it will take even more work to get to the owner’s name if that’s even possible.”

“Right now, I’m not too concerned with the owner. I want to find the crime scene.”

John nodded. “Got it.”

"And connect with Kurt. Maybe he can conduct an aerial surveillance of that area and identify some of the distinguishing features Katie mentioned, like the front porch and a bulkhead door.

"Will do."

"Tomas? My gut is telling me this guy lives here full-time. Would you look at the driver's license database and pull together a list of all the locals who fit the general description? Also, see what you can find on the car?"

Sergeant Santos nodded.

"And Noah. I'd like you to grab a few CSOs and see if you can try to retrace Katie's escape path. She's offered to help, and we need to take her up on that. It's unlikely she'll remember exactly, but you never know."

Officer Coffin nodded.

"Lastly, Rick, would you mind following up with your friends at Quantico? See if they have been able to find anything with those two partials?"

Rick nodded and pulled out his phone. "Already on it," and smiled.

"Thanks, guys. Please continue to work on this case with urgency. The kidnapper is still out there, and I worry he may try again."

CHAPTER TWENTY-FOUR

Tuna stared at her computer screen, frustrated. It was a different level of frustration than the night before - then she was worried about finding Katie alive. The pressure to perform and find the missing woman had been intense. Now that Katie was safe, they were looking for her attacker, and while the pressure was still there, the urgency had been dialed back.

Still, it was frustrating, and Tuna looked to her computer for answers. And what stared back at her was depressing. According to the latest statistics, over sixty thousand women were missing in the United States, the majority of them Katie's age or younger. While only a small percentage of those were considered stranger abductions, the thought still made Tuna's head hurt.

Why were there so many bad men out there? And why do women get the worst of it?

She had been researching other abductions in the hope that something she would read might prompt a thought or steer her in a new direction. Many of the cases she had reviewed had involved long-term confinement, and often with a sexual component. There were several cases where the hostage had broken free, in some cases years or even decades after they were first kidnapped. Sadly, a lot of the abductions ended in death. Finding the woman safe and unharmed, as they had with Katie, was the exception.

She was about to start another search when there was a light tap on the frame of her cubicle. She turned to see Sergeant Santos.

"Tomas. Did you find anything on the license search?"

He nodded. “I have a list of several hundred locals that fit the description. I did expand it to include non-Caucasians as well, just in case.”

“Excellent. Anyone stand out?”

He shook his head. “No, but I didn’t expect to. I’ve got a CSO compiling the full list with their pictures. We will have that ready in a couple of hours and can then ask Katie to look through them and see if anyone jumps out.”

“What about the car?”

Tomas shook his head. “Nothing. We have a number of nineties Chevrolet sedans registered on the island, but none are brown. Do you think Katie might have gotten that wrong?”

Tuna shook her head adamantly. “I doubt it. She seemed to have a very good recall on what she saw.”

“If that’s the case, the kidnapper must be driving on expired plates. Or no plates at all.”

“Damn,” said Tuna, muttering. “It seems like we are chasing our tails with this guy.”

Tomas was quiet, shifting from one foot to the other.

“Tomas? What is it?”

“Can I show you something?”

“Of course,” said Tuna, her curiosity piqued. “What have you got?”

“Based on what John was saying, I decided to go back and look through the records of the Inquirer and Mirror. They have an excellent online tool to search their prior editions, all the way back to the eighteen hundreds.”

“Okay,” said Tuna, slowly. “And…”

“And, it turns out he was right. That poem, the Robert Frost one with the four added lines, was first published in the community notices section in 1992.

“1992?” said Tuna, surprised.

“Yes. And it has run every year since. As John said, it is always the week after Memorial Day.”

“Okay, but don’t you think that could just be someone honoring a veteran for the holiday, like what Officer Downs thought?”

“That’s still a possibility, of course. But look at this,” said Tomas, and laid a spreadsheet on her desk.

“What am I looking at?”

“This is a list of all the deaths, accidental, suspicious or otherwise, that have happened around Memorial Day weekend since 1992.”

Tuna stared intently and then whistled softly. “All of these people died around Memorial Day?”

“Yes. All of these are from the week or two leading up to the holiday weekend. But it’s important to note that not all of them died; some were reported missing. Like this,” he said, pointing to a line on the spreadsheet. “Mary Ward, age seventy-two, was reported missing in 2002, but her remains were not discovered until 2015, thirteen years later.”

“Okay.”

“And here, in 2008, Matilde Poole was also reported missing. Apparently fell from the Hy-Line during a crossing returning from the Cape. There were no witnesses to her going overboard, and her body was never recovered.”

Tuna nodded intently, fascinated by what the sergeant was showing her.

Tomas continued. "And 1992? The year the poem first ran? That year, David Savage, nineteen, was found on the south shore, the beach by the old Naval station, by a pair of walkers. Cause of death was listed as drowning, but his blood alcohol was off the charts at a point two five."

"So he drank himself silly and went for a swim?"

"Yeah, or someone plied him with a lot to drink and then, when he passed out, put him in the water."

Tuna looked at Sergeant Santos, questioning. "Really, Tomas. Do you really think this was intentional? Not just some young kid out having fun and decides to go for a swim?"

Tomas shook his head emphatically. "No. We have had a death or missing person every year since 1992, the week or two leading up to Memorial Day. Doesn't that seem like a pretty odd coincidence to you?"

"Did you by chance look for deaths before then?"

Santos nodded. "I did. I went all the way back to the early seventies. Nothing. I mean, we had some deaths, but they weren't in the week or two before Memorial Day. Those didn't start until ninety-two."

Tuna nodded slowly, looking at the list of over thirty deaths on the spreadsheet. "Hey, Rick?" she yelled across the cubicles.

"Yeah?" came the muffled reply.

"Can you spare a minute?"

"Sure." She heard a chair scrape, footfalls, and seconds later, Rick was standing next to Tomas in the doorway of her small cubicle.

"What's up?"

Tuna handed Rick the spreadsheet. "Tomas put this together. It's a list of deaths that have occurred on the island the week or two before Memorial Day."

Rick let out a low whistle.

"And coincidentally, that poem that John said was an urban legend? That started appearing at the same time as the first death, in ninety-two."

Rick looked at the list and then slowly at Tomas. "So these deaths and the poem started the same year?"

"Yes."

He looked back down at the list. "But I'm looking at the cause of death. Most of them are explained: drowning, heart attack, exposure, alcohol poisoning, accidental. I don't see a single one listed as a murder."

Tomas nodded. "True. But what if our killer was able to disguise the deaths?"

"Our killer?" exclaimed Tuna. "You think one person killed all these people? Like a serial killer?

Rick held up his hand and turned to Tomas. "Let's not get too far in front of this. It looks suspicious, yes, and I can understand your concern, Tomas. And I also appreciate the effort of putting this together. But it seems like a stretch."

"I agree," said Tuna. "But you have to admit it, the deaths look awfully coincidental, and I thought you didn't believe in coincidences." She smiled conspiratorially.

Rick blew out a long breath. "Okay, you're right. The deaths do look to have a pattern to them. But why kill someone every year around Memorial Day? What would be the meaning behind that?" He looked to Tomas and back to Tuna.

Tomas looked at him blankly. Tuna shrugged.

"A lot of help you are," said Rick, jokingly.

"What about the FBI?" asked Tuna. "Is there someone there who could look at this and give us their perspective? Maybe they could make some sense of it?"

Rick nodded. "Sure, we have the Behavioral Analysis Unit. They look at serial killers and such, but really? I'm not sure they'd give us the time of day on this one."

"Oh come on," said Tuna. "You've got to know someone there that could take a look. At least unofficially."

He paused. "Sure. I have a friend there, Margot North. You remember her. She helped us with the Post case. We went through basic together at Quantico. She's not in the BAU, but I'm sure she could walk it by someone in the department to at least give us a topline. Maybe."

"That would be great, Rick, thank you," said Tuna.

"I'll give her a call and let you know what I find." He turned to Tomas. "Can you email me this file?"

"Yes, sir. I'll have it to you as soon as I get back to my desk."

"Thanks," said Rick, and walked back to his office.

"Nice work, Tomas," said Tuna.

"Thank you," he said and started to turn.

"Wait a minute!"

"What?" asked Tomas, concerned.

"Could it be as simple as calling the paper and asking them who placed the ads? If they have that, then wouldn't we have our suspected killer?"

"I'm one step ahead of you, detective. I already checked."

"And what did you find?"

"The Inquirer and Mirror went completely digital by 2010, so all placements in the classifieds and community announcements had to be done on their website."

"And do they have those records?"

"Most years have been archived. The lady I talked to was only able to pull up the last few years."

"And?"

"She has the order submissions, all of them were placed the Thursday or Friday before the holiday."

"And does she know who placed them?"

He shook his head. "No. The name changes year to year with a variation like John Doe, or Jane Smith."

"That's disappointing. What about payments? Can we trace those?"

"No. Looks like he used prepaid gift cards, the kind you buy just about anywhere; a convenience, drug, or grocery store."

"Damn!" said Tuna, loudly. "I thought that might have just been the trick."

"We have one more possibility."

"What's that?"

"The paper archived the original insertion orders from before they went digital."

"You mean they have the paper copies?"

"Yes. They are in storage, and we are free to review them if we wish."

"Okay, but why would they keep those? Wouldn't they have transferred them to microfiche or at least scanned them?"

"I was surprised too and asked the same question. Apparently, they have been doing a little bit each year. They just finished the year 2001, so all of the paper copies before that have been destroyed. But that still gives us nine years to look at."

"Good. If you find the insertion order, treat it as evidence. We may be able to lift prints from it."

Tomas nodded. "Of course. And just one more thing. I think how these placements were ordered supports my theory that we have a serial killer."

"How so?"

"Well, if it were someone running the poem every year to honor a friend or family member, I don't think they would go to the trouble to conceal their name or payment information. I mean, what would be to hide?"

Tuna nodded. "Tomas, I think you might be on to something."

"Thanks, detective. And if you'll excuse me, I need to go so I can email this to Rick."

"Go. And keep up the great work."

CHAPTER TWENTY-FIVE

Randy Evans was beside himself with grief, frustration, and exhaustion. He had spent the night looking, futilely, for the Gift, and she had escaped him. Now everything he loved was at risk of being destroyed. What would happen to the balance without the Gift? What would she tell authorities about her confinement? What would happen to the island if he were discovered and arrested? Who would look after his precious charge then? Guilt seared through him.

He kicked himself for trying something new.

For decades, he had been successful in maintaining the balance of his beloved island. He knew people thought him a bit strange, a single man in his mid-fifties, no wife, children, family. But they didn't understand that the island was his family. The island was his spouse. The island was everything to him - his alpha and omega. And now he had put it all at risk.

For decades, his approach had been consistent. He would take days, weeks, or even years to identify the right Gift. Then he would establish a rapport, his avocation helping to ease the initial tensions, before he would make that final offering in a way that would satisfy the island's need but without bringing unwanted attention.

That attention could have led to his discovery, but he wasn't concerned about that as much as he wanted the Offering to be special, an intimacy between him and his cherished island, and not spoiled with publicity or even awareness. He liked to fly beneath the radar.

He let out a low moan. Why did he have to try something new? You fool!

It had started with his colonoscopy, his doctor encouraging him to have one due to his age. He had delayed it several years, fearful of the process, but finally succumbed to the physician's urging. And the doctor had been right, the procedure itself was nothing thanks to a wondrous drug named propofol. The nurse had asked him to count down from ten, and the next thing he remembered was waking up in recovery. It had been magical.

Given his family background, he didn't drink or do drugs, so he was caught completely off guard by how well this medicine had so quickly knocked him out. And it got him thinking. Maybe he should use it to secure his next Gift and prepare it for the Offering.

But that plan had failed and failed miserably.

It had done its job well when he first encountered the Gift and allowed him to gain control and bring her home for the final preparations. But what he didn't count on was what happened when the propofol wore off. It was a short-acting anesthetic, and he didn't count on her waking up with an immediate desire to escape his confinement.

He knew he couldn't keep injecting the Gift with the medicine, as he had read that it could carry some health risks. Losing the Gift in his basement would have been a disaster that no doubt would have had significant implications on his ability to maintain the balance. And how would the balance have been impacted? The Gift expiring in a moldy, darkened basement? The Offering was supposed to be magical, intimate, and loving. He feared the island would have veered off balance almost immediately had that happened.

Perhaps he should have been more explicit in explaining his intentions to her. If she had understood the importance of what the Offering represented and her role in it, she might have accepted it. Even embraced it. She might have felt proud to be part of such an important undertaking.

Absent her understanding, she probably thought he was some sort of pervert. Someone who just wanted to keep her captive to entertain himself. Some serial rapist who would kill her when he no longer had use for her. He shuddered at the thought. He was not a monster like that. He had no base needs or evil intentions that he expected her to satisfy. Quite the opposite. He cherished the Gift and what her Offering would represent.

But he had failed to explain his intentions and the implications clearly.

He had tried. He had recited lines of the poem to her, the same as Mama Hickman had to him when he was just a young boy. He had left messages for her with her daily repast, hoping reading them would bring a click of recognition and an understanding of the importance of his actions and her role in them. But clearly, the words did not carry the influence, the impact he had hoped they would.

The composition's meaning was crystal clear to him, just as Mama Hickman had explained when she had recited it to him every evening. The Poem was her focal point in life. It hung on the wall of her kitchen, inside a simple oak frame, the glass smudged with spots of bacon grease, the paper inside yellowed with age.

Nature's first green is gold.

Her hardest hue to hold.

Her early leaf's a flower; / But only so an hour

Then leaf subsides to leaf.

So Eden sank to grief.

So dawn goes down to day.

Nothing gold can stay.

Her words still rang in his ears despite the fact that he hadn't heard her raspy voice in years.

"You were born innocent, Randy. You were born a good person. You were golden. Your father tried to take that from you. He was just an evil person, and your mom couldn't protect you. Their deaths freed you so you could live a better life. A life to protect those who can't protect themselves. A life that can help balance the misdeeds of others."

His relationship with Mama Hickman was a complicated one. She had, after all, taken him in when he was bouncing from one foster home to another and had given him stability, a refuge from the world. But she had her own ghosts to deal with, and that past had often spilled out to envelop him.

She, too, was a drinker.

She made ends meet with a variety of minimum wage jobs and taking in children who needed shelter from abuse, neglect, or abandonment. Some would stay for a few days or weeks. Randy was the only one to ever stay years. She drank every night, often until passing out, but unlike his father, she was not a violent drunk; she was an emotional one.

Each evening, after much of her vodka handle had disappeared, she would sit him down to recite The Poem. She never explained to him where she had first learned of it and why it held so much meaning for her, although he suspected it was the early death of her father. But she used those words to constantly remind Randy that he had a greater purpose in life. That there was more for him to accomplish outside of the tiny village of Turners Falls.

He was to be the balance.

"There are bad people out there, Randy. You need to be the one who helps keep the balance. You need to be the one who protects the gold."

Mama Hickman had kept him fed, clothed, and had made sure he went to school every day. His time with her had been safe, easy, almost pleasant. Although he never loved her as a mother, he respected her as a guardian. She provided emotional, if not financial, support and the freedom to make mistakes. One of those mistakes was being arrested for shoplifting a Sony Walkman just a few weeks after his eighteenth birthday.

True to her calling of taking care of him, she was there to bail him out. He had apologized profusely, claiming it was a friend who had taken the device, but she had remained silent on their drive back to their small house off Montague Street in Turners Falls. Once they were home, she sat him down in her small kitchen, pointed to the frame on the wall, and recited The Poem.

She followed Frost's haunting words with ones of her own. It was time for Randy to leave. It wasn't the arrest that triggered it; in fact, quite the opposite. Randy was a man now and had to venture out in the world and shoulder what she saw as his responsibility. He was to maintain the balance, protect the weak and vulnerable, and satisfy what she saw as his true purpose in life.

Now, over three decades later, he stood looking out over the scrub oak and pine of the Nantucket moors and feeling as if he had thrown it all away. All because of a new drug he experienced while a doctor shoved a camera up his ass.

He forced himself to calm down. To think.

He was confident that he would escape unwanted attention for her capture. He had been extremely careful in what he had exposed her to and doubted she had any idea of who he was or where she had been kept.

But he was just a day away from the Offering. And he didn't have a Gift. That would have to change, and that would bring risks. The island was crowded now, and people were alert. Her abduction had created a disturbance on an island that prided itself on the safety of residents and visitors.

Most wouldn't admit it, but many would be looking over their shoulders.

Wondering if he was out there.

Would they be next?

He smiled. He had an idea.

CHAPTER TWENTY-SIX

Rick had only been at his desk a few minutes when his computer dinged. He saw a new message in his inbox and wasn't too surprised to see it was from Sergeant Santos with the file listing the suspicious deaths. He forwarded the file to his contact at the Federal Bureau of Investigation, adding some personal commentary, and hit send.

Ten minutes later, his phone rang.

"Have you ever heard of Herbert Mullin?" asked Margot North, her Jersey upbringing coming through loud and clear.

"Hi Margot, great to hear from you."

"Good to hear your voice, too, RC. And thanks for sending this file. I bet you didn't know that one of my side passions is serial killers."

"Really?"

"Yeah. I'm actually an aspiring Ripperologist."

"A ripper what?" asked Rick, confused.

"A Ripperologist. It's someone who is an expert on the Whitechapel murders of 1888. Those murders were claimed to have been done by a man calling himself Jack the Ripper."

"I certainly know of the case, I just didn't know that studying it had become so official."

Margot chuckled. "Yeah, well, there are a number of people who claim to be experts and can rightfully call themselves Ripperologists. I'm not there yet."

"What's involved with that?" asked Rick, genuinely curious.

"Well, there is no formal process; it's really a matter of being recognized by other experts in the Ripper field of study. In my case, I'm working on a new theory that the killer was not a man at all but a woman."

"A woman? Really!" exclaimed Rick.

"Don't get me wrong, the majority of serial killers are male. But there have been some notable women serial killers as well. Their methods tend to be different from men - poisoning, smothering, and other less violent approaches."

"True. I remember studying Belle Gunness in one of my behavioral classes at the police academy. Unbelievable."

"Hell's Belle. Yeah, she was a piece of work. Officially, she is thought to be responsible for fourteen murders, but there is some speculation it could have been as many as forty."

"Hell's Belle? Quite the nickname. And you think the Ripper was a woman?"

"Yeah. Jill the Ripper. There's a lot of evidence pointing to the fact that the perp of the conical five was indeed a woman."

"The conical five?"

"Sorry. The conical five represent what is generally accepted as the five murders that can be linked by MO, time, and location as well as victim similarity."

"Interesting. I didn't know they had a term for them."

"They do. My theory is that she was a midwife. They were frequently covered in blood, and going in and out of the Whitechapel area at all times of night would not be unusual. Sir Arthur Conan Doyle thought so, too."

"The author who created Sherlock Holmes?"

"Yep. My paper focuses on Mary Pearcey as the killer. She has been investigated in the past, but I'm trying to bring some new connections to light."

"New connections?"

"For the last hundred and thirty-odd years, everyone tends to focus on the killer. There have been books written, movies made, and never-ending discussions online. I wanted to focus on the victims and see if there were possible prior connections between them and the killer."

"Fascinating," said Rick, impressed.

"I hope so. It's mostly just detailed research into existing bodies of work, but I really enjoy it. I'm presenting my findings at the Jack the Ripper True Crime Conference next year."

"There really is such a thing?"

"There is. There are a lot of people who follow true crime, especially the Ripper case."

"Okay. Wow. So I'm assuming your knowledge of serial murders extends beyond the Ripper?"

Margot laughed. "It does. In fact, that's why I wanted to know if you had ever heard of a killer named Herbert Mullin."

"Herbert Mullin? No, I don't think so," admitted Rick.

"Not a surprise. He was killing around the same time as Ed Kemper, Ted Bundy, John Wayne Gacy, David Berkowitz, and even BTK, Dennis Rader, so they're the ones that got all the media attention."

"So why does Herbert Mullin come to mind?"

"It's probably nothing. But as I'm looking through the spreadsheet you sent me, I definitely see a connection. I think you might have a serial killer on Nantucket."

"What?" exclaimed Rick. "Are you serious?"

"As a heart attack."

"What's leading you to that?"

"For most serial killers, their motives tend to be around the desire for control, for power, or there is a sexual or fantasy component. But I don't think you have that here. I think you may have a killer with a different type of motivation."

"How so?"

"I read through the entire list of suspicious deaths you sent me. And despite looking at thirty-two suspicious deaths, you know what I didn't see?"

"What's that?"

"Any signs of outright violence. There were no stabbings, gunshots, or blunt object trauma. No dismembered bodies. None of the usual blood and gore we see with most serial killers. All of your victims seemed to die in what could be considered accidental or natural ways."

"And you are sure they aren't? Accidental, that is?" asked Rick, cautiously.

"I am. The timing gives it away. If they were spread out over the year? Then yeah, maybe we could write them off as accidental or natural. But the fact that they all happened around the Memorial Day weekend? And every year for thirty-two years? That's a pattern."

"And then of course there's the poem," said Rick, matter-of-factly.

"The poem?" asked Margot, surprised. "What poem?"

Rick hung his head. "Sorry, Margot. I should have sent that to you as well. So you had the full picture, not just a list of suspicious deaths."

"No worries, RC. What's the connection there?"

"Someone has been running a poem in the community announcements section of our local newspaper, The Inquirer and Mirror, the week after Memorial Day. Every year since the first death on our list."

Margot let out a whistle followed by silence. Finally, she spoke. "What's the poem?"

"It's called Nothing Gold Can Stay, by Robert Frost. But the weird thing is, there are an additional four lines added to the original Frost work."

"Can you read me the poem?"

"Sure." Rick read the eight lines of the original Frost work.

"Beautiful," said Margot. "And it has run every year?"

"Yes, but that's not all of it. What I read to you was the original Robert Frost version. But whoever is placing this in the paper has added four lines of their own."

"Really?"

"Yes. Let me read them to you." He paused before continuing. "Unless a gift made in moment brief, can pause our time's silent grief, she follows those gone now, still and gray, a bequest I have done for you my dear, this day."

"A gift made," said Margot, her voice trailing off.

"Yes. And whoever placed the ad changed the name of the poem."

"Changed the name? What do you mean?"

"The original Frost poem was called Nothing Gold Can Stay. When this was placed in the paper, the name was changed to My Gift to You."

"My gift to you. Hah! I think that confirms it."

"Confirms it? Confirms what?" asked Rick skeptically.

"That gets me back to Herbert Mullin."

"What about him?"

"I mentioned different motivations?"

"Yes," said Rick. "Was Mullin's motivation different from other serial killers?"

"Yeah, I'll say. He believed he was saving San Francisco from having a major earthquake."

"What?" Rick asked, confused. "An earthquake?"

"Yeah. I know it sounds crazy, and Mullins was definitely crazy. Confirmed schizophrenic. His birthday was the eighteenth of April, the same date as the huge quake that hit San Francisco in 1906. He believed that was significant and that he needed to do something to prevent it from happening again. So he killed people."

"He killed people to prevent an earthquake?" asked Rick, confused.

"Yeah, that is what he believed anyway. As I mentioned, he was diagnosed with schizophrenia and claimed the voice of his dead father had instructed him to kill in order to save California. He honestly believed he was doing a good thing. That he was saving the people from a major catastrophe."

"But how does that connect to us here on the other side of the United States?"

"I'm just wondering if your killer believes that he is doing a good thing, like Mullin. I mean, look at the poem, my gift to you? Sounds like he is sending a love letter to the community. Maybe the gift he mentions is actually one of his victims."

Rick pulled the phone away from his ear and pinched his nose. It was almost too much. A serial killer on Nantucket?

"RC? You there?" a tinny voice said through the small speaker on his phone.

He lifted the phone to his ear. "I'm here, Margot. Just trying to absorb what you are saying."

"I'm sorry, RC. But it's just my opinion. I can run it by the behavioral guys if you want me to."

Rick sighed. "Would you mind? Not that I don't believe you, but a second set of eyes on this might be helpful."

"Of course. Not sure I'll be able to do that before Tuesday. The place is pretty much cleared out with the holiday."

"That's fine, Margot. Right now, we are focused on finding a kidnapper. We can always add serial killer to his description when we know more."

Margot laughed softly. "Sad but true. Enjoy the rest of your weekend, RC."

"I'll try. You too. Thanks, Margot. Appreciate the help.

"You bet, RC. Later."

Rick ended the call and laid the phone down on his desk. He leaned back in his chair and rubbed his eyes.

A serial killer. On Nantucket?

There was a tap on his door. He turned to see Tuna, looking anxious.

"What's up?" asked Rick.

"I heard you on the phone. Was that the FBI?"

Rick nodded. Yeah, my old FBI colleague, Margot North. She's the one who helped us figure out what had happened to the Post's car last September. Turns out she's also into serial killers."

"Serial killers? That's an interesting, if strange, hobby."

"Yeah," said Rick and let out a long sigh. "And she thinks we have one here. On the island."

Tuna's eyes went wide. "Seriously?"

"Yeah, seriously. I think we need to revisit those other cases. See if they can tell us anything about who our kidnapper, er, killer may be."

Tuna nodded. "I'll get Santos on it. He's made the list, so I'll ask him to pull the files, if there is one."

"Good idea."

"Anything on the partials?"

"Damn, sorry, Tuna, I haven't followed up on that. I'll call them right now," he said, exasperated.

"It's okay, Rick. The past forty-eight hours have been insane. Let me know what you hear."

"Will do."

CHAPTER TWENTY-SEVEN

His call went straight to voicemail. His old boss from the Boston FBI office, SAIC Hanna Fines, had connected him to a resource at the Latent Print Unit who she claimed owed her a favor and would turn the analysis of the partials from Katie's Cisco hat quickly, even over the holiday weekend. He left a message, requesting a callback as soon as possible, along with his number. He disconnected the call and laid his phone on the desk, screen down.

"Are you doing okay?" asked a sweet voice behind him.

He turned and saw the smiling face of Felicity.

"Fel, what are you doing here?" exclaimed Rick. He jumped out of his chair and gave her a big hug.

"I was worried about you, with this case and all. You left in such a rush this morning. I just wanted to see how you are doing and ask if I can buy you lunch."

Rick picked up his phone and checked the time. It was still half an hour before noon, but his stomach was growling. He realized then that he had forgotten to eat breakfast. The news of Katie's escape had blocked everything else from his mind.

He smiled. "That sounds wonderful, but I don't have a lot of time. Should we just go across the street?"

Felicity smiled and nodded. "Fairgrounds would be perfect. I love their chicken quesadilla."

Rick and Felicity walked through the detective's room, down the stairs, and out of the front doors of the NPD. Once out of the building, Rick reached over and grabbed her hand.

“Thanks, Fel. I really needed a break.” They walked quietly, comfortably, down the hundred or so yards of the bike path before turning to cross over the street to the restaurant. The traffic on Fairgrounds Road was a non-stop line of cars and SUVs bound for Surfside Beach. Finally, an older woman in a well-used pick-up stopped and waved them across. They returned the wave, skipped quickly across the road, and joined a large crowd already gathered at Fairgrounds for an early lunch.

They stopped at the empty desk. The hostess had just walked an older couple to a table. She returned with a big smile and light brown, sparkling eyes.

“Inside or out?” she asked enthusiastically, as if she would be joining them for their meal.

He turned to Felicity for the decision. It was another beautiful spring day on the island, something that Rick had failed to notice with his face buried in Katie’s case.

“Let’s sit outside.” She turned to Rick. “That okay?”

“Perfect,” replied Rick.

The hostess led them out the front door and onto the deck. A pergola covered the space and provided some relief from the sun. She sat them at the last open table, distributed menus, and retreated to her station quietly and efficiently.

Felicity looked intently at Rick. “Are you okay?” she asked again, this time with much more emotion and concern. She held her hands across the table, and he grabbed both of them.

“I am now,” he said and leaned over to give her a kiss.

She returned it softly, sat back, and gazed lovingly at him. Her auburn hair was catching the sun, and her green eyes sparkled with energy and excitement.

The server approached. “Hi, I’m Kate, and I’ll be your server today.”

Rick looked at Felicity and smiled at the coincidence. Yesterday, it would have been an unpleasant reminder of her abduction, but today, knowing Katie was safe, it was serendipitous.

“Can I get you two something to drink?” Kate asked eagerly.

“Sure. A couple of iced teas, please,” said Rick.

The server nodded and retreated to fill their order.

“It is so wonderful that she escaped. That she is safe now,” said Felicity. “Was she able to tell you who the kidnapper was?”

Rick shook his head. “Unfortunately, she never got a good look at him. I mean, she gave us a general description, age, size, and weight. And some good information on his car. But nothing definitive, so we still have some work to do.”

Felicity looked at him intently. “I’m sorry. It’s been such a brutal case, I was hoping all that would be left would be to arrest the bastard that did it.”

Rick nodded intently. “Me too. The last couple of days have been hell. Missing persons cases are the most challenging to work. The pressure is so intense, and as a cop, you are imagining that the worst possible things are happening to the victim and you have to get there quickly to stop them.”

“And you did. Katie is safe.”

He shook his head. “Katie is safe because of Katie. She is strong and determined, like you, and wasn’t going to let herself be a victim. And us?" he said and motioned to the police building down the street. "We did nothing but chase our tails."

"Oh, honey, don't be so hard on yourself."

Rick sighed and looked at his lap. Finally, he looked up and met her eyes. "Fel. I have to be honest. We were no closer to finding her this morning than we were when she was first missing. We had no clues, no idea of where she might be."

She stood, walked around the table, and wrapped her arms around his neck. He pulled them in tight, closed his eyes, and savored the embrace. She leaned down, kissed the top of his head, and then made her way back to her chair.

"You are so tense, babe. I get it. But maybe you need a break."

Rick shook his head. "I wish, hon. But not yet. Still work to do."

"I've got it!" said Felicity. "Why don't you join me for yoga tomorrow?"

Rick laughed heartily. "Me? Yoga? That's like oil and water. You know I'm not that flexible. I'd probably hurt myself."

"No, you wouldn't," said Felicity sweetly. "You can go at your own pace. The music's relaxing and my instructor, Karen, is terrific."

"Okay. Well, maybe. But I sure don't want to get up at the crack of dawn for class like you do."

Felicity beamed. "Well then, you are in luck! Karen had to cancel our early class tomorrow and rescheduled it for two. Join me! It'll be fun."

Rick smiled. “I’ll think about it, hon. But honestly, until this case is wrapped up, I’m not sure I’m going to have time to do anything.”

“I understand. And I’m sure you’ll get this guy and bring him to justice. It’s just a matter of time.”

He shook his head. “It’s worse than that.”

“Worse? How could it be worse? Katie’s safe and unharmed, isn’t she?”

The server arrived with their drinks and placed them on the table. She grabbed a pen and her order pad. “What can I get you two to eat?” she asked.

“Um, I think we’ll just enjoy our drinks for a moment. Maybe give us a few minutes?”

“Sure! Just holler when you are ready.” She turned and made her way to another table.

Rick turned back to Felicity. “She is, thankfully. But in our investigation, I think we may have discovered something else. Something far worse entirely.”

A shadow crossed Felicity’s face. “Rick, you are scaring me. What did you find?”

He paused, not sure how much he should really be telling her. But Felicity was smart, capable, and above all, strong. Maybe she could even help him sort things out.

“We may have a serial killer on the island,” he said, finally.

“A serial killer!” exclaimed Felicity. “No!”

He reached for her hand, and she took it quickly, thankfully.

"It's not like a traditional serial killer, Fel. You don't have anything to worry about, I promise you."

"Are you sure? I mean, how do you know?" Her face was pale, anxious.

"Honestly, we don't even know if there is a serial killer. What I can tell you is that Sergeant Santos identified a pattern of suspicious deaths over the years."

"Over the years?" exclaimed Felicity. "How long does he think this has been going on?"

Rick looked at her caringly. "Based on his analysis? Thirty-two years."

Felicity's mouth dropped open, her face reflecting the challenges her mind was having coming to grips with this new and awful information.

"Thirty-two years?" she whispered. "That means it started when I was just a baby." Her voice trembled. Her eyes betrayed the shock she felt knowing that her island, where she had been born and raised, was not at all what she had always thought it was. She felt violated.

Rick looked at her, his heart aching at the pain he had caused. "I'm sorry, Fel. I shouldn't have told you."

Her eyes sparked, and she sat upright in her chair. "No. I am glad that you told me. I would want to hear it from you, not read about it in the Inq and M. It's just so, so unexpected. How could we have a serial killer on Nantucket? And how did he get away with it for three decades?"

Rick smiled assuringly. "What we know, Fel, is that there has been a death, or a reported missing person, around the Memorial

Day weekend every year since 1992. When they happened, the deaths were ruled accidental or from natural causes. No one suspected there was anything more to them than that."

"So then, couldn't it just be that? You know, like Occam's Razor? The simplest solution? Why do you think it's more than that? Why do you think it's a serial killer?"

The server approached the table and caught Rick's eye. He shook his head, she smiled, and redirected back inside.

"Because in addition to the deaths, someone was putting a poem in the community announcements section of the Inquirer and Mirror. Every year, the week after Memorial Day, starting in 1992."

"What's the poem?"

"Um, what is it called? Nature's green can stay? It's by some guy called Cross."

Felicity looked bewildered and stared at Rick intently, her green eyes shining brightly. "Do you mean Nothing Gold Can Stay by Robert Frost?"

"That's it," said Rick, excited. "Sorry, my memory. And I never did like poetry. Anyway, how do you know it?"

"It's one of my favorite poems, Rick."

"Really?" he said, surprised.

She nodded emphatically. "You know I was an English Minor. We studied that poem, and for some reason, it always just spoke to me: the fleeting nature of life, the transience of beauty, how our lives rush by. It is a wonderful work of poetry. The question is, why would he choose that particular poem?"

“Well, he actually made changes to it. He added four lines and renamed it.”

“What, really? What were the four lines?” she asked, excitedly.

“Hang on,” said Rick, and pulled out his phone. It took him a minute to find it. “Okay, here. After the eight lines of the original, our killer added these: Unless a gift made in moment brief, can pause our time’s silent grief, she follows those gone now, still and gray, a bequest I have done for you my dear, this day.”

Felicity sat quietly, absorbing the words. She closed her eyes.

“Fel?”

Without opening her eyes, she asked, “And what did he rename it?”

“My Gift to You.”

She sat thinking, contemplating the words, and then opened her eyes. “So is every death in some way a gift to us? Is that what he’s thinking?”

Rick nodded. “You remember Margot North, my colleague from my Quantico days?”

“The one who calls you after her favorite soda, RC?” said Felicity, smiling.

He nodded. “That’s the one. She helped us with your mom’s case. Anyway, in addition to her cybercrime work with the FBI, she is into serial killers.”

“Into serial killers? Sounds like her,” she said with a soft smile. “And that’s what she thinks? That this ‘gift’,” she said, holding up air quotes, “has something to do with the deaths each year?”

"Yes. She talked about another serial killer, this guy in California who thought he could prevent earthquakes if he killed people. Essentially made sacrifices to appease the gods or whatever. She thinks this might be a similar motivator for our killer."

"Stopping earthquakes," she said, jokingly.

"No, not that exactly. But that maybe he thinks he's doing a good thing. That, in his head, these deaths are doing something positive for the community."

She looked thoughtful. "Were these people, the ones who died, bad?"

"Bad?" asked Rick.

"You know, were they really bad people. Like child abusers or wife beaters. Were they criminals? Like, did he think he was making our community better - or safer - by killing them?"

"I haven't looked at the cases in detail, but my gut says no. They were just ordinary citizens enjoying their time on the island. I mean, look at Katie."

Felicity nodded. "True. I don't think you could ask for a better person. So why would he want to hurt her? Kill her?"

Rick shook his head. "That's what we are trying to find out."

Rick's phone buzzed. He picked it up and looked at the screen. "I'm sorry, Fel, I've got to take this."

She smiled, knowing her decision to get into a relationship with a detective would probably mean lots of moments in her life like this.

Rick stood and walked across the deck and out into the parking lot. She watched him intently, thankful that she had found him despite the loss of her parents that had brought him back to the island. Thankful that he had trusted her with his move back to Nantucket. Thankful they were together and stronger, happier than ever.

He talked animatedly to whoever was on the other end of the call. After a few minutes, he tapped the screen and slid the phone in his pocket. He smiled, pumped his fist, and came rushing back to the table.

"What is it?" asked Fel excitedly.

"That was the Latent Prints Unit at the FBI. They found a match!"

"A match to what?" asked Fel, confused.

"Oh, sorry, babe. We were able to lift a couple of partial fingerprints off Katie's hat. The LPU team was able to clean them up and make a positive identification. We know who grabbed Katie!"

Felicity stood and embraced Rick. "That is wonderful news! Now, I know you probably need to go."

Rick nodded quickly. "Yes. I need to get back with Tuna and track this bastard down. This is by far the best lead we have. We need to get this guy."

"Yes, and you also need to eat. Tell me what you want, and I'll bring it over to you."

Rick smiled at her adoringly. "You take such good care of me. Thank you."

She smiled back. "Happy to. Now what can I get you?"

CHAPTER TWENTY-EIGHT

He ran back to the NPD, almost getting run over in the process as he dodged traffic crossing Fairgrounds Road. He stormed through the front doors, took the stairs two steps at a time, and made a beeline to Tuna's desk.

She heard the commotion and turned in time to see Rick slide to a stop at her door.

"We got 'em!" said Rick. He was out of breath, his face was red from exhaustion, and his eyes were bright with excitement.

"Who? Our kidnapper?" asked Tuna, eagerly.

"Yes! I just got the call from the fingerprints team at the FBI. They were able to match the partials on Katie's hat through AFIS. A fourteen-point match! We have him, Tuna!"

Tuna stood, nearly knocking her coffee cup to the floor. She steadied the cup and then turned to Rick. "Who is he?"

"His name is Randy Evans," replied Rick. "Last known address was Turners Falls, Massachusetts. He was arrested and printed in 1988. He was caught shoplifting in Greenfield, Mass."

Tuna did some quick math. "So that would make him mid-fifties today. That ties with what Katie said about her kidnapper. What else do we know?"

Rick shook his head. "Nothing more. That's all the info that the latent unit had. It's up to us now to figure out what he's been doing since the late eighties."

Tuna nodded, turned, and sat back down at her desk. She tapped on her keyboard to wake her laptop. Rick stood behind her, his arms crossed, ready to make an arrest as soon as they located him.

She pulled up Google, typed in the name, and hit enter. A millisecond later, her screen filled with images of Caucasian men of all ages, though the skew was more toward fifties and sixties. The name must have been pretty popular in the 1970s.

"Can you tie him to Nantucket?"

She moved the cursor to the search bar, added a plus sign, and then typed in Nantucket. She hit the return key. Once again, the browser thought for a fraction of a second and then filled her screen with images. Unfortunately, none of the men shown was connected to the island.

"Did that not work?" asked Rick. "That looks to be the same group of men it showed us a minute ago."

"It is. Hang on." She moved the cursor and clicked on the option to force the search engine to only look for entries that included the name Randy Evans and Nantucket. She hit enter. There were two hits.

"Bingo! "That looks to be our guy," he said, pointing to the image of an older, heavyset man wearing a green half zip.

"Hold your horses, Rick."

"What?"

"It says here he lives in Iowa. He wrote a story for their local newspaper that mentions Nantucket. Something about billionaires. We can certainly follow up with him, but I don't think he's our guy."

"Okay," said Rick, deflated. "What about him?" He was pointing to a second image about halfway down the page. The age was right, but the man looked very fit. "It looks like he's a sailor. That would tie with Figawi, wouldn't it? Maybe that's the connection we've been missing?"

Tuna grunted and clicked on the link. The screen changed to show a man in front of his sailboat, arms crossed, and smiling. He had the grizzled look about him from spending a lifetime on the water. Tuna read a few lines and then turned to Rick, shaking her head.

"Sorry, Rick. Dead end here as well. Looks like he lives on the Cape and has a thing about lighthouses. A couple of mentions on his social media about the lighthouses of Nantucket, but no claims of ever visiting."

Rick blew out a long breath. "Damn it!"

Tuna held up her hand. "It's okay, Rick. We knew it wasn't going to be that easy. What did you think, we'd key his name in and then his address on the island would pop up?"

He blushed. "No, not really," he said softly. "But a man can dream, can't he?"

Tuna chuckled. "Rick, you are too funny. But look on the bright side, we have a name. And we have a solid connection to Katie with the hat. We know who kidnapped her. Now we just need to do some solid detective work to figure out where he is now."

Rick nodded. "You're right, of course. As usual," he added. "Let's go back to when he was arrested. Can you access those arrest records?"

"Sure can, thanks to your friends at the FBI. Let me pull up the National Crime Information Center database and see if we can get a hit." She clicked an icon on her favorites bar and a new webpage loaded. It featured the FBI and NCIC logos and a bright white search box. She tapped in Randy Evans along with Turners Falls and clicked on the little magnifying glass icon. This time, the returns were not as fast, and the progress wheel on her browser kept spinning.

"Did it freeze?" asked Rick, concerned.

"No," replied Tuna. "I think it's just having to sort through a lot of records. There must be millions."

Her screen shifted again, and this time showed the mugshot of a thin, young man with long brown hair, a bushy, unkempt beard, and vacant, brown eyes. He was not smiling and looked like he'd been through hell.

Tuna turned and looked up at Rick. "Here's our man."

Rick leaned in and stared at the image. "Does he look at all familiar to you?"

She shook her head. "No, not at all. He could be almost anyone."

Tuna moved her cursor to the print icon and selected two copies. She hit enter. A few seconds later, the printer in the corner whirred to life. Tuna got up to retrieve the records and returned to her desk. She handed one to Rick and began studying the other.

"Looks like he was arrested just a few days after his eighteenth birthday," said Rick.

"Talk about fortuitous. If he'd been arrested a week or even a few days earlier, his record would have been expunged at eighteen. Then we would really be lost."

"True. Any other records in NCIC for our man Randy?" asked Rick, hopefully.

"Nope. Just that one shoplifting incident."

"What about the RMV? Does Randy have a driver's license?"

Tuna tapped at her keyboard. "No. No record of Randy Evans in the Registry of Motor Vehicles. That means no records for a car registration or a driver's license."

Rick looked puzzled. "It's almost as if he dropped off the face of the earth after his arrest."

"Hey, you two," said Felicity. She was carrying a large brown bag. "I brought you lunch."

"Thanks, hon," said Rick, lovingly. "It is so sweet of you."

She smiled. "Happy to. And Tuna? I wasn't sure what you'd like, so I got you a Caesar salad with grilled chicken."

Tuna's eyes lit up. "That is perfect! Thank you so much, Felicity. My stomach was growling, and I didn't want to take the time to eat, especially with this news."

"You are welcome. Now, I'll leave you two to it."

Rick leaned over and kissed Felicity on the cheek. "Thanks, babe. I'll see you tonight."

"Uh-huh," said Felicity, conspiratorially. "I believe that when I see it." She turned and left.

Rick unpacked the bag and handed Tuna a circular foil container with a plastic lid and a small clear bag with a napkin and utensils. Tuna removed the top, pushed the utensils through the end of the bag, and tucked in.

She finished chewing and then said, "Let's check the Registry of Vital Records and Statistics. That will tell us if he died, got married, or divorced." She navigated to another screen. A few more taps. "Okay. Here's his birth record."

Rick was busy with his Reuben, careful not to let the dressing fall on his shirt. He put the sandwich down and leaned in to examine her screen. "May 21, 1970. Born at Baystate Franklin Medical Center to Levi Evans, age 17, and Chloe Evans, 14."

"Fourteen?" exclaimed Tuna. "Is marriage at that age even legal?"

Rick nodded. "Sadly, back then it was. At least with parental consent. The law was only changed in Massachusetts a few years ago to prohibit marriage before the age of eighteen, regardless of what the parents said."

"Thank heavens for small favors," said Tuna, sarcastically. She took another forkful of salad.

"Anything else in the Registry?" asked Rick, sprinkling a few crumbs of rye bread. "Oops. Sorry."

Tuna wiped the crumbs off her shoulder and scanned her screen. "No. No listings of death, marriage, or divorce."

"Hmmm," said Rick. "Maybe he moved out of state?"

"Maybe," said Tuna. She clicked at her laptop and pulled up the National Driver Register. "Okay, lots of Randy Evans out there have driver's licenses."

"Can you filter it?"

Tuna tapped at her keyboard. "Okay, I've filtered by birth month and year."

"And?"

"We have two hits. Randy Evans, of Madison, Indiana, and Randy Evans, of Sharp, Nevada."

Rick leaned in again to examine their pictures. "Indiana Randy is bald and looks to be pretty short."

"Five two based on the Indiana Bureau of Motor Vehicles," responded Tuna.

"He's out," Rick said, shifting his weight and flicking his gaze back to the screen. "Nevada Randy? Anything there? I don't recognize the face, but he could be one we need to show to Katie."

Tuna scanned her screen. "This Randy has a Star of Life on his license."

"Okay. Does it say what this Randy's medical condition is?"

"He's handicapped. Apparently missing his right leg."

Rick let out a hard breath through his nose and looked away for a second, jaw tightening. "Damn. Looks like he's out too."

Tuna and Rick were quiet, frustrated that their search had ended in a dead end.

"Try the parents," said Rick, a little more forcefully than he intended.

"What?" asked Tuna, a bit annoyed.

"Sorry. His parents were young. I'm sure they are still around. If we can find them, then hopefully they'll know where their son is."

Tuna nodded. "Makes sense." She pulled up the RMV search screen and entered their names. "No licenses or car registrations for either of them."

"Really. That's kind of strange. Are they even still married?"

“Good question.” She clicked on a tab in her browser. The window was still open to the search screen of the Registry of Vital Records and Statistics. She keyed in Levi’s name. “Okay. Dad is dead. Died when Randy was pretty young. 1978.”

“Grew up fatherless? Might explain a few things,” said Rick.

A few keyboard clacks later. “Whoa.”

“What?”

“Mom’s dead too. Also in 1978.”

“They both died the same year? Car accident, maybe?”

“Could be. Do they have a newspaper there? In Turners Falls?”

“I doubt it. I think Turners Falls is pretty small. But let me check.” Rick pulled out his phone and tapped on the screen. “Yeah, no, not in Turners Falls. But Greenfield does. They are just a few miles away.”

Tuna opened a new window in her browser and typed in the search bar. Seconds later, a page of links popped up, and she clicked on the first one.

“The Greenfield Recorder. They have been in business since 1792. Wow.”

Rick pointed to the upper right corner of her screen. “Looks like they have archive access. Try putting in Randy’s name and see what happens. Maybe he had some juvenile priors?”

She tapped at her keyboard and hit enter. A number of stories appeared. All seemed to have either the name Randy or the name Evans, but none had both. She continued scrolling and was almost to the end of the list when a headline caught her attention.

Levi Evans Suspected in Turners Falls Murder Suicide

She looked at Rick and arched an eyebrow. "The date on the byline is 1978."

He looked at her intently. "Let's see what it says."

Tuna clicked on the link, and an image of a mobile home filled the screen. The yard was strewn with trash, a rusted-out car, and piles of debris. Several police officers were clustered around the front door. Below the photo was the story.

Levi Evans Suspected in Turners Falls Murder Suicide

By Jack Spears, Staff Reporter.

TURNERS FALLS - The Franklin County sheriff's department responded to a disturbance call on the 1200 block of Fellman Street yesterday afternoon, only to discover the bodies of Levi Evans, 25, and Chloe Evans, 22, in their Turners Falls home.

The preliminary investigation suggests that Levi Evans had attacked his wife with a metal baseball bat. Her body was found in the kitchen of the small home with a significant head injury. The body of Levi Evans was found in a bedroom of the house with an apparent self-inflicted gunshot wound.

The couple were married in June of 1970 and had one child together, Randy Evans, 8.

Levi Evans was well known to local law enforcement with multiple arrests for shoplifting, breaking and entering, as well as trespassing. While he spent time in the Franklin County Jail in Greenfield for these crimes, he did not have a prior record of violence.

A neighbor, 43-year-old Cassie Simmons, has lived next to the Evanses since they moved into their home in 1972.

"To be honest, I worried about that boy. The dad, Levi, was a heavy drinker, and I don't think the mom ever did much. But I did see the boy playing outside a lot," she said. "I think he was afraid to go inside. He seemed lonely."

Authorities said the investigation of the deaths remains ongoing and that no further information was expected to be released pending the formal investigation by the Massachusetts State Police Detectives Unit assigned to the Franklin County district attorney's office.

Rick looked at Tuna. "Okay. That definitely explains a few things. Losing your parents in such a violent way? Must have been incredibly traumatic."

Tuna nodded. "Absolutely. But what happened to young Randy? He was only eight."

"Could he have been taken in by a family member? Maybe adopted?"

"Most likely. But we'll need a court order to access those records. That will take a few days." She was quiet for a minute. "I wonder," said Tuna, softly.

"What are you thinking?" asked Rick. "Did we miss something?"

"I'm thinking about his arrest. That should show where he was living at the time. Can you see it listed?" asked Tuna, pointedly.

Rick scanned the printed document. "Here it is. And still in Turners Falls. Must be family."

"What's the address?" asked Tuna. Her fingers were poised on her keyboard.

"Seventeen fifty Grout's Corner Way. 01376."

She keyed in the details. A wheel spun on her screen while they looked on impatiently. After a minute, a blue table appeared with a number of entries.

"Okay, here is all the activity on that property address since," Tuna leaned into the screen, "1902. That's probably when the house was built."

"What's the most recent record?"

Peering intently at the small type, Tuna took a minute to find the information. She leaned back in her chair and looked up at Rick. "1967."

"So no activity since then?"

"Doesn't look like it. They must still live there. Or at least own the property."

"Who is it?"

Tuna clicked on the record. Her screen filled with a spinning wheel. Finally, a record popped up. "Okay. The name on the property deed is a Gayle Hickman."

"Gayle Hickman? Might be a relative? A married name?"

"Could be. Let me check."

She clicked on the tab for the vital records search. "We have a birth certificate, January 1939, but no record of a marriage or divorce."

"Hmm. Maybe she's a foster mom?"

"Possibly. But again hard to verify. Those records require a warrant, and we don't have the time."

"What does her driver's record show?"

Tuna navigated back to the Massachusetts RMV search page. A few seconds later, her screen filled with an image of a geriatric woman, very overweight, with stringy silver hair and dull gray eyes. “Says here she’s eighty-six years old, five foot four, two hundred eighty pounds. Flag on her license says she is also diabetic.”

“Can you check her in NCIC, see if she has a record?”

Tuna switched tabs on her browser and quickly tapped her keys. “Negative. Looks like she is an honest, law-abiding citizen.”

“Hmm, interesting,” said Rick. “So why did Randy Evans claim to be living with Gayle Hickman? What is the story there?”

“Only one way to find out,” said Tuna, conspiratorially.

Rick eyed her cautiously. “Road trip?”

Tuna laughed heartily. “You and I, Caton. We definitely think alike.”

Rick glanced at his phone. “If we hustle, we could make the two-fifteen Hy-Line. Grab a hotel somewhere near Turners Falls and then pay a visit to Ms. Hickman first thing in the morning.”

“Don’t you think we should call her first?” asked Tuna.

He shook his head. “In my experience, it’s better to catch them unprepared. We don’t want her to have the time to think about it or how she might answer questions. You have to think she’ll be defending him, so best to catch her off guard.”

Tuna nodded. “Okay, makes sense. I’ll run home and pack a bag. Can I give you a lift?”

Rick smiled. “That would be great, thanks.”

CHAPTER TWENTY-NINE

2019

Ariel Bird was a self-styled travel influencer who had been to Nantucket just a few times in her thirty years of life, yet claimed to be the island expert on everything from best beaches, to the latest hot restaurants, to the key selfie photo spots not to be missed. She managed to share all of this information via her many social media feeds and had several hundred thousand followers who hung on her every post. She dismissed those who claimed she was a poser, a self-seeker using the island to grow her following, or an opportunist who diminished the island's centuries of history.

No, she claimed, she was an influencer, a professional, who was only trying to build awareness of everything that Nantucket had to offer.

To Randy, she was a cancer that needed to be surgically removed from the island. She represented everything that was wrong with Nantucket today. Nantucket wasn't a photo opp to be posted on your Insta feed. It wasn't an upscale amusement park designed only for young women to use to validate their societal standing. It wasn't a trope to be used to build your followers.

He was tired of all the people who exploited the island. The people who had no clue of the island's rich history or the sheer beauty of the island. The people who were only there because it was Nantucket. They just needed their sweatshirt, their selfies, and the story of their trip to share with friends and family. And Ariel Bird took full advantage of this group.

Randy had started following her online and discovered she was going to reward Nantucket with a visit over the Memorial Day weekend. He knew he had to act and take advantage of the rare opportunity to silence what he viewed as a cause of the island's increasingly unwanted popularity.

But how? Her visibility through her socials suggested that she would land on the island with an entourage, heavily protected and difficult to reach. But the reality was quite the opposite. When he finally saw her walking down Main Street, he was startled at how little she looked like her online persona. But not a surprise, he thought, given her penchant for exaggeration.

Getting to her proved remarkably easy. A single spritz of a water and foxglove blend on her salad while her attention was focused on her phone.

She died of unexpected cardiac arrest several hours later at Cottage Hospital.

CHAPTER THIRTY

After spending the night at the Motel 6 in South Deerfield, Rick and Tuna made the twenty-minute drive to Turners Falls, stopping at a Dunkin on the way for coffee and a couple of breakfast sandwiches.

They pulled up to the curb at seventeen fifty Grout's Corner Way in Turners Falls just past nine a.m. The house was a gable-front Victorian with a broad porch extending the width of the home. The paint, originally a creamy white, was heavily faded and chalking. Remnants of gingerbread details hung drunkenly from the eaves. The porch railing was missing at least half of its balusters, and the steps leading to the front door were angled crookedly to the right.

There were a number of windows visible, each with the curtains completely closed as if the owner was afraid to let any light into the home. An upper-floor window had a piece of plywood filling the space where glazing should have been.

A lawn, desperate for a mowing, was populated by dandelions and other weeds. An asphalt driveway ran down the left side of the lawn and terminated in a rusted metal, standalone carport. A beige, early eighties station wagon, its faux wood trim peeling off, was sitting on four flat tires under the carport and looking like it hadn't been moved in years.

The only signs of life at the home was an overfilled garbage can tucked between the driveway and the house, its contents spewing out over the old asphalt.

Rick eyed the house closely, surveying the structure as if he were preparing for a SWAT team raid. He turned to Tuna.

"What do you think?" he asked.

"It looks like Ms. Hickman might not be the best housekeeper in the world. She certainly isn't going to be winning any awards from House Beautiful."

Rick chuckled. "That's for sure. Ready?"

Tuna nodded.

They got out of the car and made their way to the front door. They gingerly climbed the steps to the porch, fearful they might give way at any moment. The entry was typical Victorian, with two full sidelights framing a door with four wood panels on the lower half and etched glass above. Lace curtains antiqued by time blocked the view through the sidelights.

Rick pushed the doorbell. Nothing.

"I guess her penchant for home maintenance extends also to her doorbell," said Tuna, sarcastically. She reached past Rick and rapped her knuckles hard on the glass. She peered through the door's glass, opaque with dirt and cobwebs. "I think I see movement."

Moments later came the sound of a lock being turned. The doorknob twisted slowly, and the door opened, its hinges squeaking in protest.

An elderly woman looked out cautiously at them. She clearly hadn't undertaken any form of self-improvement since her driver's license photo had been captured. She was wearing a soiled housecoat with badly faded red and green flower print that looked like it hadn't been off her body in years.

"Can I help you?" she asked, her voice carrying the rasps of every cigarette she had ever smoked.

"Ms. Hickman?"

"Yes," the woman replied, nervously. Her face twitched. She had a large mole on her left cheek that looked to be growing hair.

"I'm Detective Tina Fisch. This is Detective Rick Caton. Can we talk to you about Randy Evans?"

Her rheumy, gray eyes showed a spark of recognition and concern. "Randy? Is he okay?"

"That's what we'd like to talk about. Do you mind if we come in, Ms. Hickman?" asked Tuna considerately. "Where we can talk in private?"

The woman looked them up and down suspiciously. She coughed loudly, snorted, spat on the floor, and then took a step back. "Suit yourself. Not sure what good it will do."

She turned and left. Tuna and Rick eyed each other as if to gauge their desire to complete this interview before they followed in her shuffling footsteps. They entered into a darkened parlor that reeked of mildew, stale cigarettes, and an undertone of alcohol. Furniture, once fashionable in the 1960's, was arranged haphazardly around the room. Several pieces were covered in plastic, yellowed by age and smoke.

They followed her way down a short hallway to a small kitchen in the back of the house. Knotty pine cabinets, coated in an orange shellac, lined the back wall, the doors hung with black strap hinges. A metal-banded orange laminate countertop extended the length of the cabinets uninterrupted, save for a stainless steel sink, piled high with dishes. The edges of the laminate were curled, exposing the cheap particle board below.

The walls were a faded yellow and streaked with bacon grease and cooking oils. A solitary turquoise pendant light fixture hung from the ceiling centered over a green Formica table with matching metal chairs. An acrid aroma filled the room that reminded Rick of spoiled meat.

"Please have a seat," said Gayle, motioning to the chairs. She sat down heavily, her face reddened by exertion.

Rick eyed the chairs, well-worn, cracked, and with numerous cigarette burns. He pulled the chair out and sat down. Tuna did the same.

"Thank you for seeing us, Ms. Hickman. What can you tell us about Randy Evans?"

"Do you mind if I smoke?" Without waiting for a response, she pulled a pack of generic cigarettes from a pocket of her housecoat along with a cheap disposable lighter. She lit the cigarette, took a long drag, and exhaled a plume of blue smoke over Tuna's head.

Rick coughed subtly while he explored the space around them. Empty vodka bottles lined the floor next to another overflowing garbage can. This one featured the packaging refuse of all types of junk food, from snack cakes to potato chips, to white bread. He was pretty sure Ms. Hickman did not follow the government's nutritional recommendations on daily sugar and salt intake.

He glanced at Tuna. She was motioning with her eyes to look behind him. He turned slightly. Hanging on the wall was a wooden frame, its smudged glass protecting a white paper yellowed with age. He looked closely and could just make out the title.

Nature's first green is gold.

A shot of adrenaline burst through him. He turned back to Tuna, their eyes meeting. She nodded slightly before turning her attention back to Ms. Hickman.

"Randy Evans? What can you tell us about him?"

"Is he okay?" she asked again, her voice wheezing.

"That's what we are trying to determine, Ms. Hickman."

She took a long drag on her cigarette and then stubbed it out in a dented aluminum ashtray already piled high with used butts. "I'm sorry, but my memory isn't good. Sucks getting old."

"When was the last time you heard from him?"

"Randy? I think it was last year. As I mentioned, my memory ain't good, especially with time. Some things I think happened just a few years ago were more like ten." She coughed, and a small cloud of spittle flew out and settled on the table.

"Did Randy visit you here?"

She shook her head slowly, sadly. "I haven't seen Randy in probably thirty years. Maybe more." She lit another cigarette.

"But you said you heard from him?" prompted Rick.

Gayle turned. "Uh-huh. Postcards. I get one from him every year, usually around Christmas, letting me know how he's doing."

Tuna nodded. "Have you saved his postcards?"

"Yes. They are very special to me. Randy was a special child."

"Would you mind if we looked at them, please?" asked Tuna, softly.

Gayle eyed her carefully, unsure of whether or not to trust this woman. Making her decision, she slid her chair back, its feet scraping against the linoleum floor, and heaved herself up. She walked slowly over to the cabinets and opened a drawer. She pulled out a stack of postcards bound by a couple of thick rubber bands and walked back to the table. She placed the postcards in front of Tuna and then fell heavily into her chair, grunting.

"Thank you, Ms. Hickman," said Tuna. She grabbed the pile, undid the rubber bands, and split the stack in half. She handed Rick one group while she began perusing the other.

Each of the postcards was some variation of a brief update of his life, hoping she is taking care of herself, and the prospect of a physical get-together in the future. The images were of various local attractions from Nantucket's rose-covered cottages, to the Gingerbread houses on the Vineyard, to the Long Point Lighthouse on the Cape. Each was postmarked from Hyannis. They revealed very little personal information about Randy Evans.

"Was Randy living in Hyannis then?" asked Rick, hopefully.

"Why would you think that?" asked Gayle. She took a final drag on her cigarette and then crushed it into the ashtray. It continued to smoke.

Rick showed the back of the postcard. "All of these are postmarked from Hyannis. So, I just assumed that he must be living there."

She shook her head. "No. He lives over on Nantucket."

"Do you by chance have his address there?" asked Tuna.

Gayle shook her head. "I'm sorry, no. I think he might be staying in a boarding house."

Rick picked up another postcard. "Randy mentions several times that he wanted to get together. I assume he means a physical visit?"

She smiled softly. "Yes. It would be so nice to see him, but it just hasn't worked out."

"Can I ask why?"

She pulled out another cigarette, but her lighter refused to cooperate. She dropped the unlit cigarette on the table, frustrated. "He said he couldn't come back here, to Turners Falls. Too many bad memories. And I don't drive anymore, haven't for years. So it just really hasn't worked out. But we'll keep trying," she added optimistically.

"And do you know what Randy does on Nantucket?"

"No, he has never shared that with me. But whatever he is doing, I'm sure he is making a difference. He always wanted to do the right thing."

"How did Randy come to live with you?" asked Rick, changing the direction of the conversation.

She turned to Rick, her gray eyes clouded and teary. "His parents died. I took him in."

"Are you family?"

She laughed briefly and then coughed. "No. Why would you think that?"

"Then why? Take him in, that is?"

"I felt bad for the boy. So young and to lose your parents like that? Plus, I needed the money."

"Needed the money?" asked Tuna.

She nodded. "Foster care. They paid me four hundred a month to look after him."

Tuna looked at Rick and back to Gayle Hickman. “It was kind of you to take him in. But wasn’t there any family to take Randy in?”

Gayle let out a cackle. “Are you kidding me? They’re all just a bunch of losers. No one wanted Randy. And to be honest, I’m pretty sure he didn’t want to go with any of them either. He didn’t have what you would call a happy childhood. At least until he came to live with me.”

Rick nodded. “Was he your only foster child?”

She shook her head, slowly, sadly. “No. I usually had a couple. Most would just stay for a month or two. But Randy? He was here until he turned eighteen. I think he was happy here.”

“And how was your relationship? Did you guys get along?”

She nodded. “For the most part. I mean, we had some challenges. Money was tight. He didn’t always want to go to school. But we got along okay. I’d like to think I saved him from going down the wrong path.”

“Did Randy ever get in trouble?”

She shook her head. “No, nothing serious. He got into a couple of fights in school. Kids would tease him about his parents. You know how they died, right?”

Tuna and Rick nodded in unison.

Gayle was quiet, unsure of how much to share. She spoke softly. “What you’ve heard or read about his parents’ death is not really the whole truth.”

Tuna shot a glance at Rick. “Not the whole truth?”

She shook her head. “Randy came home and found his mom dead in the kitchen. Levi, that bastard son-of-bitch had definitely killed poor Chloe. With a baseball bat. She was a sweet little thing who fell into the wrong crowd. Got knocked up by Levi, next thing you know, they're married." She paused and fumbled with the cigarette on the table, her fingers struggling to get a purchase. She slid it into her mouth, her gray lips holding it while she flicked the wheel on the lighter. This time, it cooperated, and she touched the flame to the tip. She took a deep drag and exhaled a small cloud of blue smoke.

"And then?" prompted Rick.

"Randy did find Levi in the bedroom, but he was alive. Had drunk himself unconscious. Passed out with the gun in his hand. Maybe he did mean to do it, you know, kill himself, but passed out before he could pull the trigger."

"And are you suggesting that Randy killed Levi?" asked Tuna, surprised.

Gayle eyed her carefully, subtly tipped her head, and took another drag on the cigarette.

"But the police report said the gunshot that killed Levi was self-inflicted," said Rick.

She nodded. "Levi Evans was a piece of shit. He was a petty thief, a vicious drunk, and pretty much made Chloe and Randy's lives miserable. The police didn't put a lot of effort into trying to figure it all out. To them, it was cut and dry."

"And you know for sure that Randy did it? Killed his father?"

She let out a sigh. "He told me, a few years later. Said finding his mom dead had made him incredibly angry. When he saw his dad unconscious, and with the gun in his hand? He told me he decided to finish what his dad had started."

"You seem okay with that, that Randy killed his father," said Rick, accusingly.

She looked at him, bristling. "Of course, I was okay with it. Levi didn't deserve to live after how he treated Randy and what he did to Chloe. I told Randy it was okay. That he did what he had to do to maintain the balance."

"The balance?" asked Tuna, confused.

She nodded emphatically as she turned to Tuna. "Randy needed to know that life was a balance. That it couldn't be one-sided and that sometimes sacrifices had to be made to maintain the equilibrium."

"What sort of sacrifices?" asked Rick, intently. He glanced at Tuna.

"Oh, you know, like nature does. Like a bee that stings an invader to the hive. The sting kills the bee, but the hive is protected. Her death is a sacrifice that saves the group. Killing Levi Evans did just that and made this town a better place."

"Biological altruism," stated Rick, matter-of-factly. Tuna turned to him, a shocked look on her face.

"Bio what?" asked Gayle, confused.

"It's a term used to describe how certain individuals in nature - like the bee you mentioned - are sacrificed to save the broader group."

"Hmm, okay," said Gayle. "Whatever you call it, I wanted Randy to believe that he could help maintain that balance. That he was a good person. That he needed to protect the weak and vulnerable."

Rick nodded. “And what can you tell us about that?” he asked, pointing to the frame on the wall behind him.

She brightened considerably, as if the mere glance at the frame gave her energy. “The poem. Yes. It has always been my favorite. Robert Frost. You know he lived in Vermont? Just about fifty miles from here.”

“And why do you like that poem?” asked Tuna, softly.

“It’s beautiful. But more importantly, it talks about balance.”

“How’s it about the balance?” asked Tuna.

“It’s about life and death,” she said, as if talking to a toddler. She took a final pull on the cigarette and crushed it into the ashtray to keep company with several dozen of its brethren. “It’s about saving the gold.”

“The gold?”

“The beauty.”

“And is that what you shared with Randy?”

She nodded. “I read him that poem every day. I wanted him to see the beauty in it, but also to understand the balance. It was up to him. That in the world of black versus white, good versus evil, he had to be the good person, the white, to save the gold.”

“Can I ask about Randy’s arrest? Just after he turned eighteen?” asked Tuna.

“Oh, that,” she said, waving her hand. “That was bullshit. His friend, who he was with, was the one who stole that tape player. Randy was innocent. Just hanging with the wrong people.”

“Is that what you told him?”

Gayle looked thoughtful, remembering the moment. “After I collected him at the police station, I brought him home and sat him down. Told him it was time to make his way in the world. He couldn’t stay here, in Turners Falls. He needed to leave the nest, find his way.”

“And did he leave?”

“Yes. It was a few days later, but he was ready. He packed a couple of bags, I gave him some money, and drove him to the bus station in Greenfield.”

“Do you know where he went?”

She shook her head. “No. But I think it was Boston.”

“And that was it? You didn’t hear from him until a postcard months later?”

“Oh, he called once or twice, just to let me know he was okay. But he didn’t get into specifics of what he was doing or where he was. I think maybe he was still trying to find himself.”

“Hmm, okay,” said Rick. “Do you know when he changed his name?”

“He changed his name? He’s not Randy anymore?” said Gayle, perplexed. “He always signs his notes to me as Randy. Why do you think he changed his name?”

“We are not sure, Ms. Hickman, but we can’t locate anyone by the name Randy Evans. We suspect he changed it fairly soon after he left you. His arrest is the last record with that name that we can find.”

“I’m sorry. I didn’t know,” said Gayle, thoughtfully. “Now I have a question for you two.”

“Of course,” said Tuna, kindly.

She lit another cigarette and took a long pull before exhaling a noxious cloud. "Is he okay? My Randy? Why are you asking all these questions about him?"

"Detective Caton and I," said Tuna, motioning to Rick. "We are working a case, and Randy's name came up. We are just trying to locate him to ask him a few questions."

"So he's okay?" Gayle asked, concerned.

Tuna nodded softly. "We think so. And we'd ask that if you hear from him, you'd let us know?" She handed Gayle one of her cards.

"Of course. I just hope he's not in trouble."

Rick stole a glance at Tuna, and she subtly shook her head. "As I said, we just want to ask him a few questions. And we certainly appreciate your time."

"Sure," she replied, coughing out smoke. "When you see Randy, please let him know I'm thinking of him. Tell him to call me."

"Of course, Ms. Hickman. Thank you. We'll see ourselves out."

They left the house, anxious for some fresh air, and made their way to the rental car. Tuna slid behind the wheel and looked at Rick. "Biological altruism? Where the hell did you learn that, professor?"

Rick chuckled. "It was a nature documentary I watched a few weeks ago. Found it fascinating. That there are a number of species that will sacrifice themselves for the greater good of their group."

"And do you watch a lot of these, um, nature documentaries?" asked Tuna, curiously.

"Well, aside from a personal interest, I think it makes me a better cop."

"A better cop?"

Rick nodded. "You know, we're animals too. So learning about certain animal behaviors, like biological altruism, can help me better understand some of the criminals we chase."

"Hmm. Okay," said Tuna, not at all convinced.

"Remind me to tell you the story of how I caught a money launderer by studying bird caching techniques."

Tuna looked at him suspiciously. "I'll hold off on calling BS on that until I hear the story. But not sure how any of this connects to the poem."

"I agree. I don't think it connects at all. But she seems to," he said, thumbing a finger toward the house. "She thinks it's all about that, and more importantly, it sounds like she drilled that into Randy's head. This balance shit. Saving the gold? Sounds like she may have some issues, besides her diet that is."

Tuna tapped on the steering wheel, impatient. "So you think our killer believes he is practicing some sort of biological altruism?"

Rick nodded. "I'm not a psychologist, but between what Margot shared with me and hearing Hickman here talking about the balance, I can believe that Randy honestly believes he is doing a good thing."

Tuna shook her head. "So we have a better understanding of his motivation, although we have no idea what he's trying to save. But we are also no closer to identifying who he is."

Rick nodded. "He is still a mystery. "

"What else can we do?" asked Tuna, expectantly, hoping Rick might have an answer.

"Let's get back to Nantucket and figure things out from there. If we hustle, we can catch the two twenty-five boat."

CHAPTER THIRTY-ONE

It was nearly three in the afternoon when Felicity walked out of the yoga studio. The class had been great as usual, and she felt relaxed, peaceful, and content. The instructor, Karen, had challenged her to try a new pose, the eight-angle. It took several tries; she kept losing her balance, but was finally able to achieve and hold the pose. She felt proud of herself for trying it and equally happy to have been successful. But her arms were sore.

She made her way across the parking lot, her purple yoga mat tucked under her arm. As usual, finding a spot for her old Bronco had been a challenge, and she was forced to use the lot across the street at the Irish restaurant, Kitty's. She and Rick ate there at least once a week - he loved the shepherd's pie - and they were good friends with the owner, Chris. She had even asked him for permission to park there when the yoga lot was full, and he had said she was welcome to use it at any time.

Traffic was heavy as people were wrapping up their holiday weekend and heading to the airport or the ferries to make their way back to the mainland. Felicity could almost feel the island sighing in relief as thousands of weekend visitors departed. A break in traffic finally came, and she rushed across West Creek Road, anxious to get home, shower, and get ready to meet Rick for dinner. They were going to the Sea Grille for dinner, and she was excited to get their grilled swordfish.

She slowed to a walk as she entered the parking lot and was a bit surprised to see a Nantucket Police Department pickup parked next to her car. As she approached, an officer got out of the pickup and advanced toward her.

“I’m sorry, ma’am, but is this your car?” he said, as he motioned toward her old Bronco.

“It is,” she said nervously. “And I promise I have permission to park here.”

He waved his hand. “No worries about that, ma’am. I just got a call that someone had backed into the side of your car and done some damage.”

“Oh, no!” said Felicity, upset. “This was my dad’s car, his pride and joy. I’ll be sick if I can’t get it fixed.”

The officer smiled. “Thankfully, it’s not bad, it’s just a scuff down the side. I don’t even know how they noticed it, but at least they were honest enough to call it in.”

Felicity nodded and walked around to the far side of the car. Her dad had restored the classic Bronco years before and had it painted a deep navy blue. Now, an ugly white scuff extended from the wheel arch to the passenger door.

The officer followed her and used a pen to trace the damage. “I’m no expert, but maybe this could be polished out. Worst case, it might need to be repainted, but I think the sheet metal is okay.”

She relaxed her shoulders, thankful that the damage wasn’t extensive.

“Your Felicity Post, aren’t you?” he said, straightening up.

“I am. But I don’t think we’ve met. You are?”

“Sorry. Kurt White. I knew your dad. Well, sort of,” he said anxiously. “I volunteered with him at the Boys and Girls Club. Flag football.”

She smiled. “My dad so enjoyed that. He loved football and really enjoyed working with the kids.”

"I enjoyed it as well. He was a good guy. I'm so sorry for your loss."

It had been eight months since her father had drowned off Great Point, and yet to her it felt like last week. It was a hole in her life she still felt every day. "Thank you, officer."

He nodded. "Would you mind stepping into my truck for just a minute? I have some paperwork for you to sign, and I can give you the details about the gentleman who hit you."

"Oh, of course," said Felicity and made her way to the passenger side of the pickup. She opened the door and hopped inside, leaving the door ajar.

He climbed in across from her and slid behind the wheel. A black storage clipboard was on the seat between them, and he picked it up, a paper form affixed to the front. He pulled the pen from his breast pocket and started writing.

"Sorry. Let me just complete this one section before I forget."

"Sure. Take your time." She looked out over the hood and watched a mom pushing a stroller while a young boy walked next to her. She looked at them longingly, wondering if she and Rick would ever take the step.

* * *

The holiday traffic had been brutal. An accident on the Mass Pike had backed up traffic for miles in both directions. What should have been a three-hour drive had turned into nearly twice that, and it was after four by the time they pulled into Hyannis and dropped off their rental. They had long given up on making the two twenty-five ferry.

They walked out of the Steamship Authority building and were greeted by the long blast of a ship's horn from across the harbor. The Hy-Line was backing out of her berth.

Rick looked at his phone. "Damn. And we missed the four-fifteen!"

Tuna placed her hand on his arm. "I know. But there's another boat in a little over an hour. So let's use that time and grab some food. I'm starving."

He looked at her and smiled tiredly. "You're right. Maybe Black Cat? I enjoyed that place a lot earlier this month when I was trying to get to the island."

"Black Cat is good, but I have a better idea. Baxter's."

"Baxter's? I haven't been there since I was training at the academy."

"It's still there and still so good."

They made their way through the parking lot of the Steamship and down Pleasant Street. It was a quick walk, and as they approached the door to the bar, they were greeted by a young man in a navy blue shirt with the restaurant's old-fashioned ship's wheel logo on the breast.

"Are you here for dinner?" asked the young man, clearly working a summer job.

"Just want to sit at the bar," said Tuna. "That okay?"

"Of course, ma'am. Right this way." He opened the door and waved them through.

Rick and Tuna entered the crowded space, the noise from dozens of conversations flooded the room. The L-shaped bar held only a dozen or so barstools, and thankfully, two were free on the corner. They made their way over quickly and settled in.

A bartender approached. "Hey, guys. I'm Josh. What can I get you on this glorious day?" He slid a couple of menus in front of them.

Rick turned to Tuna. "What are you thinking?"

Tuna looked thoughtful and then turned to Josh. "I'll do the Naukabout IPA, please. And a water when you get a chance."

"Sure thing. And you, sir?"

Rick turned to Tuna. "Naukabout?"

"It's a great local brewery. They're in Mashpee, just down the beach aways."

"Hmm. Sounds good." He turned to Josh. "I'll do the same, please."

"Excellent." Josh turned to pour their beers.

Rick looked at his phone and muttered.

"You okay? What's up?"

"Oh, sorry. I was trying to get a message to Fel to let her know I missed the boat. We were going to have dinner together tonight. Now I'm going to be late."

"And it's not working?"

"Nope. I keep getting an error. Message failed to send."

"Maybe try calling?"

"I did when you went to the bathroom. Went straight to voicemail."

"Well, given that it's a very busy holiday weekend, maybe the system is just swamped."

Rick shook his head. "Not sure what it is, but it's really frustrating."

"I get that. Do you know what you want to eat?"

"Haven't even looked at the menu."

"Well, if you're looking for a recommendation, you can't go wrong with the chowder."

Rick didn't hesitate. "Sold."

Josh came back and put their beers in front of them. "You guys hungry?"

"Starving. Can we get two chowders, please?" She turned to Rick. "Want to share some onion rings?" He nodded. To Josh: "And a large order of the onion rings, please."

"Coming right out." He grabbed the menus and left them to their beer.

Rick took a long sip. "Hmm. That is good."

"It certainly is. It can be tough to find a good West Coast IPA on the Cape. Everyone seems to prefer the hazy, New England style. But I'd rather have this."

"Me too." He took another sip and looked out the windows across the harbor, the blue water sparkling. Everyone, it seemed, was having fun and enjoying their holiday weekend. But Rick just couldn't shake the past few days and the fact that they still had a killer loose on the island.

"Do you really think she hasn't seen Randy in thirty years?" asked Tuna.

Startled from his thoughts, Rick took a moment. "I don't know why she would lie about that. Do you?"

Tuna shook her head. "No. No reason to. I mean, it doesn't sound like they were close. She was more like the manager of a boarding house. Did you notice there weren't any personal pictures of any kind? No photographs. Nothing. It seemed like the only thing she cared about at all was that framed poem."

Rick nodded. "It sounded like she was more concerned with getting the monthly checks than she was about Randy's welfare."

"Sad, really," said Tuna. "I think Randy Evans had a very difficult childhood. First, his parents' violent death, of which it sounds like he had a part in, and then spending all those years with Gayle Hickman? I don't think he ever really knew what it was like to be loved."

"Lots of people have rough childhoods, live in foster care. They don't all turn into serial killers," said Rick. "Something is different here."

She rubbed her neck. "I just wish we had learned something, anything, that would have helped to identify him. I feel like we are no closer to identifying Katie's kidnapper than we were this morning."

"Yeah. But I think we learned a bit about why he is doing what he's doing."

"The balance thing?" said Tuna, shaking her head. "I don't get that. I really don't."

Josh arrived with their food and placed it in front of them. The chowder was in a paper bowl with a bag of oyster crackers. Rick eyed Tuna suspiciously.

"Trust me, it's good. Don't let the packaging fool you."

Rick opened the oyster crackers and sprinkled a few in. He grabbed his spoon, dipped it into the chowder, and ate. His eyes went wide.

"Okay?" asked Tuna, concerned.

"Okay? This is delicious. It's like, pickup truck chowder," said Rick, excitedly.

"Pickup truck, what?" asked Tuna, totally confused.

Rick let out a laugh. "Sorry. In my family, when you enjoy something that is like the best you've ever had, we call it pickup truck."

"Pickup truck? There has to be a story there, I'm thinking? Or your family is just plain weird."

Rick took a few more bites and put his spoon down. "I promise we are not weird. My parents and I used to go to my aunt's place in Connecticut every Labor Day. One year, we saw a guy selling sweet corn out of the bed of his pickup truck on the side of Route 44, outside of Pomfret."

Tuna nodded and grabbed an onion ring. She dipped it in ketchup and took a large bite.

"So we stopped and got a couple of dozen ears. My aunt served them with dinner that night, and they tasted amazing. Everyone said it was the best corn they had ever had. So, we called it pickup truck corn, and then over time, just started using the expression with any really good food."

"Okay. Makes sense, I guess. But still seems kind of weird."

Rick chuckled. "I guess. But man, this chowder is good."

"Pickup truck good, apparently," chuckled Tuna.

Rick smiled.

They finished their food, settled their tab, and headed to the Hy-Line docks. The ferry was coming in as they made their way through Aselton Park, and by the time they reached the slip, there were already a hundred or so people waiting in line.

"I would think most people would be wanting to leave Nantucket. Surprised it's this crowded," said Rick.

"Actually, a lot of these people are locals. The Figawi race, combined with the Memorial Day weekend, really stresses the island. Everything is crowded, traffic is awful. So a lot of Nantucketers leave for the weekend. Visit family or friends on the mainland. Do some shopping. At least those that don't have to work."

Rick nodded. He pulled out his phone.

"Any luck getting Felicity?"

He shook his head. "No. I checked her location, and it looks like her phone is now offline. So now I'm thinking she forgot to charge it."

"We'll have you back on the island in a little over an hour. Hopefully, you can still have an evening with her."

Rick smiled uneasily and slipped his phone into his pocket. He didn't share it with Tuna, but he was feeling tense. It was probably just this damn case, but something just didn't feel right.

CHAPTER THIRTY-TWO

Tuna and Rick sat outside on the top level of the Grey Lady IV. The boat had just passed Kalmus Park Beach, and the captain had advanced the throttles. The large boat was cruising at thirty-five knots on a calm sea under a brilliant blue, cloudless sky. The fresh, salty air swirled about them, tussling their hair and making conversation difficult. Their seats vibrated subtly from the powerful engines whose thrum blanketed the entire vessel in white noise.

Tuna was seated to his left with a space between them. She was deep into her Kindle, enjoying a new novelist she had recently discovered. Every few moments, a gust of wind would push a wisp of brown hair onto her face, which she would unconsciously brush behind her ear.

Rick didn't have the concentration to read; his mind was too full of concern for Felicity. He sat and stared at the ship's wake, the boat generating the only waves on the water. He just couldn't shake the feeling that something was wrong. In his head, he knew it was simple; Fel had just forgotten to charge her phone. Again.

It was one of the little idiosyncrasies he had picked up since they had started dating. As a cop, he wanted her to have a phone available to her at any time should she need it. He always thought the worst: car breakdown, accident, or worse. Felicity had a different view, a convenient but not necessary device that would track her life and ply her mind full of garbage if she let it.

They had just had the conversation again the day before.

What if you break down?

We are on an island, Rick. I can pretty much walk the entire length of Nantucket in a few hours if I had to.

What if you are hurt or injured?

There are plenty of people around me. I can make it to a house or wave down a car. People are friendly here.

It was hard to reason with her. Nantucket and the people who had lived there survived without the convenience or perceived need of mobile phones for centuries. And Felicity was old school in that way. She had grown up without a phone; her parents did not provide her with one until she went off to college. And she never fell into the trap of social media and the feeling that she always needed to be connected. For her, FOMO was hearing about a run of stripers at Smith's Point while she was at work, not the latest meme, dance trend, or celebrity gossip.

So getting Felicity to carry her phone and keep it charged was always going to be an uphill battle for Rick.

He didn't mention the other reason he wanted her to have her phone charged. More from genuine curiosity than concern, he wanted to be able to locate Felicity quickly and easily. Like Katie and her friends, he wanted the security of knowing where she was. Felicity wasn't particularly thrilled with the idea, feeling like she was being tracked, but she did it anyway, knowing that it gave Rick some sense of comfort.

What she didn't know, and Rick hadn't admitted to, was that he had enabled alerts to notify him when she left her house on Monomoy Road or her office at the foundation on Main Street. It was one of those alerts that notified him that Felicity had left the house while they were stuck in traffic on the Mass Pike, most likely for the yoga class that she had tried to talk him into attending with her. But then, a little more than an hour later, nothing. The tracking app claimed her phone was offline or out of network, and he had never received the message that her battery was getting low.

The parallels to Katie's abduction were frightening.

But the one thing he did know was that the old Bronco was still in the parking lot at Kitty Murtagh's. The value of the old truck had skyrocketed in the past few years and was now worth close to six figures. Although auto theft on the island was rare, it was not completely out of the question, so her dad had hidden an Airtag in the engine compartment. After his death, Felicity had reluctantly added the device to her Find My app and had shared the information with Rick.

He stared intently at the Find My app on his phone. The blue dot of Felicity's phone had disappeared while that of the Bronco's hadn't moved in almost three hours.

Fel. Where are you?

Rick heard the engines throttle back and felt the boat decelerate. He looked across the port side to see the tip of the Nantucket Harbor jetty. A cluster of seals was sunbathing on the rocks, and a pair of cormorants sat with their wings outstretched, drying them in the bright sunshine. He glanced at his phone, hoping for a message from Felicity. It was almost six and well past when they had planned to leave for dinner. Nothing.

Tuna noticed the boat slowing and tore herself from her Kindle. "That was a quick crossing."

"For you, maybe," replied Rick, sharper than he intended. "Sorry, I'm just struggling a bit right now."

Tuna eyed him with concern. “Still nothing from Felicity?”

He shook his head slowly. “No. And the Bronco hasn’t moved either. It’s been parked at Kitty’s since before two.” He stood and walked to the railing.

Tuna slipped the Kindle into her bag and followed him. She slid next to him and crossed her arms on the railing.

“Maybe she had some car trouble?”

Rick grunted. “Possibly. I know she has had issues before. But I don’t know.”

“Maybe it wouldn’t start, and she just walked home?” said Tuna, hopefully.

“I hope you are right. But I just can’t shake this feeling that something is wrong.”

Tuna looked at him with care. “I’m sure she’s okay, Rick. It’s probably something simple. Dead phone. Car issues. With everything we’ve experienced the past few days, though, I understand why you would think something is wrong.”

He sighed heavily and turned to face her. “We still have a killer out there, Tuna. Someone who we now believe has orchestrated the deaths of over thirty people. Thirty! If our theory is correct, that he is sacrificing someone every year during this time, then he will be looking for another right now. Katie’s escape screwed up his plans.”

She nodded thoughtfully. “My head wants to believe you are wrong, but my gut thinks otherwise.”

“Even with the island on full alert from Katie’s abduction and confinement, I believe he is going to try again, most likely tonight, if he hasn’t already. He has managed to elude us for more than three decades, and maybe he is just clever enough that he will again."

Tuna looked at him intently, her brow furrowed. "We've got the entire NPD on alert. The CSOs have been briefed to notify us if they see anything that is even the slightest bit out of the ordinary. And locals, seasonal residents, and visitors are all on edge. If he is going to try and take someone else, it is going to be damn near impossible for him to get away with it."

Rick nodded and looked across the harbor. The clock on the Unitarian Church read six thirty-three. His gut churned with anxiety.

The captain brought the big boat in quickly, reversing the engines at the last minute to deftly and smoothly ease the vessel into her berth. The crew quickly tied her up and wheeled the gangplanks up to the main hatchway. The large door slid open, and passengers soon filed out, toting luggage, pets, and, for many, shopping bags.

Tuna and Rick made their way down the central staircase. The boat was barely half full, so it emptied quickly, and soon they were walking down the bricks of Straight Wharf heading for Tuna's car. She had parked at a small private lot on Commercial Street reserved for the local electrical utility. They had graciously extended overnight parking availability to the NPD and other first responders.

They reached Tuna's old Ford Explorer and got in.

"I know you're anxious to get home to Ellen, but would you mind running me by Fel's house? I was supposed to pick her up for dinner over an hour ago. Hopefully, she got my messages about being late."

"Sure, Rick, happy to." She slid the car into gear. The old suspension struggled with the cobblestones on New Whale Street and Main Street, but things smoothed out as they made the turn onto Washington Street.

"Where are you guys going to dinner?" asked Tuna, hoping to lift Rick's spirits.

"Um, Sea Grille." He glanced again at his phone. "But our reservations were for six, and I wasn't able to move them later. They are pretty much sold out."

"You could always sit at one of the bars. Ellen and I are a bit partial to the front bar by the parking lot."

Rick nodded. "Honestly, it doesn't matter much anymore. I just want to see her safe."

Tuna reached out, touched his arm, and squeezed. He put his hand on hers.

The gravel crunched under the tires as they pulled into the Post home off Monomoy Road. The driveway was empty, and there were no signs of life. Rick jumped out and ran to the front door. There was a large brass knocker shaped like a whale fluke, and he lifted and let it fall hard several times.

The house was quiet.

He turned to Tuna and subtly shook his head. She waved him back to the car.

"Any chance she thought you were meeting at the restaurant?"

"No."

"You sure?"

"Not one hundred percent."

"Get in. I'll run you over there."

It was a quick drive over to Sparks Avenue. Tuna had barely stopped when Rick jumped out of the car and ran up the ramp and through the doors, nearly knocking an elderly couple off their feet.

"Sorry!" he said over his shoulder and went straight to the hostess. "Hi, Rick Caton. I had a reservation for two at six. Do you know if my friend, Felicity Post, arrived?"

The hostess flipped through her reservation book. "Um, no." She looked up at Rick. "That reservation was cancelled."

"I know. I'm the one who cancelled it, but I wasn't sure if she got my message. We were delayed on the mainland and missed our ferry."

The hostess rolled her eyes. "Been there. Happened to me last week. Could she be in the bar perhaps?"

Rick glanced to his right. Every seat was full, but Felicity was nowhere to be seen. He pushed past the hostess stand, through the crowded restaurant, and to the back bar. Again, every seat was full, but Felicity was not among them.

"Damn!" he muttered to himself.

He thanked the hostess as he walked by and out the doors to Tuna's Explorer.

"Not there."

Tuna thought for a moment. "Let's go check out the Bronco. You said she parked it at Kitty's?"

Rick slid back in. "Yes."

Moments later, they were pulling into the small lot at the Irish pub. Every space was full. Tuna was forced to park in front of several cars, blocking them in. Felicity's old Broncho was in the last spot by the entrance from West Creek Road.

Rick got out and walked over to the car. He peered inside and tried the doors. He returned quickly to the driver's side of the Explorer. Tuna had rolled her window down.

"It's locked. And I don't see her purse or her yoga mat inside."

"Hmm. Maybe go inside and talk to the staff. Maybe someone saw something?"

Rick nodded. "Join me?"

"I'd better not. In case any of these cars need to get out," she said, pointing to several cars next to her.

"Okay. Be right back."

He walked quickly across the lot, up the steps, and into the restaurant, where he was met with the sounds of billiard balls clacking, classic rock music from the speakers, and loud conversations from the tables. He stopped first at the hostess stand.

"Hi. I'm just wondering if you saw anything with that old Bronco out there?" asked Rick, pointing to the classic truck outside.

The young girl shook her head. "Sorry, no. But it was here when I started my shift at four, if that helps."

Rick thanked her, and they made their way to the bar, squeezing into a small gap at the end. He waved down the bartender, who approached quickly.

"Rick! Good to see you. In the mood for some shepherd's pie?" said the man cheerfully.

Rick shook his head. “Thanks, Chris, but no. I’m looking for Felicity. Have you seen her? Her Bronco’s been parked in your lot since two.”

Chris smiled. “I think she might have had some car trouble.”

“Why do you think that?”

“She got into a pickup truck. One of your guys from the NPD.”

“Really?” said Rick, surprised. “When was that?”

“Um, I’d say around three-ish. We were kind of quiet, and I noticed the pickup arrived shortly before. He was talking to her, walking around the Bronco. Then she got in, and the truck drove away.”

“Did you by chance see who she was talking to?”

The bartender shook his head. “No. Sorry. I was refilling the beer cooler, so not really paying a lot of attention.”

“Um, okay,” said Rick, anxiously.

“Hey. Are you alright?” asked Chris, concerned.

Rick picked up his chin. “Thanks, Chris. Yeah, everything’s okay.” He turned and started to walk away.

“Good to hear. I hope to see you guys in here this week.”

He waved his hand without looking back, walked out the door, and made a beeline for Tuna’s Explorer. He placed his arms on the roof and leaned over her window.

“Chris says she got in an NPD pickup truck,” said Rick. “But didn’t see who she was talking to. Thought she might be having car trouble.”

“Just like I told you,” said Tuna. “I knew there wasn’t anything to worry about.”

"I'd still feel better if we could reach Fel."

"Well, let's see. The department has a total of four official pickups. Most of the NPD vehicles are SUVs. And I know one of the pickups is out of commission."

Rick eyed her curiously.

"Hit a deer on Polpis last week. Officer Taffey was returning from a call. It's at Nantucket Auto Body getting the repair work done."

"Okay. That leaves three. Do we know who would be driving them?"

"Officer White for sure. He has one assigned to him for the drone work. But I'm not sure about the other two. Hang on a minute." Tuna pulled out her phone and tapped the screen. "Tomas, it's Tuna. Who's assigned the NPD pickups this week?" She cupped the phone with her hand and whispered to Rick, "He's checking the vehicle log."

Rick grunted.

"Yeah, I'm here. Okay, thanks, Tomas. Yep, Kurt, we knew about. Okay, John Downs, and Lawrence Stanley? Oh, that's right, he was working that B and E case out on the South Shore. Thanks, Tomas." She disconnected the call and then turned to Rick. "Okay, we have three officers to chase down. See where they took Felicity."

"Can we call them right now?"

"Of course!" Tuna tapped her screen, put the phone on speaker, and placed it on the dash. It rang a few times before a deep voice came on the line.

"Lawrence Stanley."

"Lawrence? It's Tuna."

"Hey, T, how are you? Seems like ages since I've seen you. Any luck with the stripers this spring?"

"Sadly, no. Ellen and I worked Eel Point last weekend but got skunked. You?"

A gravelly chuckle at the other end of the call. "Yes, ma'am. Hit them at Smith's Point on Thursday at sunrise. Got some great fish. A bunch of schoolies and even a forty-pounder."

"Forty pounds?" exclaimed Tuna. "It's early in the season for the big guys. You lucky son of a bitch."

A laugh. "It's talent. All talent," said Lawrence, chuckling. "Anyway, I know you didn't call me for the fishing report. What can I do for you?"

"We're looking for Felicity Post. Any chance you helped her with her old Bronco at Kitty's earlier today?" Tuna eyed Rick, who was leaning into the window, eager to hear the response.

"No, sorry. I've been working the South Shore today. We had that burglary here late last week, over by the airport. Just keeping an eye on things and seeing what clues I can scare up. Probably just a bunch of kids, you know?"

"Okay, thanks, Lawrence. How about some fishing next week?"

"I'd love that, T! Let me know when you are available, and I will find you some of the best stripers on the island."

"Thanks, Lawrence, I'll look forward to that. Later," said Tuna and disconnected the call. She turned to Rick. "Let's see what John has to say." She tapped her screen and held it in the palm of her hand. Officer Downs picked up on the first ring.

"Downs, here."

"John. Tuna."

"Detective. Are you calling for an update on the Chapman case? I've been pulling old insertion orders at the Inq and M. Tomas put me on it. I've secured four from the years 1999 through 2002. The handwriting is similar on all four, but the names vary. All generic. John Smith. Paul Miller. Frank Robert. Steve Jones. And all paid with a money order."

"A money order? Talk about old school."

A grunt of acknowledgement. "They are the OG form of anonymous payments. And believe it or not are still used today."

"I guess gift cards and Bitcoin haven't taken up all the shady payments business," said Tuna with a laugh. "Anyway, thanks, John. I appreciate the update, and sorry it's been a dead end. But also wanted to check with you and see if you helped Felicity Post earlier today. She was having car trouble over at Kitty's."

He cleared his throat. "No, ma'am. I've been in the Inq and M storage unit since late morning. Just now finishing up here."

"Okay. Thanks, John. Let me know if you find anything interesting."

"Will do."

Tuna disconnected the call and turned to Rick. "Okay. That answers that. She must have gone with Kurt, but let's confirm."

Once again, Tuna picked up her phone and tapped the screen. Rick put his elbow on the door and leaned in. A few rings, then voicemail.

"Hi, this is Officer Kurt White of the Nantucket Police Department. I'm sorry I can't answer your call right now, but if you leave me a message, I'll return it as soon as I can. Thank you."

Tuna left a message to call her as soon as possible, but didn't mention the reason. She disconnected and then followed up with a quick text to Kurt with the same message.

Rick eyed her curiously.

"What? Belt and suspenders. Just want to make sure he gets the message."

Rick smiled grimly, tapped the roof, and walked around the front of the Explorer. He hopped into the passenger seat. "Now what?"

Tuna looked over at Rick intently. "I know you, Caton. You're not going to rest until you know Felicity's okay. And I can't rest until I know you're okay. So let's head over to the station. Maybe we can find out more there."

Rick nodded. "But don't you have plans with Ellen tonight?"

She smiled wearily. "Yes, but that can wait, and Ellen will understand. This is far too important. Plus, to be honest, I'm concerned as well." She started the engine and headed towards the government center on Fairgrounds Road.

CHAPTER THIRTY-THREE

2023

The cottage on Orange Street had been renovated three times in the last decade, each new owner trying to outdo the last with reclaimed beams, imported stone, and increasingly elaborate kitchen fixtures that were rarely used for anything more than plating takeout.

Evan Pike was its most recent steward.

A venture capitalist from Palo Alto, Evan had purchased the property sight unseen, wiring the full asking price within hours of the listing going live. He told anyone who would listen that Nantucket was "undervalued from an experience standpoint," whatever that meant. He split his time between conference calls and carefully curated dinners, where the food came from Michelin-starred restaurants, and the conversation revolved around disruption, scaling, and exits.

He had no interest in the island beyond what it could offer him. To him, Nantucket was a backdrop. A brand. Something he could boast about to his Silicon Valley coworkers.

To others, he was harmless enough. He tipped well. Kept to himself. Didn't cause trouble.

But to Randy, that wasn't the point.

The island had rules, whether people like Evan Pike understood them or not. And lately, there had been far too many like him.

Too many who arrived, consumed, and left without ever truly being there. Too many who reshaped the island in their own image, sanding down its edges until nothing authentic remained.

The imbalance was growing.

Randy had watched Evan for weeks. Observed the rhythms of the house. The renovations had been thorough, but not careful. Modern gas appliances installed into an aging system. Lines extended, fittings adjusted, inspections rushed.

It didn't take much.

A minor adjustment made late in the day after the crews had left. Barely perceptible. The kind of thing that could just as easily have been the result of a careless contractor or the natural settling of an old house resisting its latest transformation.

He made the change on a Tuesday.

Evan returned that evening after dinner in town, slightly drunk, slightly sunburned, already on a call with the West Coast as he stepped through the front door. He never noticed the faint smell. Or if he did, he dismissed it. Another quirk of an old home dressed up as something new.

He went to bed late.

Sometime in the early hours, the concentration reached its peak, and the explosion shattered windows up and down the street. A low, concussive blast that rattled the island awake. By the time the fire department arrived, flames were already licking through the roof, fed by timber that had stood for over a century.

It took hours to bring it under control.

The official report cited a gas leak. A tragic accident, likely tied to recent renovations. Incredibly lucky that it hadn't spread to the other houses nearby. There was talk of inspections, of liability, of whether the contractors had cut corners.

Evan Pike was found in what remained of the bedroom.

The Inquirer & Mirror ran the story above the fold for two days. A cautionary tale about the risks of modernizing historic homes. Letters to the editor debated preservation versus progress.

Then, as always, the island moved on.

Balance had been maintained.

CHAPTER THIRTY-FOUR

It was nearly eight by the time Rick and Tuna made it back to the detective's room at the NPD. Outside, the late May sunset was finishing a gorgeous display. The sky was a deep purple, and the early stars were just starting to emerge. Venus, the brightest object in the sky, kept company just over the northwestern horizon while just below her a low bank of clouds reflected the last golden light from the dying day.

They made it to their offices, Tuna settling in behind her desk. She checked her phone. No new messages. She moved the mouse to wake her laptop and checked her email. A note from human resources to double-check overtime hours during the holiday weekend, the weekly activity report, which showed a spike in DUI arrests and drunk and disorderlies, and an announcement about a new employee, Detective Rick Caton, joining the department on June first.

"Hey, Rick?"

"Yeah."

"Your new employee announcement is out. It's official. Congratulations!"

Tuna heard his desk chair scrape. Seconds later, he was at her door. "They really put out an announcement about me?" he asked, curiously.

"They did," said Tuna. She angled her flat screen to give him a better look.

He leaned in and read the one-page announcement. Finished, he stood up and laughed. "They make me sound like some financial wizard," he said, smiling.

"Well, you did have a few major arrests during your time with the Financial Crimes Unit at the FBI. We're just happy you were willing to let all that glamour and glitz go to join us here on our little island," said Tuna, giggling.

Rick put his hand on her shoulder. "I can't tell you how happy I am to be back, Tuna. Happy to be back on Nantucket. Happy to be back with the NPD and working with you. And happy to be…" his voice trailed off.

Tuna reached up and put her hand on Rick's. "She's okay, Rick. I'm sure of it."

"Anything from Kurt?"

She looked at her phone and then at Rick, shaking her head. "Nothing."

"Damn." He paced outside her cubicle. "What else can we do? Can we put out a BOLO?"

"Rick. I think it's a bit early for a be on the lookout. She probably knew you were going to be late and grabbed dinner at Brotherhood or Rose and Crown. For all we know, she could be taking a cab back to her house right now."

Rick nodded slowly. He wanted to believe that was the case.

"Anyway, I'm sure we'll hear from Officer White any minute."

Rick stopped in his tracks and turned to Tuna. "Wait. What did you just say?"

Tuna looked at him, perplexed. "I said, I'm sure we'll hear from Officer White any minute."

He stared intently at Tuna.

"Rick, what is it? You're scaring me."

"Officer White," he muttered.

"Yeah. What about him?"

Rick paused to speak. "Do you remember what Gayle Hickman said this morning about Randy Evans? That in the world of black versus white, good versus evil, he had to be the good person, the white, to save the gold."

Tuna looked at him intently.

"The white, to save the gold," he said slowly and emphatically.

Her eyes went wide with recognition. "You think Kurt White is Randy Evans?" she exclaimed.

Rick was suddenly energized. "Yes! I mean, think of it. His age fits. His body type fits based on what Katie told us. How long has he been on the force?"

"A while. He had been with the NPD for at least a decade or more before I joined in 2005. In my work with him, I've found him to be a decent if unambitious officer."

"Well, I originally joined in 2009, not too long after you, and I don't remember him at all," said Rick. "I know I was only on the force a few years, but I'm wondering if he intentionally kept a low profile."

Tuna eyed him knowingly. "I think the timeline fits, if we believe all those deaths are related." She dug through a stack of papers and files on her desk until she found what she was looking for. "Here. This is the list Tomas put together. It shows the first death in 1992. That would put Kurt in his mid-twenties at the time."

"What else do we know about him?" asked Rick. "And where does he live?"

Tuna spun in her chair and grabbed her keyboard. She navigated to the internal network and pulled up his personnel file. She scanned it quickly and then tapped the screen with her pencil. "Okay, joined the NPD in 1991 as a CSO. Got his degree and joined as a deputy officer in 1994. Made patrol officer in 1998 and his current role, police officer, in 2010."

"And nothing since 2010?"

Tuna scanned the screen again and turned back to Rick. "Nope. I told you he was unambitious. And frankly, he's a competent officer but definitely not detective or management material. Plus, he really seemed to find his place in the drone unit."

Rick grunted and pointed at her screen. "What's his home address?"

"Um, home address is listed as thirty-one Western Avenue, Nantucket."

"Why does that address ring a bell?" asked Rick, thinking. He put a finger to his chin.

Tuna pulled up her browser and keyed in the address. "Ah, that's it. The Star of the Sea Youth Hostel."

"Star of the Sea?"

"Yeah. Don't you remember it? It's the old lifesaving station out by Surfside. It was converted into a youth hostel in the 1960's and was quite popular with young people coming to the island. It was clean, affordable, and an awesome location. It closed as a hostel back in 2020 and was just sold a few years ago to an investment group."

“He was living at a youth hostel?” said Rick.

“Think about it. He arrives on the island back in 1990 or 91, when Gayle Hickman told him to find his way. Finds the hostel. It’s clean and cheap. Stays there for a few years until he can afford his own place.”

“But why not change his address on his personal record?”

“As you said, Rick. He’s keeping a low profile.”

“What does his driver’s license say?”

Tuna spun back to her laptop and pulled up the Massachusetts RMV website. “Thirty-one Western Avenue.”

“Wouldn’t he have to change it?” asked Rick, confused.

Tuna shook her head. “Not if he didn’t want to. Probably got his license while he was staying there. No reason to change it. I doubt anyone at the RMV would have challenged him. They just keep renewing it every five years.”

“Damn.” Rick started pacing again. “Oh, shit!”

“What?” asked Tuna.

“Felicity! We’ve been so focused that we forgot Kurt picked her up earlier. What if she is his next sacrifice?” exclaimed Rick. He was breathing heavily and pacing the floor, his hands clenched. “Oh, Fel.”

“Okay, Rick. Stay calm.” She picked up her desk phone and rang the duty desk. “Tomas? We need to find Kurt White ASAP. Can you put out a notification to all officers?” She paused. “Yes, we need to find him immediately. We believe he may have taken Felicity Post. Yes, I know. Not one hundred percent certain, but it looks that way. Okay. Thanks, Tomas.” She hung up the phone and turned to Rick. "He's sending a notification to all officers. We'll find him."

Rick looked anxious and unsteady. "What about his truck? Any way to track it?"

A slow smile spread across Tuna's face. She snapped her fingers and pointed one at Rick. "LoJack."

"LoJack?"

"LoJack. It's a vehicle tracking device. We put them on all the NPD vehicles a few years ago. We got some grant or something. Honestly, I never understood the need on a small island, but it was free, so why not?" she said, shrugging her shoulders.

"Could he have disabled it?" asked Rick, nervously.

Tuna shook her head. "I doubt he even knows it on his truck. And it's not easy to get to. It's tucked up inside a wheel well."

"Okay, so where's his truck?"

"Good question." She picked up her phone and called the duty desk again. "Tomas. Can you come up here, quickly? Thanks."

She turned to Rick. "I don't know how to access the system. I've never had a reason to use it. But Sergeant Santos can help us with that."

They heard footsteps on the stairs and then walking quickly across the room. "Detectives," said Santos and nodded at Rick and Tuna. "The notification just went out. I don't have anything to report. Sorry."

"Tomas, thanks, but it's not that. Can you access the LoJack tracking information for NPD vehicles? Is there a website or something?"

The sergeant nodded. "Actually, it's an app. Let me pull it up." He tapped on his screen, furrowed his brow, and then looked back at Tuna. "Sorry, it's updating. I guess I haven't used it in a while."

Tuna smiled.

Santos' phone dinged.

"Okay, update complete," said Tomas. He tapped the screen. "I'm assuming you want to know where Kurt's truck is?"

"Yes," said Rick, eagerly.

"Got it." He tapped the screen a few more times. "Looks like its most recent location was just off Pout Pond Road."

"Pout Pond Road? Never heard of it," said Tuna. "Where is that?"

Tomas looked intently at his phone. "Um, it runs off Polpis, just east of Island Lumber, and goes past Altar Rock." He held out his phone. "See, just after Altar Rock, it rejoins Polpis just west of the Windswept Bog trailhead."

Rick looked at Tuna knowingly. "That can't be a coincidence."

"No. It can't. It's him," said Tuna. "Tomas, can you text me the coordinates of Kurt's truck?"

The sergeant nodded enthusiastically. "Absolutely." He pulled his phone back and tapped it a few times. Tuna's phone dinged. "You have it."

"Thanks, Tomas. Please notify the team and ask them to meet us at that location," she said, pointing at his phone. "We are heading there now."

Tomas nodded. "Yes, ma'am. Consider it done."

To Rick. "Let's go!"

CHAPTER THIRTY-FIVE

Tuna and Rick scrambled out of the detective's room and took the stairs two at a time before bursting through the front doors. They ran across the lawn to the parking lot and jumped into Tuna's old Ford Explorer. She started the engine, put the gear in drive, floored the gas, and pulled quickly out of her parking spot, spraying dirt and gravel at the cars parked behind her.

"I need you to navigate me! I have no idea where this putt-putt road is," said Tuna. She was gripping the steering wheel at ten and two and staring intently out of the windshield.

"Got it!" said Rick, pulling up his phone. "And it's Pout Pond Road." He tapped the screen a few times. "Pout Pond is actually the first right after Island Lumber. But as I'm looking at it, the road is narrow and tight. So, we can head down Polpis a few miles and cut over. That will be the fastest way."

Tuna nodded and turned on her lights and flashers. She didn't have a lightbar on her car and wanted to make herself as visible as possible to everyone on the winding road. Although the speed limit was thirty-five, she pushed the old SUV to nearly twice that. Rick sat nervously in the passenger seat, one hand on the grab handle above the door, the other clutching his phone as if it was about to be wrenched from his fingers.

Her phone dinged. She pulled it out of her breast pocket and handed it to Rick. "See what that says. It might be from Tomas."

Rick pinned his phone under his leg and grabbed Tuna's. He tapped the screen to wake it and then held it to Tuna's face to unlock it.

"Yes, it's a text from Tomas. He says all available units are responding," said Rick, excitedly. "But he thinks we're the lead vehicle. The other officers are driving in from downtown or Madaket."

Tuna nodded. "Okay. Good. How are we doing until our next turn?" She slowed for a tight corner just past Moors End Farm and then got back on the gas, the tires squealing in protest.

Rick looked at her intently. "You know, it's not going to do Fel or anyone any good if you kill us," he said, anxiously.

She chuckled. "You're right. I'll slow down. A bit."

"Our turn is coming up. One point seven miles to Altar Rock Road. It'll be on the right and a very tight corner."

"Just give me a countdown as we approach."

Rick nodded. "I'm on it."

"Do you really think Kurt is Randy Evans?" asked Tuna. "I understand the white reference and that connection. But a Nantucket police officer being behind all of these deaths? Don't you think that's a stretch?"

"It's unusual for sure. But think of it. Being in that role would give him access to just about anyone. I mean, who's going to question a cop when he engages them? It would be an excellent cover for a killer."

"True," said Tuna, reluctantly. "But I hate to think it's one of our own."

"One and a half miles to go. Yes, it will be difficult to manage the publicity if true, but the more important thing is that we get to him and confirm if he is Randy Evans. And does he have Fel?"

Tuna nodded.

"A little over a mile. Get ready to turn."

"Why do you think he's doing this? The sacrifices?"

Rick watched the Lifesaving Museum pass by on his left, the building blurred by their speed despite Tuna's assurances to slow down. "I wish I knew, Tuna. I wish I knew." He looked at his phone. "Okay, one mile. About ten more seconds based on your current speed," he said, sarcastically.

She eased off the gas a bit, the Explorer slowing down. "Sorry. I just want to get there as soon as possible. In case…" her voice tailed off.

A shadow spread over Rick's face. "Fel. Yes. You are right. What the hell am I thinking? Floor it!"

The throttle pedal squeaked a bit as Tuna pressed it to the floor, the Explorer soon nearing eighty.

"Okay, we are two-tenths out. Slow down. It's a narrow road and the corner's tight. I don't want to miss it."

She moved her foot from the gas to the brake and slowed the car quickly.

"There!" said Rick, pointing ahead. "There's the turn."

"Got it!" said Tuna. She pushed harder on the brakes and smoothly turned the truck onto a dirt road. The rear end fishtailed as she got back on the gas. A plume of dust followed them.

Her phone rang. Rick unlocked the phone and answered.

"Detective Fisch?"

"Hi Tomas. It's Rick Caton. Tuna's busy driving. What is it?"

"He's moving."

"Kurt?"

"Yes. He left his house on Pout Pond Road about three minutes ago. Just passed Altar Rock Road and driving east on Ponds Road."

"Damn," said Rick, and turned to Tuna. "He's on the move. Heading east." He looked down at the mapping app on his phone. To Tuna: "Okay. We'll be making a left turn in about a quarter of a mile onto Pond Road. We'll be right behind him." He juggled her phone. "Tomas, you still there?"

"I am."

"I'm going to put you on speaker. Please continue to track Kurt and guide us to him."

"Yes, sir." A pause. "It looks like he just turned right on Polpis."

"Where the hell is he going?" asked Tuna.

Rick shook his head. "No idea. Maybe back to Windswept Bog? Could that area have some special meaning to him?"

"I suppose. But why? He didn't do anything to Katie there except kidnap her."

"Hmm. True. Maybe he was interrupted. Maybe his original plan was to do something there, and he had to abandon that plan? Maybe the hat and the jon boat were not a distraction?"

Tuna slowed the Explorer down, the tires skidding in the dirt, and barely made the left turn onto Ponds Road. The read end slid out, and she deftly added gas and steered into the slide.

Rick looked over at her, admiringly. "Nice move. You been taking drifting lessons?"

She smiled, lightly. “Had a go-kart growing up. My dad made me a little race track in a big dirt parking lot. I spent a lot of time going sideways. It was fun.”

“Huh. Learn something new every day,” said Rick, impressed.

“Okay, heard you talking. Windswept Bog is not his destination. He just passed it,” said Tomas, on the speaker.

“Thanks,” said Rick. “Polpis is a few hundred feet ahead.”

Tuna nodded. “Got it. Hang on.” She slowed the truck dramatically, took a quick look left for traffic, and hit the gas, the rear wheels struggling for traction and leaving a short black strip on the pavement. “Where is he now, Tomas?”

“Just made a left turn on Wauwinet Road.”

“Wauwinet Road?” mumbled Rick. “Where is he going?”

The Explorer was hurtling down Polpis when four deer popped out of the hedge and ambled into the middle of the road. Tuna saw them and jammed on the brakes as hard as they could go. Her old SUV didn’t have ABS, so all four wheels locked up, the tires squealing on the pavement. Startled at the sound, the deer disappeared as quickly as they had arrived.

The Explorer came to a stop, slightly askew and crossing the center line.

Tuna, breathing heavily and adrenaline coursing through her, looked over at Rick. “You good?”

“Not really. That was almost a disaster.” He looked shaken.

“You guys okay?” asked Tomas over the speaker.

“Yeah. Just had a close call with some deer,” said Rick.

Tuna blew out a long sigh, adjusted herself in the seat, and got back on the gas, knowing they had lost valuable time to Kurt. Soon, the SUV was pushing sixty.

"So why Wauwinet Road?" asked Rick.

She thought for a moment. "Great Point," said Tuna, matter-of-factly. "I think he's going to Great Point."

Rick nodded. "Makes sense. Unless he's got another property out this way."

"Either way, he's got a couple of miles on us," said Tuna, pushing down harder on the gas pedal. A minute later, she switched her foot to the brake and knocked her speed down by thirty before taking the slight turn to the left onto Wauwinet Road.

The pavement immediately narrowed, and the curves increased, hiding the road beyond. Tuna was forced to slow down lest she accidentally drive off into a hedge. Or into an oncoming car.

"We're not going to catch him," said Rick, discouraged.

"Hang in there, Rick."

"He just passed the hotel," said Tomas from the speaker. "He's now on the dirt road leading to the Point."

"Got it," said Tuna.

Rick turned to her. "Don't we need to take air out of the tires? If we don't, once we get on the sand, the truck is really going to have a hard time."

Tuna shook her head. "A little hack I learned. The NPD keeps all oversand vehicles at twenty-two PSI. I tried that, but the Explorer struggled, so I dropped them to twenty. Worked like a charm. It's a nice balance between driving on the street, but then you can go right on the sand. Saves a lot of time and hassle."

Rick looked at her intently. "We were just doing eighty on under-inflated tires?"

"Um, maybe," said Tuna, glancing quickly over at him. "Sorry."

"I never knew you were such a risk-taker. And if Kurt's already passed the hotel, it doesn't sound like he'll need to either?"

She shook her head. "No. As I mentioned, all the department's four by fours maintain tire pressures at twenty-two PSI. Safe for the street but still allows rapid access to the beaches when necessary."

He nodded. "Should we see if there are any other assets we can utilize to get to the Point faster? Boat or helicopter, maybe?"

"A boat from the harbor, even if it were ready to go right now, would take at least thirty minutes. Even more if it was low tide and they couldn't take the cut out in the jetty. And the closest helicopter is on the Cape. So we are the lead."

"Damn," said Rick, pounding the dashboard. "If he's got Fel."

"I know," said Tuna, taking a hand off the wheel and touching his arm. "We are going to get him. And Felicity is strong. She's a fighter, like Katie."

"I hope so," said Rick, emphatically.

* * *

The white Ford F-150 pickup of the Nantucket Police Department made its way quickly down the rutted dirt road leading to the beach access entry for Great Point. The road had huge swells and ruts that tested the suspension as well as the patience of the driver. Occasionally, they would encounter a particularly harsh impact, and he would wince, thinking of the prize he carried in the back for his beloved island.

Several minutes later, the road eased into the sand, and he crossed through the gate. The truck automatically switched into four-wheel-drive, and Kurt eased the pickup onto the sand, following the tracks laid by dozens of vehicles before him. He increased his speed to twenty MPH, five over the posted limit. He knew the rangers here were pretty strict, but suspected they wouldn't bother him given his truck's livery.

He veered to the right where the path split between the inner and outer routes. The route to the left followed the inner trail through the beach grass and alongside several ponds. It was a pretty drive, but being one lane, could slow one down significantly if you had to back up to a turn-out area to allow for opposing traffic to pass. He didn't want to take that chance. Time was of the essence. He could feel the island stirring beneath him. She was out of balance, the weekend having taken its toll on her.

The right took him to the beach route, along the water, and it was his favorite. It could be quite narrow at high tide, but always provided stunning views both across the water and of local sea life. He followed the track, pushed the truck through some particularly heavy sand, and emerged on the beach, the dark waters of the Atlantic extending out thousands of miles in front of him. Kurt got into a smooth track close to the water and got on the gas. The big pickup was soon doing thirty.

Above him, the sky had turned a purple black, the last vestiges of light just barely visible on the western horizon. A heavy blanket of stars spread over him, some brilliant, some faint. The high beams pierced the darkness and lit the sand in front of him. Seagulls, resting by the tracks and disturbed by the truck, flew up through the light. To his right, breaking waves effervesced, the surf a ghostly glow against the dark blue, almost black, ocean.

He put his window down, laid an arm on the edge, and took in a deep breath of the salt air. God, he loved this island. And he hoped, desperately, that his gift wasn't late. He had felt the balance shifting under his feet as the Memorial Day weekend had progressed. Too many people. Too much drain on the island's limited resources. It was tilting, reeling, and pitching away from its natural balanced state, and he was worried.

He prayed his Gift would help.

The sand was smooth, and the pickup made its way easily north toward Great Point. Over time, the waves and tides had created large, gentle swells and dips in the beach. For each, the truck would rise gently a few feet before descending, like a whale breaching for air. He nudged the speed up to thirty-five. He looked at the clock. He still had time.

Thankfully, the beach was quiet despite the busy holiday weekend. Officially, the Point closed at dusk; the only exceptions were for active fishermen. But this was May, and the fishing season was young. A handful of cars had passed him, heading back after a day on the beach. Most drivers waved as they passed, respecting his position. His was the only vehicle on the beach heading out.

As he was nearing an area known as The Galls, another white Ford F-150 emerged from the darkness heading on the opposite track. It dipped its high beams, and as it neared him, he saw the window roll down, and an arm emerge, holding out a hand. It was a ranger for the Trustees of the Reservations, the group that managed and monitored the Point and surrounding areas.

Kurt, suddenly nervous, slowed the truck and stopped. The other pickup pulled up opposite him. A bearded man looked at him, concerned, from across the sand.

"Evening, officer. Everything, okay? Do we have a problem out here that I'm not aware of?"

Kurt forced himself to relax and held up his hand. "No, not at all. I'm not out here on official business. Thought I might try my luck for some stripers tonight."

The ranger, relieved, eyed his truck up and down. "Hmm, okay. Where's your gear?

"It's actually in the bed, under the cargo cover. I have a new setup I'm anxious to try. It's light tackle, so it should give a really good fight."

The ranger shook his head and chuckled. "It's a bit early for stripers at the Point. But I know the urge can be hard to resist. Good luck. And do keep an eye out for the seals. There is a particularly large colony of them on the eastern edge of the Point. I'd keep your distance if I were you."

Kurt smiled and tipped his head. He heard a loud thump from the back of the truck as if someone had kicked the bed.

Did the ranger hear that?

Across the sand, the window on the white pickup was closing as the bearded man lifted a hand to say goodbye. He accelerated slowly away.

Kurt followed the taillights in his rear-view mirror. He saw the lights slowly move up and down as the truck crossed the swells and dips of the beach. The headlights painted long strips of light across the sand, rising and falling with the truck's movements.

He closed his eyes and took a deep breath.

Relax.

He slid the gear into drive and eased the truck back up to thirty. In the distance, he could see the simple white beacon of the Great Point Lighthouse flashing every few seconds. He knew he was getting closer, only a mile or so more.

His lights cut through the darkness and highlighted a rising dune covered in beach grass, signifying the end of The Galls. A few thousand feet further, the track veered to the left, and he was forced off the beach. Years ago, when he had first started with the NPD, the beach to the east of the lighthouse had been a popular spot for beachgoers as well as fishermen. And a fast and easy route to the tip of Great Point. But a series of storms in the early 1980s had not only taken out the original lighthouse, which had stood since 1818, but had also significantly narrowed the beach.

As a result, it had been closed to vehicular traffic, and instead, he had to make his way past a large pond and through the dunes to the harbor side of the Point. The route forced him to slow down significantly and was really testing his tolerance. His gut kept urging him to go faster, but he fought that down. The sand here was heavy, and even though he had a good four-by-four, it was still possible for him to get stuck if he wasn't careful. And getting stuck meant getting caught.

He worked the truck through the narrow trail. Looking up to the right, he could just make out a pair of weathered, gray shingled houses. He wondered who lived there and was envious of their situation. Secluded. Desolate. Quiet. Alone.

That would be the perfect place for me.

He sighed heavily. Maybe when this Gift was delivered, fortune might bestow on him an opportunity to purchase one of the homes. Maybe if he sold his property on Pout Pond Road, he could afford one of them. He shook his head, knowing that if he were honest with himself, that was never going to happen. But he could dream, couldn't he?

Five minutes later, after navigating a series of tight bends and deep puddles, he emerged on the western edge - the harbor side - of Great Point.

His lights splayed across the sand, revealing large swaths of pebbles and shells that littered the beach, a few seagulls, and not much else. A popular spot during the day, thankfully, now it was deserted. He drove the truck slowly northward toward the Point until he was stopped by a wire fence. The thin, metal cable crossed the beach from the dunes to the waterline. Spread across a handful of metal posts, the wire had some red and yellow nylon ties to make it more visible. Each of the posts featured a small sign stating that any further travel by motor vehicle was prohibited.

He got out of the truck, walked to the post nearest the water, pulled it up, and created a space just wide enough for his pickup. Returning to the truck, he drove through the gap in the fence and crossed the last few hundred yards to the absolute tip of the island.

As the ranger had warned, a large colony of seals was bedded in along the water to his left. He kept his distance, not wanting to upset the herd, and parked his truck at the Point, but with an ample gap. He turned the engine off and rolled down the window. Only the sounds of breaking waves, the wind through the beachgrass, and the occasional grunt from a seal broke the silence.

In front of him, he could make out the Great Point Rip, that spot where the Atlantic met the waters of Nantucket Sound. It was a confused patch of sea with waves building, cresting, and breaking over each other, again and again, and extending out into the ocean for miles. To the west, along the thin black line where the sky met the sea, the top of a pale circle had broken through. The full moon was rising.

It was magical.

And it was time.

CHAPTER THIRTY-SIX

The old Ford Explorer was just minutes behind Kurt's F-150, but to Rick it felt like hours. He urged Tuna to drive even faster down the curvy, narrow road, suffering a few close calls and a lot of ugly glances from opposing traffic.

The road straightened, and they flew by a line of trucks and SUVs waiting patiently on the left side of the road for their turn to refill their tires after a day on the beach. The Explorer speeding drew plenty of stares from the group and a few motions to slow down. Tuna ignored them.

She backed off the throttle as they neared the Wauwinet gatehouse and coasted through the stop sign there, going just under double the posted limit. Rick glanced ahead and saw an upcoming speed hump and then back to Tuna, his eyes wide. She smiled, pushed the gas a little harder, and managed to get the Explorer airborne, if only by a few inches. Crashing back down, she flew by the hotel and nearly collided with a Jeep coming the opposite way from the beach.

She raised her hand to the horn and flying finger of the other driver and tore down the heavily pitted dirt road leading to the beach access point. The suspension of her old Ford struggled with the swells and dips of the road and alternated from being airborne one second to crashing back down the next. Tuna maintained a tight grip on the wheel and stared determinedly at the road ahead.

Rick did his best not to vomit.

The beach access point was just ahead, and a white pick-up was parked, blocking the entrance. They could just see the back of a heavy-set man behind the pickup moving from one side to the other.

"Is that Kurt?" asked Rick, excitedly, pointing at the truck.

Tuna squinted as she eased off the gas pedal. "I don't think so. It doesn't look like one of ours. Maybe with the Trustees?"

Tuna slowed to a crawl as she approached the other truck. The ranger, hearing the Explorer, walked around the side of his pickup, holding up his hand and shaking his head. He approached Tuna's window.

"Sorry, ma'am. The Point closes at dusk except for those actively fishing."

Tuna held up her badge. "I'm Detective Tina Fisch. This is Detective Rick Caton. We are on urgent business, looking for one of our officers. Did you by chance see one of our pickups tonight?"

The ranger looked at the badge and across at Rick. "Yes, I did. I passed him just north of marker three, in The Galls. I'm Charles, by the way. With the Trustees."

"Thanks, Charles. Could you tell if he was alone?" asked Rick, anxiously.

The ranger nodded. "Yes, sir. We did talk briefly. He said he was heading to the Point to try his luck for some stripers."

"And you didn't see a woman with him?" asked Tuna.

The ranger shook his head. "No, ma'am. He appeared to be alone. But…"

"But what?" asked Tuna.

The ranger looked across the dunes covered in beach grass to the harbor. In the distance, the lights from town sparkled in the clear air of the evening. He turned back to Tuna. “I don’t know. He sort of gave me a weird vibe.”

“Weird how?”

“Well, for one, he didn’t have any visible fishing gear. He claimed it was in the bed under the cover, but unless he had a two-piece rod, your typical equipment is not going to fit in that small bed. And to be honest, he didn’t look dressed to fish.”

“Anything else?” asked Rick.

The ranger paused and looked around, unsure.

“What?” prodded Tuna gently.

“It’s probably nothing, but I just got this feeling that he was hiding something. I can’t explain it. But I don’t think he was going to the Point to fish.”

“Thanks, Charles. We really appreciate your help. Can you please move your truck? We need to get out there as soon as possible. And there are several more NPD vehicles on the way. We’d appreciate it if you could direct them to the Point.”

“Yes, ma’am. I’ll keep a lookout for them. You two be safe.” The ranger ran back to his truck and pulled it forward.

Tuna raised her hand in thanks and slid through the entry. She ran her hand to a dial on the dashboard and turned it from 2WD to 4WD. She leaned back on the bench seat and put her foot down. The Explorer jumped forward and was moving quickly across the sand. When she reached the split between inner and outer routes, she veered right and headed for the beach.

The Explorer struggled a bit in the heavy sand of the trail, but as soon as they emerged on the beach, the sand lightened, and the Explorer gained speed. Tuna planted her foot on the gas, and soon the truck was nudging fifty, sand spraying from the tires. Rick grabbed the handle above his door and held on for dear life.

Tuna forced herself to ease back on the gas. The swells of the beach were pronounced, and she was concerned that if she hit one at the wrong angle and speed, it would force her into the water. With the rest of the NPD still several minutes behind them, the last thing she wanted to do was lose control and plunge her truck into the surf.

"I hope we are not too late," said Rick, anxiously. "I'll never forgive myself if something happens to Fel."

Tuna glanced at Rick. "We are going to get her, Rick. I'm not going to let anything happen to her."

Soon they were flying across The Galls, the Atlantic to their right, and just a few hundred feet away on their left was Nantucket Sound, the lights of town twinkling in the distance. Tuna swerved to miss a handful of seagulls sleeping in the track. They scattered quickly as the tires of the Explorer passed by inches from their roosting spot.

Rick looked out his window and saw the moon emerging from the water. "Look at that, Tuna. Is it a full moon tonight?"

She leaned forward and looked out of the windshield. "Not quite. It's close to ninety-five percent. Full moon is in a couple of days."

Rick eyed her curiously. "Ninety-five percent? Are you sure it's not ninety-six?"

Tuna smiled grimly, staring straight ahead. "With all the fishing Ellen and I do, we follow the moon phases pretty closely. Have a chart on the fridge that I check just about every morning."

"Okay. Well, I wish we knew what the hell Kurt was thinking. And doing. Why would he hurt anybody? It just doesn't make sense."

"You know what doesn't make sense to me?"

"What's that?"

"There's no violence in the deaths. No blood. No gore. I was looking at Tomas's list. The causes were almost natural, as if he respected his victims ."

Tuna swerved out of the track to miss a large log that had washed up, and almost lost control getting the old truck back in the track.

"That was close. Sorry."

"It's okay. Just get us to Fel in one piece. Anyway, what you are saying about the deaths? Margot said the same thing. All the deaths are free of blood and gore," said Rick.

Tuna stole a glance at him. "Yeah, but why? We have alcohol poisoning, drownings, heart attacks, exposure. But no blood. No gunshot wounds. No knife lacerations. No blunt force. I think he wants to kill, but in as pleasant a way as possible for him."

Rick grunted. "I guess. But it's still murder, no matter how you frame it."

"Yes, it is. And we will make him pay."

The white light of the Great Point Lighthouse blinked in front of them. Wisps of fog occasionally dimming the beacon. Tuna peered intently through the windshield, trying to locate the turn into the trail to head to the harbor. She slowed as her high beams were becoming almost unusable in the increasing fog, bouncing the light back in her eyes and obscuring the trail ahead. She switched to the low beams and was able to make out the cable and posts blocking access to the beach side by the lighthouse. She picked out a section that gave her the most room between posts and hit the gas. The Explorer caught the wire mid-grill and pulled the posts out of the sand. Soon they were trailing behind the SUV like just married cans following newlyweds.

"What the hell are you doing?" asked Rick, surprised.

"Saving at least five minutes, maybe more. If he's at the Point, this is by far the fastest route. It gets awfully narrow in spots, so we may get wet."

She kept the truck as close to the dunes as possible, trying her best to avoid the surf. Rick could hear the waves crashing just feet from his door and gripped the handle above him even tighter. The Explorer leaned heavily to the right as the dunes sloped steeply toward the water.

Rick thought for sure they were going for a swim.

Tuna eased the truck across the sand and corrected the steering to overcome the gravitational pull of the incline. As they passed the lighthouse, the sand flattened, and the beach widened. She got back on the gas.

Even in the darkness and the fog, they could feel the space in front of them expand, and soon they were flying across the open beach just a thousand feet or so from the Point.

"There's his truck," said Rick, excitedly, pointing. He squinted through the windshield. "But I don't see Kurt or Fel. Where do you think they are?"

"We'll know soon enough," said Tuna. She pinned the gas to the floor and covered the distance to Kurt's pickup quickly. As they got closer, other details emerged. The driver's door was open, the interior lights were on, and the tailgate was down. But neither Kurt nor Felicity was visible.

Tuna pulled up behind the NPD pick-up and aimed her lights on the vehicle. They both jumped out of the Explorer and ran to the cab. The wind was freshening and making talking difficult.

Rick ran around to the tailgate and peered in. There was a makeshift foam mattress laid on top of the metal frames where Kurt's drones would normally have been. He felt the foam. It was warm. And he caught a brief whiff of perfume.

"I think Felicity was in here."

CHAPTER THIRTY-SEVEN

Randy slid the shifter into park and got out of the Nantucket Police Department pickup. The fog had been building, and he could barely see more than a hundred feet in front of him. The cool droplets of the mist settled on his skin and dampened his clothes. He stretched and took a deep breath of the salt-tinged air. It filled his lungs and gave him life.

He looked out over the water and watched as the waves crested and fell, the tide rapidly moving from his left to right and out toward the Cape. He knew that the rip extended miles out to sea as the waters of the Atlantic and the Sound fought each other for control. He turned and could barely make out the beacon from the lighthouse through the fog. The cry of a gull and the grunt of a seal could just be heard over the waves.

He had been saving this spot for something special. It was stunningly beautiful, secluded, and if he timed the tides right, the Gift would be carried miles out to sea. This pleased him, and he knew deep down it would please the island as well. Balance would be restored.

He smiled. It was time.

He kicked off his shoes and threw them on the driver's seat before walking to the back of the truck. He opened the tailgate and could just make out the feminine outline of his Gift. She was still, likely still knocked out from the propofol he had given her at the house. It had been a heavy dosage, and he was initially concerned it might be too much for her to handle. But as he watched, she stirred. She was waking up.

He rushed back to the cab and grabbed his backpack. He unzipped a pocket and withdrew the syringe he had prepared at home. He would administer this as he led her into the water. She would sleep peacefully as the tides took her. It was such a beautiful scene in his mind that he wanted to cry. He tucked the syringe in his pocket and returned to the back of the truck.

Moving almost silently on its ball bearing slides, he pulled the metal frame out. Where normally his drones would be nested, Felicity Post lay on a makeshift foam mattress. The cool air and fog worked together to hasten her recovery. Within minutes, she sat up and looked around, confused.

She saw him standing by the frame. “Kurt? Where the hell am I? How did I get here?”

He smiled warmly. “It’s okay, Felicity. It’s time. And it is going to be wonderful.”

“Time? Time for what?” she asked, confused. “I don’t know what I’m doing here, but I would appreciate it if you could get me home.”

He held out his hand. “Here. Let’s get you out of there. Maybe you’ll feel more comfortable if you can stretch your legs a bit.”

Felicity took his hand and stepped down out of the truck. Her legs felt unsteady, and Kurt had to catch her from falling.

“Sorry. Just feeling a bit dizzy.”

“I understand. But that will pass quickly.”

Felicity eyes him cautiously, her memory gelling. “Wait. You picked me up at Kitty’s earlier. Said my car had been damaged.”

He nodded. “Yes. Thankfully, it was only superficial damage.”

“So why are we here?” she asked, a tinge of fear in her voice.

"Welcome to Great Point," he said solemnly. "Tonight, we bestow upon Nantucket a great gift."

"What! Gift? What are you talking about?"

"Nature's first green is gold, her hardest hue to hold. We need to help Nantucket. Save her."

"Save her? From what?"

"Her early leaf's a flower; But only for an hour." He began to circle her, speaking softly, calmly, reverently. "We need to restore her balance."

"Kurt. You're scaring me. What is going on? Balance? What are you talking about?" Felicity looked around her anxiously, hoping to see something or someone that could help her.

"Then leaf subsides to leaf. So Eden sank to grief."

"I'm sorry, I don't understand. What are you doing? And why are you quoting Robert Frost to me?"

"So dawn goes down today. Nothing gold can stay." He paused. He looked at her with love and admiration in his eyes.

"I love that poem, too, Kurt. But don't understand what it has to do with us being here right now."

He stopped walking and stared intently at Felicity. "Frost's poem is beautiful indeed. Nothing gold can stay. Mama Hickman read to me every night. She taught me about the balance and how I had to protect the gold."

A gust of wind blew, the mist swirling between them. She could barely make out his face as the fog thickened.

"Protect the gold?" asked Felicity, confused. "What's that got to do with Frost's poem?"

"I made it better."

"You made what better?"

"His poem. I carefully crafted four lines to allow it to reach its maximum impact. I think Frost would have been pleased."

"Four lines?"

"Yes. Four lines. They turned a great poem into a perfect one. It came to me when I realized what I must do with my life. My calling was to protect this island we all love. I was young, finding my way, and then I landed here and found Nantucket. And I was home. For the first time in my life, I felt needed, loved, and respected. Nantucket gave me that!" he shouted through the wind.

Felicity watched him intently, and for the first time, fearing for her safety. "I agree, Nantucket is a wonderful place." She wanted to keep him talking in hopes that help would eventually arrive.

"And then I saw everything she was going through. The people, the development, the violations, the disrespect. They were hurting my Nantucket, and that's when I realized that a Gift must be offered to her every year to restore the balance. Demonstrate that she is loved. Respected. Honored." He spoke quietly and emotionally.

"Tell me those four lines," asked Felicity.

Kurt smiled and swelled with pride. "I'd be delighted to." He paused and turned his body as if he were getting ready for a formal recital. He took in a breath and spoke slowly and earnestly.

"Unless a gift made in moment brief

Can pause our time's silent grief

She follows those gone now, still and gray

A bequest I have done for you my dear. This day."

Felicity listened intently. "Beautiful, Kurt. Honestly. I think you captured the pace and meter of Frost perfectly."

He beamed at the compliment. "Thank you. I thought so too. You know, I never went to college, never studied English or poetry. But those lines? They came to me, like a vision. I just wrote them down and was done. No editing or changing."

"That's impressive, Kurt. It really is." She looked back through the fog, hoping to see some help coming her way.

"And now it is time."

"Time?" asked Felicity, nervously, turning back to him.

"Unless a gift made in moment brief can pause our time's silent grief. It is you, Felicity. You are the Gift. You will help restore the balance of our beloved island." He withdrew the syringe and showed it to her.

Felicity's eyes went wide. "Oh, no. Please don't do this, Kurt. Please."

He extended his hand. "Come with me, Felicity. I promise I won't hurt you." He grabbed her elbow and began leading her down to the water.

Felicity, still weakened by the injection, struggled to pull her elbow free, but he had a firm grip and pulled her along. He guided her across the sand, and soon they were standing near the rip, the waves rolling up inches from their feet. Felicity could see the waters criss-cross in front of her and hear the breaking waves farther out. It was a confused and dangerous sea.

"Please don't be frightened."

She jerked her arm away and turned to him. "Tell me why you are doing this? Why do you want to kill me?"

"It's not death. It's a Gift."

She shook her head. "I don't understand. Why a gift?"

"Too many people. Too few resources. The balance is off. Only a Gift can restore that."

She shook her head furiously. "I love Nantucket as much as anyone. I was born and raised here and just recently moved back full-time. I know the island has its challenges, but killing me isn't going to help anything."

He winced at the word killing. "It's not a killing, it's a Gift."

"Don't do this, Kurt."

"I'm sorry. But I was born to do this. To be her protector. It is my destiny. My reason for being. And I promise, it will feel wonderful."

Movement caught his eye. Kurt turned and looked across the sand, past the lighthouse, and saw through the fog the headlights of a vehicle approaching rapidly across the sand. He felt a surge of adrenaline. He was running out of time. He grabbed her forcefully at the elbow and pulled her into the surf. He lifted the syringe and moved to plunge it into her arm.

A small wave broke across her feet, the cold water waking and energizing her. She twisted out of his grip and ripped her elbow out of his hand. She backed up quickly, out of the surf, trying to put as much distance as possible from him. Felicity scrambled backward, not taking her eyes off Kurt. Her feet tangled in some seaweed, and she fell hard in the sand. Grunting, she used her arms to quickly get back up and continued to slowly retreat from him.

Kurt looked up at her, dejected. The vehicle was almost upon them, and he realized that he had lost her. He had lost the Gift. Again. And most likely, he was going to be caught. Not that he had ever felt like what he was doing was wrong, but he knew others wouldn't see it that way. They didn't understand what it took for him to maintain the balance. The years he had invested in taking care of his charge so residents and visitors alike could enjoy their lovely isle. No. They couldn't see the gold. They would never see the gold.

He stood alone in the surf, the syringe in his hand. Despondent. He had failed.

Felicity watched safely from the shore. She turned and saw the vehicle pull up next to the pickup. She couldn't make out who it was in the fog, but then she heard a familiar voice.

"Fel!"

Rick!

She let out a whoop of delight and ran as fast as she could through the sand toward the lights. She nearly collided with Rick, who was running just as fast towards her.

He embraced her hard.

"I am so happy to see you!" he said excitedly. He pulled back and kissed her passionately, his hand in her hair pulling her toward him. She returned the kiss enthusiastically.

Tuna walked up to them, smiling. "Okay, you two."

Rick withdrew and looked at Felicity intently. "Are you okay? Are you hurt?"

She shook her head. "No, I'm fine. Just confused. I don't understand what Kurt was doing."

Tuna touched her arm. "We can talk about that later, just glad you are safe. Where is he?"

Felicity motioned toward the surf. "He was just standing out in the rip."

"Is he armed?" asked Rick, concerned.

"Not with a gun. But he has a syringe. I don't know what's in it, but if it's the same stuff he gave me, it will knock you out quickly."

Tuna ran back to the Explorer and came back with a high-intensity flashlight. She turned it on and played it out over the water. Through the heavy fog, they could see Kurt standing ankle deep in the surf, waves breaking around him. He was motionless, staring down at the water, his arms dangling.

Rick and Tuna walked slowly toward him. They stopped at the edge of the surf, just yards away. He was framed in the spotlight, the gray waters churning around him.

"Kurt. It's over. Please come out. Let's go back to the station and talk things through," encouraged Tuna. She held out her hand.

He looked up at them, his face blank, and slowly shook his head.

"Kurt. Please? We'd like to understand," said Rick.

He looked up at them. "You'll never understand. It's about the balance."

Rick glanced at Tuna and back to Kurt. "Nature's first green is gold," he said loudly over the surf.

Kurt's eyes went wide. "How do you know that?"

"We talked to Gayle Hickman this morning. She explained it to us. Your parents' death. The poem."

A large wave broke just feet from Kurt and almost knocked him over. He straightened up, glanced at the syringe, and then back at Rick. "Is she okay?"

Rick nodded. "Yes. And she'd love to see you." He paused. "Why don't you come with us, and we will see if we can get you two together."

Kurt showed little interest in the proposition and even less in giving himself up.

Tuna stepped closer. "Come with us, Kurt. Or should I say, Randy? Let's go back to the station and talk. Get you some dry clothes."

He looked at Tuna and held up the syringe. A smile spread slowly across his face. The mention of Mama Hickman stirred a thought, and it all became clear to him. Neither of the two women he had selected was intended to be the Gift. That's why they escaped. It was just nature's way of telling him he was wrong.

No, the women were not meant to be the Gift. The island had other ideas. It wanted Randy.

Of course. How could I not see it? I am the Gift.

"Kurt?"

He smiled at Tuna, turned away, and walked deeper into the rip. Soon, the water was up to his waist, and he continued pushing his way out, the waves lapping at his chest.

"Should we stop him?" asked Rick.

Tuna shook her head. "It's too dangerous. The tides are brutally strong right now, and we simply don't have the equipment."

"Kurt! Randy! Come back. You are going to drown!" shouted Rick.

Randy Evans ignored him. As he moved farther and farther out, the fog slowly embraced him, hiding him from the police who had so rudely interrupted his evening. But he knew now that he could restore the balance. He knew what he had to do. He turned toward the beach and, satisfied they could no longer see him, took the needle and plunged it into his thigh. He briefly winced, but as the drug entered his system, he felt the warmth overcome him. It was a feeling of love. Of forgiveness. Of beauty.

He spoke quietly. "Unless a gift made in moment brief can pause our time's silent grief."

Flashes of his life on Nantucket played through his mind. Walking across the moors on a cold winter day. The smiling faces of the residents during Daffodil Weekend. Rose covered cottages in Sconset. The feel of sand beneath his toes. The sounds of gulls. The cobblestones of Main Street. The old windmill. He had protected it all. He had devoted his life to maintaining her balance. And he was prepared to make the ultimate sacrifice for her.

"I follow those gone now, still and gray. A bequest I have done for you, my dear… This day."

He smiled contentedly, closed his eyes, and slid under the water.

* * *

Tuna paced the beach, shining the light out over the water. All she could make out was the churning breakers of the rip and the occasional seal. Kurt was nowhere to be seen.

Several NPD vehicles had arrived at the Point, and Rick was briefing the team on the activities of the evening. Tuna walked back up the beach and joined them.

"Any luck?" asked Rick, hopeful.

She shook her head. "No, I think he's gone."

A silence fell over the group as they each absorbed the shocking news about their fellow officer, both in his apparent involvement in the suspicious deaths and now likely drowning.

Tuna broke the quiet. "The Coast Guard has been notified. But given the fog and sea conditions, I'm not sure what, if anything, they can do. This won't be a search and rescue effort, but I suspect just a recovery."

Heads nodded. A hand went up. It was Officer John Downs.

"Yes, John," said Tuna.

"How did we not know?" he asked emotionally. "Are we really to believe that Kurt has been killing people every year for over thirty years? And then just killed himself?"

Rick stepped in. "I know it's difficult, John, but remember it's just a theory. We have no definitive evidence that Kurt was involved in any of those deaths. It certainly warrants further investigation, but it could just be an uncomfortable coincidence. That said, what we do know is that he was involved in the kidnappings of Katie Chapman and Felicity Post. Why he kidnapped them remains an open question and will be further investigated." Rick sighed heavily, shifting his weight. "And we know that he apparently just injected himself with something while out in the Great Point rip. So, sadly, yes, it does appear that he killed himself."

Officer Downs nodded solemnly and looked down at the sand.

"Okay, everyone. I think we are done here. We will regroup in the morning and discuss next steps and responsibilities in the investigation. Rick and I really appreciate your quick response in getting here, though I'm just sorry it was for nothing," said Tuna.

Heads nodded quietly as the group disbanded and retreated to their vehicles to make the seven-mile trip across the beach back to Wauwinet. It was dark, foggy, and getting cold.

Tuna turned to Rick, who was standing next to Felicity. "Rick. You and Fel take the Explorer back. I'll drive Kurt's pickup."

"Are you sure, Tuna? I'd be happy to do that."

She smiled thinly. "Thanks, but I think I should do it. Besides, you aren't even official yet. I doubt our insurance would cover you if something happened, like if you hit a deer?"

Rick smiled. "Thanks, Tuna. See you tomorrow?"

She shook her head. "I'll see you on June first, Rick. Until then, try to relax and settle in."

He nodded and reached for Felicity's hand. Together, they walked over to Tuna's Explorer. Rick managed to untangle the wire and metal posts that they had dragged up the beach and placed them in the back, careful not to disturb any of Tuna's fishing gear. Closing the hatch, he helped Felicity into the passenger seat. He gave her a quick peck on the cheek, closed her door, and walked around the front of the car. He stopped briefly and nodded at Tuna. Their first official case together had certainly been a challenge and one they would talk about for years. But for now, he was happy to know that the people of Nantucket were safe and Felicity was back in his arms. He waved, hopped in the driver's seat, started the car, and pulled away.

Tuna returned the wave and turned back to the water.

They would have work to do, no doubt. Work to understand what Kurt had done and why he had done it. Nearly three dozen cases to review, analyze, and somehow find the connections to Kurt White. The resource demands on her team would be significant. And to what end? Confirm that a member of the NPD had been systematically killing people for the last thirty-plus years? Yes, the public would want to know. They would demand to know. How did the Nantucket Police Department miss these deaths? There would be investigations. Depositions. Stories would be written in the Inq & M. Heads would probably roll. The department she knew and loved, the people she could entrust with her life, would likely never be the same.

She shook her head. Maybe, just maybe, the public didn't need to know.

After all, the deaths over the years hadn't raised any suspicions. They were seen as normal, if sad, acts of life. Maybe the right way to manage the narrative was to share that they had identified Randy Evans as the kidnapper of Katie Chapman, thanks to terrific work by the FBI's latent prints division, and excellent investigative work by the NPD. Sadly, in their attempt to arrest him, he had run and committed suicide at Great Point. No motive was ever discovered, but the island was safe. There would be no more kidnappings.

And Kurt White? Kurt's thirty-plus years on the force had earned him a well-deserved retirement. He decided to move to Florida to pursue his love of fishing.

Tuna stared out through the fog. She would have to have a long talk with the chief to convince her. Sometimes, when it comes to the public, what they don't know won't hurt them. Transparency isn't all it's cracked up to be.

She turned and walked back to the pickup. She slid the frame back in the bed, careful not to disturb any evidence, and closed the tailgate. She went around to the open driver's door and saw Kurt's shoes on the front seat. A sudden wave of sadness passed through her, not just for the apparent victims of his time on the island but also for Kurt himself. He must have suffered from some sort of mental illness and one that no one, including her, had noticed. Maybe if they had they could have gotten him the help he needed and saved dozens of people. She shook her head slowly, grabbed Kurt's shoes, and moved them over to the passenger footwell. She brushed the sand off the seat and hopped in. She adjusted it so she was closer to the steering wheel, fastened the seatbelt, and started the car. She flicked the headlights on and backed up.

As she turned, her lights lit up the large colony of seals. Many of them were awake and watching her with interest. She flipped them the bird.

"That's for stealing the striper off my lure last week," she said angrily.

She honked the horn to emphasize her point and drove slowly past the seals, cursing under her breath.

CHAPTER THIRTY-EIGHT

Thursday after Memorial Day

From the May 28th Inquirer & Mirror.

Kidnapper of Visiting Cambridge Woman Apparent Victim of Drowning

By Sarah Robsons | srobsons@inqym.com.

(May 25, 2026; Updated May 26) - The suspected kidnapper who kept the island in fear over the recent Memorial Day weekend has apparently drowned. According to reports from the Nantucket Police Department, fifty-five-year-old Randy Evans, originally of Turners Falls, MA, attempted to elude police by swimming into the rip at Great Point this past Monday evening. He was wanted for questioning by the NPD based on testimony provided by the kidnap victim, Katie Chapman, of Cambridge. Ms. Chapman successfully escaped from confinement and was able to provide detectives with critical information that led to the identification of Randy Evans as the prime suspect.

"We owe Ms. Chapman a huge debt of gratitude," stated Nantucket Police Chief Jodi Calpers. "Due to her bravery and quick wits, she was able to escape her confinement and provide us with the critical information necessary to identify her kidnapper."

Details on Randy Evans and his life on Nantucket are sketchy at best. There is no apparent record of him arriving on the island, and no witnesses have come forward with knowledge of his time here. According to the NPD, the house on Paut Pond Road where Ms. Chapman was confined was a rental, owned by a Trust. Attempts to contact the owners of the property to date have not been successful.

In a statement released by Katie Chapman, she wanted to express her gratitude for the NPD, Detectives Rick Caton and Tuna Fisch in particular, and looks forward to returning to Nantucket in the fall for her honeymoon.

"This kidnapping was a shocking, but isolated event," stated Chief Calpers. "We hope that locals, seasonal residents, and our visitors can put this incident behind them and enjoy the rest of the summer. Nantucket remains a very special place."

We will continue to monitor the investigation and will provide updates as information warrants.

In the same paper, the same day, a notice ran in the Community Announcements section.

My Gift to You

Nature's first green is gold,

Her hardest hue to hold.

Her early leaf's a flower;

But only for an hour.

Then leaf subsides to leaf.

So Eden sank to grief,
So dawn goes down to day.
Nothing gold can stay.
Unless a gift made in moment brief
Can pause our time's silent grief
She follows those gone now, still and gray
A bequest I have done for you my dear. This day.

It would be the last time the poem would appear.

CHAPTER THIRTY-NINE

One Week After Memorial Day

The week since that fateful evening at Great Point had gone by quickly for Rick, and before he knew it, he was parking his new car, a navy blue Ford Explorer, in the lot at the Nantucket Police Department. His experience in Tuna's old Explorer had been a key driver of his purchase, but unlike her car, he wanted the latest technology that cars thirty years newer offered.

He jumped out, grabbed his backpack, and hustled to the front door. Walking into the lobby, he stopped to talk with Tomas Santos, getting the scoop on the weekend's activities and the upcoming docket. Fortunately, the island seemed to have put Katie's kidnapping in the rearview mirror, and police actions returned to their summertime norm: DUIs, youth in possession, a few burglaries, and a handful of disorderly conducts.

Thanking Tomas, he headed up the stairs to the detective's room and angled over to his cubicle. He tapped his newly applied nameplate by his door, dropped his backpack on the floor, and headed over to the coffee machine to feed a caffeine deficit.

"Rick!"

He turned to see Chief Calpers walking his way. "Chief."

She approached and extended her hand. "Welcome to your official first day," she said, emphasizing official. "We are so glad you are here."

"Thanks, Chief. It is really good to be back."

"How was your week?"

Rick shrugged. "Pretty quiet, to be honest. But it was good."

"So glad. I also wanted to thank you for all your hard work on the Evans case. We didn't have a chance to debrief after the incident at Great Point."

Rick shifted, looking concerned. "I'm just sorry it ended the way it did. I really wanted to have the opportunity to interview him. Really try and understand why he did what he did."

"Agree, but I think it was probably for the best."

"For the best?" asked Rick, confused.

The Chief nodded. "Tuna will share the after-action review with you and the decisions we made to manage it longer term. But I hope you'll agree we made the right call. I certainly would have loved to have your input on the discussion, but didn't want to impose on you again."

"You know I would have been happy to come in," said Rick, a bit defensively.

The Chief raised her hand. "You don't need to convince me of your dedication, Rick. When we pulled you into the Chapman case, you dropped everything and jumped in with both feet. I saw that and really appreciate it. I knew you were going to be a great asset to the NPD, but you have proved it once again."

"Well, thanks, Chief. I appreciate the feedback."

"I'm looking forward to working with you, Rick. My door is always open. Please don't hesitate to let me know if there's anything I can do to help you settle in."

"Thanks, Chief." He turned and headed to the coffee machine. He pulled a mug that stated he was the number one police officer and filled it. He added a little creamer, took a sip, and winced.

Tuna was right. The coffee has gotten worse.

He took another tentative sip and then headed to his desk. He fired up his computer and, for the first time, opened his official NPD email. A handful of unreads greeted him, including the weekly activity report from the Memorial Day week, which showed a number of drunk and disorderlies, as well as details on both Katie's kidnapping and Randy Evans' apparent drowning. His new employee announcement was there, which he read again and smiled. And several emails from other NPD officers welcoming him back to the force.

There was a light tap on his door.

He turned to see Tuna standing there with a warm smile, her notebook tucked against her chest.

"Welcome back, officially that is, Rick." She stepped in as he stood and hugged him.

"Thanks, Tuna. It feels good. So how was your week?"

She rolled her eyes and looked over at the chief's office. "To be honest, it was a tough one. I'll give you all the details. But first, we have a call. A body was discovered on Quidnet Beach."

Rick raised an eyebrow. "Kurt?"

Tuna nodded. "Most likely. The caller didn't give a lot of details, but the description and location fit. Grab your stuff. I'll drive."

"Actually, Tuna, let me drive," said Rick, grinning.

Tuna scoffed. "I'm not riding on the back of that damn E-bike of yours!"

"No need, Tuna. I'm a big boy now. I have my own car."

She smacked him on the arm. "Finally! What did you end up getting?"

"An Explorer." Rick grabbed his backpack and followed Tuna across the room.

"Huh. An old one like mine?" she asked hopefully.

Rick shook his head. "Nope. Brand spanking new. I think you'll like it."

"Don't count on that, Caton. You know I'm a Luddite. If it's got any of that fancy technology, I'm out." She laughed lightly.

They made their way down the stairs and out into the parking lot. Tuna stopped in front of Rick's new car and let out a low whistle. "I love the color. Tough to keep clean, but looks great when it is."

Rick unlocked the doors, and they hopped in.

Tuna looked around, admiring the interior. "Fancy. And that new car smell. Pretty sweet ride."

"Thanks." He pushed the button to start the engine. "So tell me about the after-action report." He glanced behind, backed out of his spot, and accelerated quickly.

Tuna let out a long sigh. "As I mentioned, it was a tough week. We spent the day Tuesday reviewing everything we had on Kurt, er, Randy. It's amazing how little we knew as a group about a man who was part of this department for so many years."

"Really?" asked Rick.

"Yeah. No one ever socialized with him. No one had ever been to his house. It was like he kept himself in isolation, only interacting with us when his position required him to."

"Honestly, that kind of fits my impression of him. Very much a loner. Low profile."

"Yes. And I think in many ways that helped us reach the decision we did."

"What was that?"

Tuna watched out the window as the moors passed by. They were heading down Polpis, and she thought back just a week before she had been flying down this road in her thirty-year-old Explorer, hot on the tail of Randy Evans. Finally, she turned to Rick. "We've decided not to go public with what we know about Kurt and the suspected deaths."

Rick turned in surprise. "Really?" he exclaimed. "That surprises me, knowing the chief is pretty old school and straight-laced when it comes to keeping the public informed."

"She is. And it was a tough sell. But I had Tomas review his spreadsheet with her and showed her how all the deaths appeared either natural or accidental. She challenged those conclusions, though, and asked us to review each case and see if we would still come to that decision today."

"That's a lot of work."

"It was. Thankfully, we had Tomas and Officer Downs working it, and they were able to review the files, the medical examiner reports, and what witness statements we had. Essentially, they came to the same conclusion. There simply wasn't enough evidence to support a prosecution of Randy for those crimes at the time. And certainly not now."

"Humph. So he just gets a pass then?"

"I guess, if you want to call it that. But it really is the right move. If we had come forward with our suspicions, there probably would have been serious blowback. People would want to know how we missed it. There would be investigations, accusations, and incriminations. The trust in the NPD would have been shattered. And to what end? What good would it serve?"

Rick nodded thoughtfully but was quiet.

They passed Wauwinet Road, and Rick prepared to slow down, knowing the turn to Quidnet was coming up.

"It took some convincing, but in the end, she agreed with my recommendation that it would do more harm than good. So she asked the handful of us who know the details to keep them to ourselves. There'll be rumors, of course, there always are. But long term, we agreed this was the best approach to ensure the island moves forward."

"So what is the official position then?" He put his blinker on, slowed, and made the left onto Quidnet Road.

"You saw the Inq and M article on Katie's case?"

"I did. Anyone who read it would say there are still some loose ends on who he really was, how he got here."

Tuna nodded. "Yeah. But with Katie safe and Randy dead, I think the story will just naturally fade away. And we decided to keep Felicity's kidnapping out of the narrative. More for her benefit, as I know she wouldn't want that sort of attention on her."

"I know she appreciated that. And thankfully, she doesn't remember much of the whole thing. One minute she's in Kurt's truck in Kitty's parking lot, the next she's waking up at Great Point."

"Good. I'm really glad."

Rick turned onto Sesachacha Road and followed it to the end. He pulled up behind an ambulance and two other NPD vehicles and slid the transmission into park. He killed the engine and turned to Tuna. "And Kurt White? How are we handling his disappearance?"

"I hate to say this about a person, but I really don't think he will be missed. It wasn't just the NPD he kept his distance from. He didn't interact with anyone, apparently. So we will close out his employment file stating that he retired. The benefits he earned will be donated to charity, anonymously, of course. And if anyone asks, Kurt moved and is now living in Florida."

"That certainly makes this whole thing cut and dry," said Rick. "Almost too easy."

"It actually makes me sick, personally, Rick. What this man did for over thirty years? The people he killed? I wish we could bring him to justice, I really do. But in light of this," she said, pointing to the beach, "it's the least worst outcome."

"Least worst?" asked Rick, cracking a slight grin.

She cuffed his shoulder. "Alright, Caton. Don't give me crap about my word choice. Anyway. You ready?"

"Yeah."

They walked past the other NPD vehicles to the end of the road, where it dead-ended at the beach. A small group of gawkers had set up camp at the entrance and were being restrained by a couple of CSO's. Rick and Tuna nodded and made their way through the group and out onto the beach. A few hundred yards to the south, they could see a huddle of people surrounding a privacy screen. The sand was heavy, and it took a few minutes for Tuna and Rick to reach the group.

"Detectives," said Officer Downs, nodding.

"John," said Tuna. "What have we got? Is it Kurt?" She peered over the screen and could see the body half-buried in the sand. Kurt's serene face stared back at her, his eyes closed as if he was sleeping. To Tuna, he looked content.

Downs nodded. "Yes, ma'am. He was found by a beachcomber. She's the lady there in the yellow jacket," he said, pointing to an attractive older woman standing uneasily apart from the group, her long gray hair tussled by the wind.

"And is she the only one who saw him?"

Downs nodded. "We think so. She mentioned that the beach has been pretty quiet this morning."

"Good." She motioned to Rick, who followed her over to the woman.

"Ma'am. I'm Detective Tina Fisch. This is Detective Rick Caton. We understand you found the body?"

She nodded. "Yes. I'm Claire Bullock. My husband and I have a rental for the month just down Sesachacha Road."

"Can you tell us what led you to the discovery?" asked Rick, empathetically. He saw in her face how upset she was.

"Um, I walk the beach every morning. Usually, my husband joins me; it's our routine, but he had a conference call today. So I was on my own."

"And what time was this?" encouraged Tuna, gently.

"About nine. Normally, we walk down to Sankaty Head and back. It's roughly three miles round trip, so good exercise. And beautiful too," she added.

"It is that," Tuna agreed. "And when you found?" she asked, motioning back to the body.

Claire's eyes followed and then abruptly turned away. "I saw a large clump in the sand. I thought it was probably a dead seal. There are so many around these days. But then I noticed the clothing. I got a little closer and could see the face. Tangled in some seaweed. That's when I called nine-one-one."

"Thank you, Claire. I know this must be really difficult for you."

She nodded and dabbed a tear on her cheek. "I'm not sure my walk on the beach will ever be the same."

Tuna reached out and put an arm on her shoulder. "I hope you can put this behind you, Ms. Bullock. It's too beautiful a setting not to be enjoyed."

She nodded and sniffled. "Is it him?"

"Him?"

"The kidnapper. I read in the Inquirer and Mirror that they thought he drowned off Great Point."

Tuna nodded slowly. "Most likely. We will need confirmation, of course, but that's our working assumption."

She huffed, suddenly indignant. "Good riddance. Anyone who can do that to a young woman? Doesn't deserve to live."

Tuna and Rick exchanged glances.

"And why was he wearing a police uniform?" asked Claire, now offended of the body's actions in life.

Tuna forced herself not to look surprised.

Rick stepped in. "We believe the kidnapper, Randy Evans, was trying to disguise himself to make him less threatening to the public. And potential victims."

"Impersonating a policeman?" said Claire. She turned back to look at the body on the beach. "What a bastard," she mumbled.

"He was not a nice guy," agreed Tuna. "Is there anything else you can tell us about your walk?"

Claire shook her head. "No. Just that," she said, nodding her head toward the group.

"Well, thank you for your time, Ms.Bullock. Here's my card. If you think of anything else, please don't hesitate to give me a call."

She took the card. "I will." With one last glance back toward the body, Claire turned and headed back to her rental.

Tuna watched her go and then turned to Rick. "That was close. Good catch."

Rick nodded. "I hope it worked. We don't need her talking about finding a dead policeman at Quidnet."

They walked back to the group just as the zipper zinged closed on a black body bag. Two officers and a medic picked it up and struggled to carry the bag across the sand to the ambulance. Officer Downs was folding up the privacy shield and looked over at them.

"Thanks, John," said Tuna. "For getting that privacy shield up quickly. We certainly don't need anyone posting pictures on their socials."

Downs nodded. "Of course. Just so sad. I still can't believe he did what he did."

"I know, John. I think it's going to take a while for all of us to process this."

He smiled grimly, gathered the privacy screens, and walked back to his truck.

Tuna stood, her arms crossed, and watched John struggle through the heavy sand. She turned to Rick, “It’ll probably be a day or two until we get official confirmation, and then we can close this case for good.”

“Thirty years…” said Rick, his voice fading. “And over thirty victims. It still scares the crap out of me what could have happened to Fel.”

She touched his arm. “I’m sure. And speaking of Fel, you guys have any plans tonight?”

* * *

Tuna was on the grill when Rick and Felicity arrived at her home off Swift Rock Road. She was prepping the grates with olive oil in anticipation of several large striped bass fillets that were waiting patiently on their teak dining table.

“Rick! Fel! Thanks so much for coming.”

Felicity leaned in and kissed Tuna on the cheek. “Thanks for having us.”

“Of course. You doing okay?” asked Tuna, concerned.

Felicity nodded. “I am. Thanks. Where’s Ellen?”

“She’s inside making the salad. Why don’t you go say hi and maybe grab a drink? I just have to catch up with Rick on a work thing.”

Felicity’s shoulders slumped. “Work? Really?”

Tuna smiled assuringly. “It’ll just take a minute. I promise. Then we can celebrate Rick’s first day back with us.”

"Okay. But please don't be long." Felicity walked across the patio and through an open slider into the house.

Rick watched her go and then turned to Tuna. "What's up?"

She put down her BBQ tools and stepped back from the grill. Her old leather satchel was sitting in one of the chairs. She opened it, pulled out a small green book, and handed it to Rick. It was well-worn, with a spiral binding, and had a number of red highlight flags protruding from the pages.

"What's this?" he asked curiously.

"It's Randy Evans' diary."

"What?" exclaimed Rick. "He kept a diary? How did you get it?"

"It was part of the evidence collected from his house on Paut Pond Road. I didn't even realize we had it until just after you left the station today. Noah Coffin brought it to me. He was in charge of the search and cataloging of evidence."

"And?" asked Rick, leafing through the pages. "Have you had a chance to read it?"

"No. I looked through it quickly, but as you can see, Noah flagged several pages he felt were specifically important."

"Does he talk about the deaths?"

"He does. And explains why he did it. In his perverted mind, he really did think he was saving the island."

Rick shook his head. "Just don't get it. And never will. But thankfully it's over."

"It is. And hopefully, that," she said, pointing to the diary, "might answer some of the questions we have. And then we can close the Evans' case for good."

"Let's hope so."

Tuna sighed deeply and looked at him.

"What?" asked Rick, curiously. "Is there something else?"

She shifted from one leg to the other, her arms loosely crossed.

"What is it? You're worrying me."

"Peter Bois called me on my way home."

"Peter Bois?" said Rick, his hand rubbing his chin. "Why would the head of The Jack Tate and Tristram Coffin Foundation, not to mention Fel's boss, call you? Looking for a donation?" He chuckled nervously.

"Well, you remember he's a financial genius, right?"

"Of course. His help with the Charles Post drowning last September was critical. What did he want?"

Tuna was quiet, unsure.

"Tuna. What is it?" asked Rick, anxiously.

"He didn't get into the details, but he suspects ongoing corruption at The Lighthouse Circle."

"That's your mom's charity, isn't it?"

Tuna nodded soberly.

"Oh, shit."

Author's Notes

Thank you for reading *Last Seen on Nantucket*. I hope you found the story entertaining and that you will take a moment to leave a review wherever you purchased your book. Good reviews are the lifeblood of aspiring writers, so I hope you'll let other readers know how much you (hopefully) enjoyed the book.

I'd also love to keep in touch and invite you to join my reader list. Sign up and receive *The Island Behind the Page*, a free 16-page companion guide to the real Nantucket behind the fiction.

I'll take you behind the stories with an insider's look at the island's extraordinary whaling history, the landmarks that shaped the books, the real locations behind the fiction, and the characters who refused to leave once they arrived. It's the guide no map of Nantucket can give you.

Sign up at www.garthjeffries.com

Those who know me know that I have the utmost respect for the Nantucket Police Department and the men and women who serve the island community. The character of Randy Evans / Kurt White as a member of the NPD is purely a fictional literary device created to serve the story and should not be interpreted as any reflection of the department or its officers. The Nantucket Police Department would pursue a case like this with professionalism, integrity, and unwavering dedication to protecting the community.

For the Robert Frost fans out there, I hope you'll forgive me for the use of his classic poem, *Nothing Gold Can Stay*. My high school English teacher, Robert McGlynn, whom I named the protagonist after in ***Not All Bodies Stay Buried***, was one of my favorite teachers of all time. He was also a friend of Robert Frost.

Mr. McGlynn's classes instilled in me a love of Frost's work as well as a desire to write (fiction - not poetry). By leveraging the Frost poem *Nothing Gold Can Stay*, it is my way of honoring both of them for helping me develop that love of writing.

Finally, but most importantly, a thank you to my "team" for always being there, ready to help. To K for your ideas, feedback, and proofreading. Also, for your tolerance when my head is in the clouds thinking of storylines, character development, and plot twists. And to M for help crafting storylines and making my prose sing.

And as always, I like to express my gratitude to the men and women in the military, the Coast Guard, our first responders, and all our healthcare providers. Thank you for all you do in keeping us safe, healthy, and free.

Garth Jeffries

Siasconset, MA

May 2026

www.ingramcontent.com/pod-product-compliance
Lightning Source LLC
LaVergne TN
LVHW100507110826
845146LV00002B/545

* 9 7 9 8 9 9 5 9 1 9 4 1 4 *